ISBN 978-1-330-88815-5
PIBN 10117397

This book is a reproduction of an important historical work. Forgotten Books uses
state-of-the-art technology to digitally reconstruct the work, preserving the original format
whilst repairing imperfections present in the aged copy. In rare cases, an imperfection in
the original, such as a blemish or missing page, may be replicated in our edition. We do,
however, repair the vast majority of imperfections successfully; any imperfections that
remain are intentionally left to preserve the state of such historical works.

POLA NEGRI AS THE SPANISH DANCER.

THE
SPANISH DANCER

Being a translation from the original French
by Henry L. Williams of

DON CAESAR DE BAZAN

BY

VICTOR HUGO

As dramatically told in the stage play
by Adolph D'Ennery and P. S. P. Dumanoir

WITH A FOREWORD BY

GLENDON ALLVINE

POLA NEGRI EDITION
ILLUSTRATED WITH SCENES FROM
THE PARAMOUNT PICTURE

G R O S S E T & D U N L A P
PUBLISHERS   NEW YORK

Made in the United States of America

FOREWORD

Some Remarks About Novels That Become Motion Pictures

By Glendon Allvine

The story-teller nowadays does not necessarily write with one eye on the screen, but, on the other hand, he cannot shut out from his mind's eye all images of his characters as the camera might reveal them. A very few creative authors still refuse to recognize the films as a new medium of expression.

Some authors to-day are actually writing in front of the camera—devising their plots and characterizations right in the moving picture studio. Most of them, however, are doing their creative writing with only slight concessions to the technical demands of motion pictures.

Homer Croy insists that he wrote "West of the Water Tower" with no thought whatever that it might make good screen material. When Jesse L. Lasky tried to buy the picture rights of the novel of small town life the author insisted there was no picture in his story—a judgment he revised some months later when he saw the picture in the making at the Paramount studio on Long Island.

"The Covered Wagon" came from the pen of the late Emerson Hough without any thought, on the author's part, of its picture possibilities. Mr. Hough had had one unfortunate experience with a lesser producer who filmed one of his earlier stories. And as a result he was "off" all picture producers. Yet James Cruze took this novel of the winning of the West and gave it an epic sweep which will make this story live forever, giving the world a better understanding of the hardy pioneers who pushed over the Oregon trail to establish a new empire of the Pacific Coast. Mr. Hough lived to see his story hailed as one of the great pictures of a decade, and died with a kindlier feeling toward film folk. This one picture revived the interest in all of Mr. Hough's writings and caused "The Covered Wagon" to leap again into the six best seller class of novels.

In his experience with the films Mr. Hough reached the depths of despair and the heights of triumph. Few other authors have run such a gamut from failure to success in the screening of their stories. Some authors have only kind words for the movies; others are loud in their denunciation. Their readers likewise go to extremes in their attitude toward film versions of books.

Readers of popular fiction sometimes complain that their entertaining novels have been ruined by the people who make motion pictures. No sooner do I finish reading a novel that gives me a definite idea of intensely human characters I have visualized from the author's words than along comes a movie director and mangles the pictures I have built up in my own mind. He seems to have no respect whatever for the image my mind has devised and the chances are that his ideas do not coincide with the mental images worked out by any of the many thousands who have read the novel.

And yet how do I know that I am completely right? Perhaps he does have a right to his own ideas even as I have a right to mine and there may possibly be good and sufficient reasons why a story comes through the picture mill in a form so different from the story I got from the printed page.

My contempt for the movies was second to none when I emerged from college weighted down by two degrees. What puerile, childish efforts these movies were! What silly, stupid things the picture people perpetrated!

Yet such was my curiosity about the mysterious ways of the makers of photoplays that I set about to learn, as best I could, how they got that way. A motion picture has so many ingredients that the process of devising film entertainment is most complex. It may not be inappropriate to discuss here some of the problems involved. Perhaps some reader whose feelings have been outraged may at least understand some of the mental processes that went into the translation of a novel into a film.

Nobody ever wrote a motion picture in the sense that Booth Tarkington, for instance, writes a novel. Even Mr. Tarkington, perhaps the foremost of living American novelists, feels his own inadequacy in reconstructing his story as a stage play and usually calls in Harry Leon Wilson to help him adapt it to the requirements of the theatre. Mr. Tarkington, in telling his story for the screen, likewise requires assistance from specialists in that medium, whose work is often evident on the screen. If there be less of Tarkington at least there is more of a photoplay.

A very few novelists, notably Rex Beach and Rupert Hughes, who have taken the pains to study the complexities of a motion picture production, have achieved considerable success in telling their stories in screen form. Yet either of these creators of fiction feels that a printed book bearing his own name carries over more of his personality than a motion picture, written, directed, supervised and edited by the author. There are actors and cameramen and bankers and audiences to be considered, and what they do to a story is often the despair of authors with paternal regard for a brainchild.

Even the title is often lost in the shuffle from the printed page to celluloid. Consider, for instance, Barrie's "The Admirable Crichton." That story, to the despair of the followers of the whimsical Scot, emerged on the screen as "Male and Female." That was many years ago but people still cite it to illustrate the stupidity, not to mention the cupidity, of picture producers. "Male and Female" is admittedly a box-office title, but the Bible is full of box-office titles. And who shall say that the Bible is not as good a source as Barrie from which to lift the quotation "Male and Female created He them." You can quote scripture even to sell a motion picture.

There is just one reason why "The Admirable Crichton" was a bad title for a film and that is that very few people, even now, are quite sure of how to pronounce Crichton. Let us imagine a young man taking his girl to the movies. On one side of Main Street the electric lights invite him to view "The Admirable Crichton" and on the opposite side the bulbs blaze out the admonition "Don't Tell Everything." Now he doesn't want to admit to the girl, who is perhaps smarter than himself, his hesitation about pronouncing the title of the one picture and so he avoids embarrassment by suggesting they go across the street to see "Don't Tell Everything." Just multiply that one incident by 100,000—you multiply almost everything by that number in the movies—and you can appreciate that the earnings of "Male and Female" might have been very considerably less if handicapped in America by the name, which Barrie, in far-off Scotland, tacked on to his excellent narrative.

I am by no means contending that picture titles are always legitimate or in good taste, but in considering successful titles let us remember that the outstanding music success of a decade was "Yes, We Have No Bananas."

Avoiding a discussion as to whether or not that title means anything, at least we are reasonably safe in assuming that to an American audience "Don Cæsar de Bazan" means nothing. Don suggests a Spanish person although Cæsar, I believe, was a Roman; and Bazan sounds like a trade name some advertising man might devise for a depilatory. In my estimation, the Famous Players-Lasky Corporation displayed excellent judgment in assigning to this story, for American consumption, the simple yet dignified title, "The Spanish Dancer."

That title, I learned, was chosen from many suggested in New York while the film was in production in California. And throughout the months the studio people were laboriously grinding out the 387 scenes that blend into the nine reels of this celluloid entertainment, the advertising and publicity men were attempting to establish in the public mind that title, "The Spanish Dancer." On seeing "The Spanish Dancer" on the screen it is interesting to speculate how many minds have exerted their influence on the story that Victor Hugo imagined in France almost a hundred years ago.

It happened that an actor, Lemaitre by name, had set his heart upon playing the part of Don Cæsar de Bazan, a minor character in Hugo's great dramatic poem "Ruy Blas." Victor Hugo had agreed to expand the rôle of Don Cæsar so as to make it the starring part in a stage play suitable for the talents of M. Lemaitre, but Hugo had incurred the displeasure of both the monarchists and imperialists and so everything he had written or intended to write was banned.

Enter Adolphe D'Ennery and P. S. P. Dumanoir, who adapted the story to the needs of the Parisian stage. Both were dramatists of repute and D'Ennery's fame subsequently reached America as the author of that venerable opus known wherever stock is played, "The Two Orphans."

Enter now two other dramatic craftsmen, June Mathis and Beulah Marie Dix, who adapted the story to the screen and the needs of Pola Negri. For as Victor Hugo wrote the stage play to fit Lemaitre, who played Don Cæsar, so June Mathis and Beulah Marie Dix wrote their screen story to put the emphasis on Pola Negri, who is the central figure in the Paramount picture.

Miss Mathis will be remembered as the author of the continuity of "Blood and Sand," which brought Rodolph Valentino to the peak of his popularity. In their collaboration on "The Spanish Dancer" they have developed a script which retells Victor Hugo's story in the most vivid fashion possible.

Their script so pleased Jesse L. Lasky, on whom rests the responsibility for the selection and production of Paramount pictures, that he assigned it to Herbert Brenon, who had previously directed many film successes. Mr. Brenon, realizing that neither he nor any living person had any first-hand information about the Spain of three centuries ago, began doing research work in the libraries of Southern California and Northern Mexico, but since he could not find there all the authentic historical data needed for the telling of his screen story, he crossed the continent to the Metropolitan Museum of Art where a week's work netted him excellent results. Finding that

The Seventeenth Century village was built in the mountains of California for a scene in "The Spanish Dancer," in which several thousand persons appear. The actors ate and slept in the tents while on location.

other data were available at the Smithsonian Institute at Washington, he went to the capital for further research work. Photographs were obtained from old prints which served as the basis for the elaborate backgrounds, native customs were studied and blended into the plans for the picture, with the result that when Director Brenon actually began the shooting of his first scene in the picture he was thoroughly steeped in the atmosphere of Spain of the seventeenth century.

To play the part of Don Cæsar de Bazan, Mr. Brenon selected a popular actor of Spanish parentage, Antonio Moreno. This was an almost inevitable selection since Mr. Moreno has many of the ingratiating personal qualities that Victor Hugo attributed to Don Cæsar. For the rôle of that old reprobate, King Philip IV, the director chose Wallace Beery, a competent actor whose villainy on the screen is well known to theater-goers. Kathlyn Williams was assigned the part of Queen Isabel. Gareth Hughes, always good in juvenile parts, was chosen for Lazarillo. Adolphe Menjou, a 100% villain, was selected to create Don Salluste. For the part of the Marquis de Rotundo Mr. Brenon selected Edward Kipling; for the Cardinal's Ambassador, Charles A. Stevenson; for Diego, Robert Brower; for Dib he chose Robert Agnew. The part of Don Balthazzar went to a girl, Dawn O'Day.

Meanwhile designers and architects had adapted from the many Spanish prints dug out of the museums and libraries a whole village which was built in the mountains of Southern California. Nowadays carpenters and plasterers and masons get big wages, and the labor costs in building a village are great, even though the village be an uninhabitable one for motion picture purposes. A studio statistician has figured out that these reproductions of old Spanish castles actually cost more than did the original castles in Spain from which the sets were modeled. Labor back in seventeenth century Spain was very cheap. Then you could build a castle in Spain almost as cheaply as you can dream about one now.

An interesting photograph is included in this book which shows, better than any words can describe, the size and beauty of the great old Spanish buildings grouped about the Catholic church. The hundreds of extra people who appear in this big scene are but specks on the picture compared with the huge sets built only to be photographed. In the foreground are seen the tents in which the actors lived while on location far from Los Angeles.

Out on this location most of the scenes for the picture were filmed, for it is essentially an outdoors story. But the elaborate garden fête in which four hundred ballet dancers appear was rehearsed and photographed in the famous Busch gardens in Pasadena. The colorful gypsy encampment was established on the Lasky ranch near Hollywood.

When most of the outdoor scenes had been photographed Director Brenon retired to the huge stages of the Lasky studios in Hollywood where the interior scenes of the picture were photographed. Finally, after many months of activity, the actual camera work had been completed. There remained then the complicated and tremendously important work of cutting, titling and assembling the film for one finished print. Out of about 75,000 feet of film which had been exposed and developed it was possible to use only about 9,000 feet, or nine reels.

Each of the 387 scenes in the photoplay, it must be understood, were photographed several times and sometimes as many as a dozen times to get the best emotional effects properly lighted.

On Hector Turnbull, author of "The Cheat," Miss Negri's previous picture, rested the responsibility of editing the seventy-five reels of film down to nine reels. After several weeks of work he got it down to 8,400 feet.

Then, for the first time, the director saw the net results of his months of work, and he was happy to learn that people with a viewpoint more detached than his considered it good. Some rate it Mr. Brenon's greatest achievement. Almost every one ranks it as Pola Negri's best picture since "Passion" and the finest of her American work.

Maritana lives again, reincarnated in another generation by means of a new toy which Victor Hugo, with all his creative imagination, could not foresee.

GLENDON ALLVINE.

PREFACE.

An entertaining little tale is attached to the springing into life of that charmingly unique character, Don
Cæsar de Bazan.

About 1830, all art in Paris—literary and theatrical—
became involved in the revolution concurrent with the
political one. Dramatic authors claimed rights which
no former playwrights, pets of princes and adulatory
slaves of kings and wealth, had dreamt of.

More terrifying still, these young writers dropped
threadbare subjects ridiculing absurdities of peasant,
trader and retired bankers, and exposed aristocratic
vices and evil passions. Laying outrageous hands on
the royal robes, they dragged the monarchs into stage-
light and showed what "a poor forked radish" is your
Peter, Charles or Louis "the Great."

Victor Hugo, by tearing off masks and cloaks and
dissipating perfumes and vapors, incurred hostility of
rulers and their hangers-on, particularly by his "Ruy
Blas." In this powerful drama, a queen of Spain is
compelled to yield the tribute of admiration to a con-
summate statesman, fervent patriot, astute pleader and
intrepid war-maker, although he was basely born and,
before he donned court suits, wore the footman's liv-
ery.

At once, Hugo had his revenge for the suppression,
since "Ruy," excluded from Paris, triumphantly made

the tour of Europe, being saluted with music in the Land of Song. Italy made him an operatic hero—her crowning triumph.

Before it was brought out, it had won its place. This was at those readings customary at the time. After the friends heard and praised, they forced the managers to sue for it. Such was the enkindled desire that the French Theatre, the chief, clamored for it.

At the first reading of "Ruy Blas," to the actors, the "old sticks" eyed each other in dismay; never could they hope to represent this whirlwind in a doublet, this sirocco under the velvet cap, this virile young spirit who, spurning his lackey's coat as the butterfly rejects the cocoon, assumed the imperial mantle and held his head with peers and senators. Upon which the author, smiling in his sleeve, relieved them of anxiety, and filled them with spite, by saying that he had found the ideal, in "the Great Frederick!"

All laughed, for this actor of the petty theatres, was the unknown—Lemaitre ("the master," prophetic name!), but the appreciative knew him well. He had, like Kean, played every *rôle* from king to harlequin; but poverty was keeping him down; all his courage was needed to hold a grim face before those sultans of the stage who frowned at "M. Hugo's foundling out of the popular side-show." He sat like Marius brooding over ruins, for his failure would be death to his long-nourished ambition.

Readers of "Ruy Blas" remember the plot: in the first act, one is startled and hesitates to admire, though inevitably loving a rakish figure, a Spanish Mercutio, a young and slender Falstaff, care-free, lively, generous, fearless, but honorable to his sword's point.

Don Cæsar de Bazan, for this is that immortal hidalgo, who, stepping out of Lope de Vega, appears again only at the last scene.

Lemaitre, absorbed from the inrush of this devil-may-care, courtly ragamuffin, was thoughtful throughout the rest, and only brightened as Cæsar, the irrepressible, shot up with all his glamour at the last.

It was the modesty of his rank. Afflicted by this gloom, the author said with feeling:

"Do you not approve?" The others had split their gloves. "Is not the part good enough for you? I am grieved, for I thought often of you while writing 'Ruy.'"

"'Ruy Blas?' you thought of giving me, 'Ruy'—the leading part; on in every scene! I—play 'Ruy?' Oh, Victor, my friend, for 'Ruy' I will do anything for its creator!" Then pausing, as when a favorite dish is borne away, although the successor is a daintier still, he longingly said: "But I should have been satisfied to play that captivating Don Cæsar!"

Unhappily for his prospects, the censor said that the Royal House was interlocked with Spain; that the vague queen, enamored of a footman, must be the king's blood-relative. "Ruy Blas" was "strangled in an hour."

Lemaitre was in despair; must he leave town to "star" in the forbidden piece?

Two authors came to his aid. It was when Hugo, by his republicanism, won the hate of both monarchists and imperialists. His works were doubly banned.

The authors were Dumanoir and Dennery. The first once monopolized our stage, but his works were given under the translators' names. Dennery wrote the "Two Orphans;" no pale copyist has kept his name off the bills. Boucicault called him "the foremost of playwrights;" no more can be said.

They talked with Lemaitre thus:

"Hugo is outlawed, but he winks at us making for you'

a three-act drama of his 'Don Cæsar de Bazan.' Thus, he and you will be again the popular idol!"

Eclipsed in the tragedy, Don Cæsar reappeared more vividly than ever. In the original, genius had shot out two or three gleams; here skilled intellect burned steadily, but as brightly.

The longer-lived hero—promoted to eternity, in fact—strode amid the grotesque imagery and lurid amosphere of "Old Madrid," with the fullness of action of "Gil Blas," the rich colors of Velasquez, the variety of Cervantes, and the polished wit of a good-humored, yet caustic, Paul-Louis Courier.

"There is always something great, pleasing or curious in a popular attraction," and Don Cæsar proves himself all three.

To us "the Cid" is nothing, and this Cæsar is "the most famous of Castilians."

In this creation, Hugo paid a debt to humanity in sterling metal, impressed with poetry, genius and originality.   H. L. W.

The venerable "Castle in Spain" had its brief day in California, while Antonio Moreno enacted Don Caesar in "The Spanish Dancer."

DON CÆSAR DE BAZAN.

CHAPTER I.

THE DANCING GIRL.

Everybody knows that the Escurial, royal palace of Spain, is modeled to remind the architectural student of the gridiron on which St. Lawrence was carbonized.

But it is not as widely known that it served as the bed (to many a royal tenant) through sleepless nights and melancholy days.

Perhaps as miserable as any under that golden sorrow, the crown of the monarch of the Indies and still wealthy Spain, was the consort of King Charles the Second.

"Celestial choirs" from the noted convents and chapels, the court buffoon, the merrymakers who had cheered multitudes on the trestles of the itinerant stages, all had failed to cheer the poor, declining queen.

As a last resort, a stage had been erected in the outer yard, facing her suite windows, on which were given entertainments by traveling mountebanks. At night, fireworks from Italy, home of such brief glitter, lit up the gloomy gardens.

But nothing dispelled her tedium.

"In order to distract her," said the master of ceremonies, "we shall be driven distracted."

At last, at their wits' end, they descended to the lowest form of popular recreation, the outcast "antics," jokers and ribalds of the byways.

On the balcony, protected from the sun by awnings trimmed with silk fringe and heavy with bullion tassels and cords, the royal dame, amid her ladies and other attendants, deigned to look down over the fans at the latest company raked together no longer by the master of the revels, but the lieutenant-royal of police.

This time, Don José de Santarem, the "civil" inquisitor, as he was playfully entitled, smiled complacently as his "troupe" made their profound bows on the platform. The queen had actually smiled at the preposterous attire and ell-wide grimaces of the merry Andrew.

The queen's saddening features were much improved by this passing alleviation of her growing dullness. She was never beautiful, but before she became thin under the Spanish sun, she had been comely and prepossessing. Only one Spanish trait was hers, the immoderate munching of chocolate, which began to spoil her teeth.

In laughing at the jester, she forgot her habit of keeping her lips closed to hide her teeth.

"You have done it," whispered the royal physician to the chief of royal police, half-enviously. "This is as well as can be! If this band of marauders and thieves have more such farces in their quiver, faith! your excellency will turn her mourning into blitheness, and make the ailment I treated her for so vainly, into a schoolgirl's malady!"

"It will do, doctor!" replied Don José. "These Egyptian clowns are death to all rigorists and precisians! Ah, if you who speak to the crowned ones in a corner, could but tell what worm bit the fruit—what weight has pulled our lady down——"

"Hum! you will not believe what all your spies must

have failed to report, since you have an empty budget! It is a rare complaint among royal ladies, espoused in the cradle to the future mate: she adores her husband!"

"It is a miracle!" sneered the criminal-lieutenant.

"When he is by, she cannot take her eyes off him!"

"That has been noted!"

"If he smiles upon her, she can be gay all the day!"

"So he has ceased to smile? He has flown off the hinges?"

"This palace game of *ombre* ought to be known to your lordship," returned Dr. Rhubarba. "I can only say that I felicitate you, for your gypsy tomfools have worked more heal than my doses of Saracen's wound-wort——"

"Yes, goldenrod does not cure the heartache!"

All eyes were fixed upon the man who had caused the drooping lady to cheer up.

Don José had not a friend among them. When he first presented himself at court, he was lofty and distant, having come of the Santarem stock which had coined money while other nobles fought in the protracted wars of the empire. Now, proud men please neither princes nor pages. At the outset, placed among the mere "cloak forms," soon it was observed that he rose by little without ever being put down a step.

"He has the slow pace by which steeps are climbed," said the old courtiers.

Then it was perceived that his red hair was darkened by using the lead comb and that his yellow complexion assumed plumpness and color, as he furnished his table more lavishly and entertained.

He who had been a "funeral mute" in the olden apparel of the ascetic Charles V., black, dulled lace, few jewels, short feathers, unstretched collars, began to follow the latest French fashions.

The inconspicuous manikin became a popinjay.

Still, on being raised to the degree of the king's police lieutenant, he relapsed into the somber costume becoming the dread office.   But still he paraded his gold chain of office, his jeweled badges of orders, his incrusted swordhilt of some knightly companionship, and his rings—signet and ornamental.

Delighted inwardly at his success, he smiled in his short, brown beard, and muttered.

"Now, Momus has had his triumph—let us see how music and dancing will move the forlorn woman!"

On the stage, at the back of which sat the musicians and comrades of the performers, to encourage them, in the Eastern mode, by throwing out praise in their own language, the music of "pig's-head" keyed-instruments, lutes, cymbals and African-stringed drums, abruptly changed from the lively strains.   To the decorous, measured notes of a slow march, in walked, rather than danced, the "stars" of the wandering company.

Men and women, all young, all good-looking in their way, serpentine in grace, showing teeth too sharp and white, eyes too black and flashing, feet and hands too effeminate, the gypsies were so choice that they seemed living models of the Bacchus and Antinoüs which the ancients liked to cast in golden bronze.

So beautiful and fascinating were they that courtiers crossed themselves and some uttered "Get thee back, Satan!"

The queen, her mood changing with the music, became enrapt.   She leaned her fan on the balustrade, covered with a magnificent brocade, and her chin on her jeweled fan-handle.   She fixed her eyes on the new set of performers.

They sang in chorus one of the Arabian poem-fables

lingering in Spain after the Moors were driven out. This was to prepare for the dance to follow.

Discreetly the other actors withdrew to the sides of the stage, where they squatted down and kept reciting the melodious verses.

The two dancers were superb.

The male, wearing a half-mask of black felt, which showed up his floured face and his mustache smothered with the farina, presented a statuelike effect. His dress was tawdry and gaudy, but worn with the freedom and even the display of a nobleman at a coronation.

He bore himself with perfect fearlessness, as if to be under royal eyes were an everyday experience.

He was taller than the gypsies, better built at the shoulders, and his hands and feet were in proportion to his height. He wore an old long sword, flapping on his calves, but he must have been more used to its carriage than even to the lute, with which he tinkled the time to their step, for it did not once embarrass him.

But with all his upright and pliant form, his alacrity and strict time-keeping, he served but as a foil to his partner.

She was already famed, for a cry of "Maritana!" had hailed her appearance on the boards from the crowd of palace servants and populace allowed to congregate in the yard before the platform.

Maritana was not swarthy, but it was difficult to judge her natural complexion. Although she was not overlaid with flour, as in her companion's case, she was daubed with rouge, her lips were made thick, and the upper one almost painted up to her nose, while immense earrings and a jeweled comb thrust through her dull hair added a barbaric accent, which marred her natural beauty.

Nevertheless, this harmonized with the surrounding Zingari, and assorted also with her wanton dance.

Without understanding the story chanted, one might guess that the two were depicting in dumb show the chase of a gazelle by a lion on the plain. There were bounds and flights, escapes and captures, which kept the spectator in turmoil.

With excellent art, just when the fugitive, exhausted by such desperate efforts to avoid her fate, sank on one knee at the side, and the captor's arms enwreathed her head, which had dislodged the abundant tresses from the coils and the comb, she became human. She lifted her glorious blue eyes, enlarged by the fever of action, and as if disdaining to sue to this human lion, she appealed to some divinity—one which knew what love was and would intervene on her behalf.

Her ruddy lips opened and there was exhibited such a burst of purity, crystalline intonation and fervency of feeling that her own companions seemed spellbound.

The queen was no mean artiste in music. Her teacher was a professor from the Veronese Academy of Music, and she reveled in emotional music.

It was not astonishing, therefore, that all heard her sigh with satisfaction. She rose without the aid of her maids, and, leaning over the gilded and cushioned rail, and detaching a heavy bracelet from her arm, let it drop with a vehement motion.

At this golden bait, all the wanderers evinced their rapacity. A hundred hands were held up. But the male dancer, as he had displayed agility in his steps, was to be in the second place to no man now. Like lightning, he had unsheathed his long sword, and, leaping up at the same time, he thrust the blade so dexterously at the gleaming, falling object that it entered the circle and it glided down to his wrist.

A cheer greeted this clever rapier trick. Almost all the men were judges of sword-handling.

His bound had carried him to the stage edge, but, poising himself as he alighted in an elegant pose, he whirled round, bowing at the time to the donor, and, reversing his blade so that the golden ring ran down, he, as deftly as in catching it, let it slip off upon the hand of his partner, just as a hoop is caught in the game of "grace."

Maritana, all blushes through her rouge, her eyes like unquenchable stars, made an elaborate courtesy to the benefactress, and was about to make a triumphant exit when a sign from the queen stopped her short.

Almost instantly a chamberlain, with a smiling mien, went over to the stage, and sweetly said:

"By favor of the queen, you are to have an audience of her majesty!"

Her redness fading, her feet no longer nimble, the dancing girl, with slower and slower step, followed the official as he conducted her within doors.

All the spectators, gentle and simple, held their breath and forebore comment even in whispers.

"Oh, my brothers by adoption," said the gypsy's partner to the men, in trepidation, "fear not! Maritana's honey in the mouth will save her back from the lash! She is born to stand in the smile of Heaven!"

Don José, however proud, had deliberately thrown himself in the way.

"It is a blessed morning, Maritana!" said he, meaningly.

She stared at him, her sight beginning to clear as she believed that she was not to meet the foil after the true metal; she was too bewildered to recognize the speaker or distinguish him, but she blurted out:

"As many to you, my lord!"

Then her eyes became downcast.

The queen had faced around on the balcony as she was

brought. She had enframed herself in the long window. She looked imposing in her robe, her coronetlike comb and her jewels. The immense Hall of Battles, through which the poor dancer was led, was thronged with great lords and great ladies. Not one but wore a historic name and historic gems.

Accustomed to the open air, the perfume almost made the gypsy swoon. But luckily, her weakness was ascribed to timidity and became a pariah's approach to a monarch.

"Now, Heaven help me!" murmured she, bowing low.

The queen admired this humility and bashfulness in one whom at a distance she had presumed to be of the usual brazen herd.

Looking at her so near and with womanly eyes, she perceived what exquisite beauty was under this paltry, gaudy mask; she saw the down of virgin modesty under the red paint; she saw in those eyes trained to look boldly into the tormentor's visage the shrinking of the virtuous and proud, though reduced out of their sphere.

"Your name, child?" said she, softening her voice.

"Maritana."

"But the rest?"

"There is no rest to us, madam! simply Maritana."

"Do you belong to Spain—to Madrid?"

"The Gitana belongs nowhere—she is a creature not of the earth, but of the air!"

"It is true that you dance as though you were fed upon it! and you sing like the bird from the heavens, which reposes never on the sordid ground, but sleeps poised in midair!"

"I am likely to take my last repose there!" returned Maritana, wittingly, but without sarcasm, as if her fate was ruled from birth.

"You! Oh, fie! Shame to the hand which would

At the Busch Gardens in Pasadena. Four hundred ballet dancers and others were there. The musicians not not only played for the dancing but also for Pola Negri and Tony Moreno in "The Spanish Dancer" scenes.

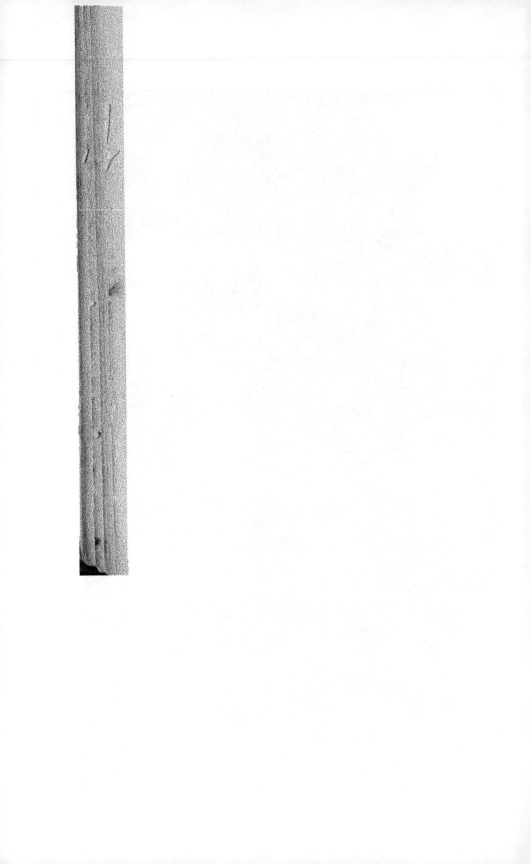

lead you to that halter. Look! here is a rope alone fitted for your neck."

Slowly unwinding from her own shoulders one of those prodigious ropes of pearls which were in the treasuries of Spain and Portugal at that period, she gravely put it upon the neck of her *protégée*, who bent low at the priceless present, altogether eclipsing the bracelet.

"Oh, your majesty!" she faltered.

Her real color came and made the rouge pale.

"Look!" cried the queen to her court painter, "is not this scene counterpart of that when the navigator Columbus returned from the Indies and presented the Indian princess to the court of Queen Isabel? But that this goodly heathen has blue eyes, and I do not believe her hair is as ebonlike as it seems, she would resemble the dusky belle-savage!"

Maritana, as if the pearls weighed her down, suffered a hundred pangs in feeling that the persons viewed her as a pagan.

"Hear ye, all!" cried her patroness. "my lords of the State and the Church! I adopt this waif and will strive to make her enter the pale. Maritana, remember that the Queen of Spain takes you under her personal care, and that it will fare ill with him who undertakes to harm you or prevent your elevation to the place of a Christian dame! I have spoken! Let those who love me, love this poor errant child, and assist her stumbling feet on the road to salvation!"

There was a murmur of approval on the men's part, and they solemnly lifted their dagger hilts and took the royal vow. Maritana had enchanted them. Their dames were not so enthusiastic.

"Am I, then——" began the gypsy, conjecturing that she was a kind of state prisoner—a queen's ape.

"To remain actually under my hand? It might be better so, but no; I would not so soon break the fetters that may bind you to those who have at least brought you to this age without defacing your loveliness!"

It was the popular belief that the Egyptians disfigured their captives, while being as fond to their own offspring as any parents. It might be presumed that Maritana, therefore was a true Bohemian. Her reply as she regained courage would emphasize that belief.

"Please, your majesty, while grateful for such right-royal bounty to the fullness of my heart, I beg respectfully to desire not to be sundered wholly from those with whom I have always dwelt. I am not a house-dweller. Like the swallow I should die if not allowed to be ever on the wing. But if it is to please your kind and charitable majesty, why, let me die in your gilded cage. I live but to die for your majesty."

"Prettily capped—this answer delights me better than your clutching at the offer. Go your way, child, though among the briars. It is a narrow and devious way, no doubt, but it may lead sooner to happiness than the broad walks and the wide doorways of the palace. Go, yes; but, Maritana, remember the queen is your godmother if you renounce the fellowship of the beguiler and the slavery of the sinners. I would esteem it the brightest page in my life if I might have it accredited to me that I saved your soul from the Evil One, and your person, so charming, from association with these fauns and dryads of the brake."

It was a prudent speech, for the churchmen, who had begun to look black at the gypsy, were glad to have this sop thrown them. The Archbishop of Madrid spoke to his almoner, and his voice was audible on purpose.

"Look after this spark, which must be plucked from those brands, fit only for the burning," said he.

"My first gentleman-in-waiting," pursued the royal

speaker, "accompany the girl to her friends. No more
singing, no more dancing, for lucre. They may sing if
they like, but it is to be gratuitous, and out of fullness
over the entertainment with which I express my grateful-
ness at their having given me pleasure this red-letter day.
A feast to the Egyptians!"

Maritana retired with this additional kindness to show.

"By all that is holy," thought Don José, "this is mix-
ing the one-hundred elect with the thousand excepted.
This is something to give my time to."

At his slight beckoning, a clerk in the throng approached him stealthily and listened to him without having the aspect of doing so.

"Look to that gypsy!" said the lord. "Keep her in
sight, for she has enchanted the brooding queen. You
must not let her quit the kingdom, or in my turn I will
have you followed and chastised, though you sail round
Cape Aiguillas."

"I marked the whole, my good lord! As sure as that
I am the last scion of the once noble and high-placed
Nigueraelas, I will watch well. But she will not flee!"

"No?"

"A gypsy will stay and fawn while there are still
crumbs of the cake once given. That girl will be coming back to take singing lessons of the queen's instruc-
tors in the harmonies and the orbo!"

"Let me clasp hands with him, then! for I want that
castaway to learn a song by which I may fill my pouch!"

It was well that he had not attempted to pursue the
quest in person, for while the gypsies and their friends
were being feasted in the yard, an usher warily came up
to the lieutenant-criminal, whom few accosted openly,
and said, with deference:

"My Lord of Santarem, the queen would see you in
the orangery at sunset this evening."

It was a private audience, such as grandees craved and hidalgoes danced attendance for.

"Ho, ho!" chuckled Don José. "I may yet live in one of Madrid's ten or twelve palaces! Sparks issue from the clash of adamant and steel; so may some particles of value strike off by the meeting of misery with mightiness."

He bowed assent to the messenger, and betrayed by his high step that he thought the first ministership might not be far out of reach.

CHAPTER II.

THE QUEEN'S CONFIDANT.

Four lines of orange trees, borne in gigantic troughs, formed the Orangery of the Escurial. The bells of the *Capella Mayor* and of the Petty Chapel were tinkling for vespers while the police minister held his tryst. He did not feel impatience, for queens cannot keep appointments like shopkeepers' apprentices, their hours being at business or pleasure, as the kind of queen may be.

"What!" cried he at last, as the long vista was obscured by a dark, shapeless figure. "Is it off? A murrain on it—I have not so many opportunities to advance myself to my goal as to lose this one with calmness! Ah, yes, it is the royal confessor! Good-even, Father Consalvo!"

"Good-evening, my lord! What a sacrilege!"

"What, my smoking an Indian *cigarro* under the royal fruit?"

"No, no! that rout, that pagan rabble out there carousing under the windows of the Major Chapel! One can scarce hear the holy canticles amid those heathen jingles from the hoarse throats of sinners."

"Oh, the gypsies revelling at the queen's expense. What says the king about this adoption of one of that desperate spawn?"

"The king? Your lordship ought to know that the king never has a moment to listen to any complaint."

"I am aware of that—poor monarch! as much to be pitied as a mortal like ourselves, between French intrigue and German pertinacity! 'Fore Heaven! it is impudent to pester a king in his mid-life to name his successor! They say—his grooms in waiting—that he sleeps, when he does sleep, with one hand under the bolster!"

"To keep it on his crown, there?"

"You are a wag, father!"

"I never was in more earnest when I say that it is the queen who sleeps with her hand under her pillow, but it ought to be with the key of the secret postern under it!"

"Ho, ho! is she going to lend it to her new caprice, this wanderer, who is to be finished in music and made the female David to our Saul?"

"That is the knot!"

"What, the gypsy!"

"Or the stiletto to loosen the knot!"

"What knot?"

"The charm tying up our sovereign. The buzzing goes that he is absorbed in some single passion! and the Lord deliver the realm from a ruler with but one thought!"

"My amen to that! What is the thought, my reverend?"

The old priest let his cowl fall a little. He smoothed his smooth chin in its three folds and answered, with a merry twinkle of his small gray eyes:

"One that he does not share with his confessor!"

"Ask your brother, the queen's confessor, then! He will withhold nothing from you—you are *Nicolaites* in such matters—you hold everything in common."

"But this is not a common thought."

"Strange that it is not known to—to the general!"

The priest looked hard at the noble, and, accepting its true meaning, replied gravely:

"That is the rub; the General of the Inquisition has

made inquiries and learned nothing. The king's excursions are secret as the voyages of the Venetians!"

"Carlos has become silent?"

"No, the same garrulous one, but great speech goes with a little conscience!"

"Save us! Is it seeking the stone to turn all to gold?"

"Spain has the gold! The crumbling palace needs stones to repair it more than ingots."

"Would he be too fond of hunting? Does he contemplate making Andalusia a hunting forest? Would he revive hawking and waste level Teruel into one plain?"

"He hunts and he hawks, but not game and bird of our known hide and feather! Save us!"

"I dare not guess! He was 'the Wild Prince' in his youth, and what youth took on, age is used to! You think that when he slips out of the gateway in the south wall, he goes to meet——"

"Certainly none comes to meet him, for we have watched!"

"Oh, if your lookouts, who are, I own, more valuable than mine, since mine work for filthy coin and yours for the heavenly pay—if your lookouts descry nothing, mine——"

"Oh, if it be a worldly lure, your men will the sooner trace him to the decoy!"

"The decoy? No, Carlos is no follower of that *ignis fatuus*, woman! I should have perceived that long since! Depend upon it, he confers with some philosopher who has the draught which renews life, which foretells how a dynasty ends, which gives the glib tongue to deceive a French envoy, and the strong fist to impress the doughty German!"

"My lord," said the other, seriously, "we have concluded that the man who unravels this tangled skein may

have all our votes in case he aspires to be the prime man
of the kingdom."

Silently the noble's eyes expressed his content. He
had reached the point when, himself overtasked, the
friendly push would lift him where he could grasp the
parapet and draw himself erect upon it.

"My good father," said he, still breathlessly, "I understand you. The motto is: 'Help you, and Heaven's
ministers will help me!' "

"You will win at the Primero, sir!"

"Ah, if it were chess, with the bishops supporting the
queen——"

"What is your last word?"

"That I leap at the offer—I am nothing without your
approval, holy father."

"So instruct your lime-hounds."

The man drew up his cowl and glided in his sandals
noiselessly away under the arches which made the palace
resemble a cloister.

Don José resumed his vigils, pacing the long rows
steadily, while musing, and humming an old Moorish
song of love and battle.

Presently two workmen, gardener's assistants, emerged
from a toolhouse in an angle, and, without more than
glancing at the amateur sentry, proceeded to trim the
trees.

Then, convinced that the lone gentleman was rather
in favor of their movements than opposed, they ran
along out of its cover a singular, but useful, engine.

Novel to him, he had the curiosity to go in that direction and observe their proceedings.

This engine was such as are used in lofty buildings to
enable a painter or cleaner at ease to get at the heights.
A platform, surrounded by a small rail, to prevent one's

The Spanish Dancer.

A Paramount Picture.

being shaken over the edge, was worked upward by a screw turned by a cogwheel and crank.

"What is that Jacob's ladder for, my friends?" inquired Don José, disturbed by the occupancy of this trysting ground. "Do you expect thus to reach a footing in paradise?"

One of the men, with the gravity of common folk, responded, as he bowed with his cap off:

"Your lordship, while many a gallant has mounted among the angels, as he accounted them, by this ladder, it is used by us daily to let the man, thus elevated above his fellows, trim and prune the trees without injuring the least of the twigs or the fruits, which are counted. If your lordship will but be patient, we should not be surprised if his desire to add to his lore were amply gratified."

The platform at the surface of this engine, controlled by the men at the winches, steadily rose until it reached the level of the second story.

"How ingenious!" cried Don José; "the most dainty page could thus hand a billet to the lady of his master's love!"

"Or the maid of the beauty could descend to earth to bless the gallant with the reply!" returned the spokesman of the pair. "But the best is yet to come. See!"

A tall window opened like a door of two folds, at the level of the platform, and a woman threw inside the surrounding guard a mantle, which carpeted the boards. Almost immediately, as if this means of rising and falling had been employed more than once before, a lady, for her richnes of cloak with its furred hood denoted that much, stepped out of the window upon the stage. Her attendant had raised the rail on that side in its socket and now replaced it.

"Lower!" cried the maid, but in a repressed tone.

With the same care and mechanical regularity with

which they had wound up the platform, the two men reversed the winding beam, and the human load was safely brought to the ground. Don José stepped forward and offered his arm to help the lady step down upon the gravel of the path.

The men, convinced that their work was momentarily finished, said not a word. They retired into the tool-house, where something like a hoe handle, but possibly a musketoon barrel, indicated that they were watching the gardens—for moles!

"Your majesty does me much honor," cried the police lieutenant, who had time to fortify himself for this interview during the operation.

"Why are you apprehensive?—alack! You need not fear that the king will surprise us! He is not here at this hour. It is that of his disappearances!"

"Well, your grace, if you do not know—who can call our liege to account for his hours' disposal?"

"Is it my place, sir?"

"No, not if, as I doubt, he but goes to counteract some cabal, some imbroglio in which his personal inspection is indispensable."

"I did not believe him so adventuresome!" she lightly scoffed.

"If he personally thwarts a plot, what glory and example to do-nothing rulers!"

"The only plots in hatching are to replace him with a French prince or an Austrian archduke! Never, my lord, will he believe a Spaniard will hold out his hand to a foreigner, unless the national knife be in it!"

"Well, the fascination of gambling——"

"You jest! a king need gamble only at his own tables; there, he may rely on always winning! No, he is playing, I think, a game where the king of hearts is to be warped from his liege!"

"Oh'o!" coughed Don José, almost speaking his gladness.

"What do you say?" said she.

"That the idea, saving your respect, is ridiculous! though I lose my portfolio for my frankness!"

"I hear——"

"Backstairs gossip—court-alcove tattle!"

"I have other advices, not beneath my notice and quite credible as well as creditable."

"But still there is no court beauty so disloyal, so inimical to her sex, to wifehood, to ordinary rules of amity, as to—oh, this treachery would be infamously ungrateful to your majesty."

"What the inquisitor does not spy, and what you are blind to, my informants——"

"From the moment your majesty has a police of her own——"

"Your resignation is hypocrisy! I do not believe you to be an obstructor. But without warning to me, you allow my king to be absent for hours from the palace without his reasons and whereabouts being discovered."

"To be sure, if no lady of the land would dare to rival your majesty, there may be one embodiment of disrespect, who, failing to vie with the incomparable by fair means, employs foul ones."

"Certainly, there are black arts as well as black hearts to use them!"

"Precisely; love-potions, powders, talismans—my police seize them by the basketful every month! This will go on as long as my petition is not heeded, that the quarter where lodge all the practicians of evil devices, witches, sorcerers, Egyptians——"

"You are coming to the fire!"

"Ho! a gypsy——"

"Well, is it not written in the annals that one of your kings was entangled with a gypsy?"

"Let me see; Don Pedro, the Cruel, was in love with Maria Padilha, one of that branded race——"

"In love? A king love a rejected one!"

"I should say, infatuated! When one is captivated by an inferior, love is not in the chapter; it is infatuation!"

"Yes, the Church cannot deal with love, which is a blessed emotion—but infatuation is to be proceeded against by bell, book and candle!"

"But, my gracious lady, if the gypsies——"

"If the gypsies bewitch my lord, why should I applaud their stupid gambols and speak encouragingly of that daughter of Herodias who dances for my heart! It is because the queen wishes to learn what your police and the spies of the Holy Tribunal fail to gather. And at the fountain-head, likewise. If I stoop to making a low creature like that gitana a pet, a plaything, a puppet, a magician's speaking-head to say 'my queen!' at a pinch, it is because I expect her to betray what goes on at midnight in that camp of pests and miscreants which you, indeed, ought to be let stamp out."

Don José, in the thickening darkness, felt that his blazing eyes revealed his sudden admiration for the woman whom he had thought made of wax, but who through jealousy had become flesh and blood.

"Admirable!" said he. "Well, I grant that my emissaries would bring me a dozen of these skipjacks who would own to everything, snatch purse and betake themselves to their native Africa, but none would be the one at whom the king has deigned to throw the handkerchief."

"I would it were for her to be strangled with!" said the vindictive woman.

"But since such a siren would not boast of it to us

outside of her diabolical tribe, how single out the true
offender? All are alluring, all good-looking in 'their'
alien mode, all daughters of the father of lies and mother
of blandishments!"

"What the inquisitor and your subordinates fall short
of, I require of you."

"It is not for me to shrink from the signal and ap-
preciated task, great lady," said Don José, shuffling,
"but, as it may offend the king to whom I owe my
post——"

"A hangman's post! what better? Suppose we find
you a higher and ennobling one! What do you say
to the premier's?"

The plotter pretended a surprise not felt, considering
that he had already the formidable support of the priest-
hood promised him. Recovering hastily, he joyously
replied:

"As that would give me power to be usefully employed in your majesty's service, I should rejoice and
kiss the hand which gave me the place."

"Then, while I try to prevail over this girl, you, on
your part, must penetrate to the heart of that den of
thieves, and witches' cave, and seek out the enticing
evil!"

"I venture in the ghetto?"

"You are not fit for the head of the police unless
you have dared to wade in that crime and guilt!"

"Oh, I have obeyed my duty," replied Don José,
afraid that he had been spied by the secret agents of this
woman who might, indeed, have organized a police superior to his—that is, the king's.

"Oh, I have had your daring and intrepidity reported
to me! You have not hesitated to insinuate yourself
where none but those of the league of dishonesty dared

to go.   Run the gantlet for me this time; a good errand
if ever a chief of police was set to one."

"To gratify a queen, a lady!" said he, bowing. "I
would do anything."

"If it is through your guidance that the king is led
back to his place, his last step will be over the portfolio
of the prime minister—you understand!"

"I am your majesty's devoted servant," said he.
"May my rise be as artistically successful," added he,
watching the lady mount the platform, and the men,
who had come out of their concealment, repeat the
operation of sending up the stage to the palace windows.

The queen entered her rooms.

When alone, she went into the praying-closet, but
instead of praying, she muttered:

"I do not wholly trust that ambitious spirit. I am
going to manage my own police, and chief among them
will be this gypsy girl, who, unless I much underrate her
intelligence, knows what goes on in the Jewry among
these pernicious outcasts."

She looked at a mirror set in the cover of her missal,
irreverent concession to mortality! and continued to herself:

"Oh, to be face to face with this rival!   It is the lowly,
that too often debase the exalted to their dusty level!"

CHAPTER III.

SERPENT AND DOVE.

As Madrid was the center of Spain, so is its Grand Plaza the heart, full of lifeblood and fire, of Madrid.

This was an epitome of the whole city.

In the cathedral, the church; in the grand mansions, the nobility; in the shops and stores, the merchants and bankers; in the hovels of the back streets and winding alleys, the lowest orders.

Between a fountain, due to the Saracens or perhaps the Romans, and a drinking-den, two contrasts of provisions allowing the toper and the temperate to suit their tastes, opened the dirty maw of the ghetto, the sink into which was poured at dusk all the cripples, the ailing, the contaminating, the denounced, the outlaws, the espewed and the revengeful of humanity.

It was toward evening; beggars and musicians, bearers of Oriental and African musical instruments, hideous in tune and exasperating when out of tune, limped home to their burrows. But as was the order among these brothers of the lute and "loot," all took a halt before the wine-house.

Here hobnobbed the still honest, ill-paid soldier, the thief whose pence was the residue of the gains the receiver made of his hard-got spoil, the wreck and the youth just embarked on the perilous voyage.

While the lime-frothed wine flowed, and the children groped in the gutter for crusts and half-gnawed bones, Maritana, returning from her day's performances, darted upon the old stone block guarding the entrance of the court from the coach wheels, and began to sing, while the varied instruments accompanied her as well as the voices of the chorus.

Those who had witnessed her vocalism at the palace would have comprehended that a great artist is inspired by the company. What there was chaste and soaring in her verse under the royal eyes, was free and tantalizing with her cronies around.

> "*Pahli* (brothers), tread a merry measure!
> We're the boys who furnish pleasure
>   Cheaper than what tapsters bring!
> But for us there'd be no laughter—
> Maybe there comes none hereafter—
>   So be jolly; let Care swing!"

"*Viva los Egipchios!*" said the young man who had been Maritana's partner at the palace dance, and who, taking off his tattered sombrero, went the rounds to collect of the vagrants as they had collected of the burghers.

"Are you going indoors so early, Maritana of my heart?" said this volunteer attendant, pouring the coins of all sorts into her kerchief, which she took off and tied it up as in a bag.

"No, I am going to the bridge to catch a breath of fresher air. It is like the plague in the passages to-night. I am depressed as if a calamity overhung us."

"Can I still be your cavalier?"

"No, I would rather be alone." She paused at a stand where a harridan, draped in second-hand clothes, and wearing a gaudy Indian scarf over her gray head, was selling black beans cooked in oil. She grasped a handful, hot though they were, and laughing in the hag's face at the idea of payment, bounded off.

"Ah, they are fresh, Maritana," reproached the woman, "and what is two coppers to you who amass fortunes?"

"Pay her Cæsario!" cried the girl at a distance, to her

cavalier, and she disappeared in the crowd on the plaza, mixed, of every degree.

"Pay her! It is all very well to say pay, but——" the man went playfully through the mockery of running his pockets through. "Why, she has taken the collection with her."

"Not to throw it into the Manzanares, mark you," said a gypsy.

"A pound of pence would make our river overflow its banks," retorted the ragged knight, repeating his forlorn search.

The toothless beldame looked up and mumbled with a grin:

"Beseeching the liberty, my lord, let this go over to your account. Lord ha' mercy on the downfallen. I knew your father's house when the butler courted me. Never shall it be said that the Count of Garofa, who has the born right to wear his hat before the king, should want to fill that hat with fried beans, and Dame Disconsolada should require cash for it."

"Oh, you, too, know me! Why, I might as well have my title branded on my shoulder, like most of you carry the town-mark! But you are mistaken, pretty dame. We have acquaintances at court, now, in the kitchen, and we have money in some of our pockets. Tomaso!"

He called out to a young gypsy of elegant manners who passed on a horse which, halt and fagged, would on the morrow sell as a magnificent Arab courser at the horse mart, thanks to the gypsy jockeying.

"Tomaso, pay Dame Disconsolada ten crowns for me! Against my steward next sending my rents to town."

All laughed at the rider as he stopped, and, drawing some silver out of a satchel, tossed the pieces upon the pile of uncooked beans before the frying-pan.

"T-ten crowns!" repeated the old woman, unable to

believe her senses, for she supplemented that of sight
by feeling without being convinced.

"Why, so! Because you trusted the lady and the
broken-down gentleman? Remember, Tomaso, at my
next haul!"

"Your honor is too good," replied the horseman, riding off negligently.

"I wish," said this associate of the riff-raff, whom the
bean-fryer had hailed as the Count of Garofa, one of the
oldest peers of the United Kingdoms, "I wish the lass
had not carried off the bag. I fear that she may fall the
prey to highwaymen."

This was the cream of jokes. Rob a gypsy in the
sight of her tribe and all their allies! And dark coming
on, by the same token!

And Maritana, their idol! If a hair of her head were
brushed the wrong way, why all Madrid had not the garrison to prevent the outcasts wreaking vengeance.

"I suppose I had better go look after her."

"Go and look after her, brother," said a dilapidated
blackamoor, who was "Duke of Egypt;" that is, king of
the pariahs for the season. "Though you have not yet
jumped over the beggar's staff with her and drawn the
straws out of the beggar's wallet to learn from futurity
how many years you should live together, you are, Don
Cæsar, of my bosom, brother of the girl and ours. Go in
peace!"

But as Don Cæsar de Bazan, Count of Garofa y Bel-
orda, for he had not usurped the proud titles, started on
his chivalrous errand, he was startled to see the girl hurriedly returning.

Her face had turned pale, her steps were unsteady, so
that she almost tripped in the wretched hollows, and her
hands twitched with terror. Out of them she designedly

poured the beans, at which she had been pecking like a pigeon, when she quitted the alley mouth.

"What the devil is pursuing her, that she throws the black beans behind her to stall off the pursuit!" cried Don Cæsar, long enough familiar with these birds of the night to know this superstitious counter-charm. "Why, there is a fellow, in a cloak worth snatching, following her as the fish follows the bait! And, zoons! another cloak in the recess of the goldsmith's a-watching both with eyes like coals."

He carried a hand round to his long sword hilt, and, without drawing it, proceeded to intervene between the dancing-girl and this too fervent admirer.

But, abruptly changing her intention, the girl not only ceased to retreat, but, disengaging a tambourine hung by a ribbon at her girdle of gilt metal, in proof of her being an outlaw, she faced the pursuer with this extended as a sexton holds out the alms box.

Her defender stopped, but retained hold of his rapier.

The second cloaked stranger remained in his concealment, and watched with the burning eyes the gypsy's colleague had remarked.

"I had forgot," said the dancer, to herself. "I must make up a great sum to enable me to follow the instruction which the queen's singing-master assures me is necessary to fit me for a rise out of this hateful mire." Then retracing a few steps, so that the follower had to stop not to run up against her, she said, sweetly, overcoming her scruples:

"If you please, though you did not come in time to hear the ballad—maravedi?"

"A maravedi, forsooth!" said the gentleman; for he was one, by the richness of his habiliments under the cloak which had in itself betrayed his degree to the experienced Don Cæsar. "I scorn to pay such melody with copper!"

His scornful gesture was mistaken by the dancer, who murmured disappointedly:

"Ah, am I losing the charm of gleaning coin from purses?"

But as the stranger, perceiving the mob at the ghetto entrance very forbidding, rapidly turned to flee, she heard a heavy piece fall and rebound on the Basque drum, and she exclaimed:

"Gold! A piece of two pistoles—seventeen shillings! Oh, I cannot tell how many silver crowns, without the abacus! I can buy a new psaltery with this! And I was afeard to wait for that noble, generous caballero, because he looked at me so hard and ardently."

The spy in the doorway watched after the donor with a startled mien.

"By the hope of my life, that is Don Carlos! The royal adventurer steers his bark into rocky seas. This is his weak side, his foible, is it! He has fallen in love with this waif, this bit of tinsel afloat on the kennel pool! And do I censure him? Not I, for faith!—it is no hard confession—I am enamored with her up to the eyes myself!"

"If this police spirit in the goldsmith's archway stared at me as he did at that liberal virtuoso," observed Don Cæsar, fidgeting with his sword handle, "I should feel inclined to spit him to that doorway, which is of good ironwood out of Brazil; but methinks this fleeing one is of importance. I must learn how he bestows himself."

But the chase was not so easily carried out as projected.

Hardly had he put this plan into execution than his way was impeded by the purest of accidents or the best arranged of obstacles. First, a passenger parting with a friend, with a prodigious bow, backed into him; and then two mulatto women, carrying a huge buck-basket loaded with linen, forced him into a wide detour; and, finally, three soldiers of the Foreign Guards, linked arm in arm, and swaggering over the space, brought him to a standstill, or he would have had a triple quarrel on his hands.

He was forced to desist and see, at a distance, the ostentatious rewarder of vocalism disappear in a horse-litter waiting at a corner under an illuminated shrine.

"If it is one of the four sword-bearing saints!" ejaculated the baffled defender of the gitana, then may St. George, Michael, Peter, or Abdiel—I am forgetting my beads among these infidels! and I a *vidame*, champion of an abbey, as an inheritance! may these saints bring me to meet that rogue again! We shall see if his *bilbo* is as long as his infernal purse, which has made Maritana's eyes start out of her head! She is beauteous—she is witty, and she—but she is covetous! I begin to believe she is a born gypsy, and not a stolen Christian babe!"

Hiding this conclusion from its object, he returned to her side. She gave him a handful of small pieces, saying:

"Pay for the beans, and distribute the rest with the comrades! This is my birthday!"

"The deuce it is!"

"Did you mark the giver of that doubloon?"

"I did not pay any heed! Just a gallant who had won a gold-washed groat at a gambling-house!"

"Washed? As well say he was no genuine gentleman!" and she gave a little scream of fright in handling the denounced coin.

"Oh, if he had been a courtier, I should have recognized him!" said the downfallen count, earnestly.

"Not a nobleman—not a good doubloon!" muttered

Maritana, sadly. Suddenly shaking off her moodiness, she exclaimed, joyously, or at least relieved:

"Here is a goldsmith! We shall learn in a trice whether this is sham and, consequently, the giver another counterfeit of his betters."

Don Cæsar paused, but, unfortunately, he heard a loud whoop of intense enjoyment.

"The rogues—they have had a heaping harvest! They have had the host of the Water-porters' Arms broach a fresh barrel of that goodish Miravel wine, as strong as its castle!"

He considered that his partner was following and hastened to join the revellers.

Maritana proceeded up into the deep overhang of the goldsmith's, which was the fair title for a shop where valuables were left for security, the safekeeper kindly providing for the owner's immediate wants by a small loan out of all proportion to the value.

But no sooner had she entered this kind of trap, when she was stopped by the man in a cloak, who, letting it drop aside, showed that he was splendidly clad in bright colors and rare cloth; a gold chain gleamed, and his sword had a magnificent handle. The feather in his conical hat was also of price.

"A gold coin!" cried he, as if he had not seen how it had been thrust upon her. "Let me appraise it."

"No, I——"

"Pooh! you can trust me more than that! a trifle to what your musical gifts earn you—and what the honorable patroness whose assistance you stupidly reject will shower in a hundredfold! But, to prove that I am above robbing you, take this!" he said, giving her a heavy gold piece.

"It is the same!" she cried.

"It is the fellow. Out of the same royal mint, look
ye?"

"Thank you; but, sir——"

"It will buy you music books to spell over the lute you
yearn for!"

"Yet, I fear——"

"What?" and he laughed with forced mirth, for he
sought to please her; "my powers of divination? Oh,
I can leave those tricks to you and your tribe."

"I shrink from the tempter!" continued she, shuddering while unable to tear her sight from the glittering
coins.

"Is that the name you have for me already?"

"No, no," she went on, in a dreamy way. "It is this
arch-tempter! When I was a child and played under
the cart, and strayed into the copses around our iso-
lated camp, my step was light, my smiles many and
bright, and my song as free as the robin's—all showed
that I was as devoid of care as of dread. But now——"

"What is there fearsome in 'Now,' pray thee?"

"The hopes and fears of womanhood oppress——"

"You talk of womanhood—a child, yet! for you are
not over sixteen or seventeen at furthest, eh?"

"I do not know. Look not into a gypsy pedigree!
Am I a gypsy, even? Sometimes, their treatment of me
seemed to point out that I was not of their blood.
There are secrets of the Zingari which they do not
let the women into—from which they exclude me, any-
how!"

"You are fair enough to be dropped out of the spheres
above. Your song is as if out of a seraphic mouth.
You may be noble, for these brownskin tutors of yours
are famous as child-stealers; but this oppression! why,
oppression, when you ought to have heart and song
and step light and blithe? If you find more reward

than ever falling like the gold, it is because you deserve the higher recompense for delighting that moping, morose creature—man."

She shook her head as if she did not understand the
drift.

"No, I am no longer a girl. I know that I am a
woman and that I am a fair one, too!"

"The fairest of the fair!" cried he.

"Then, being a woman, I must welcome the bearers
of incense to be burnt at my shrine."

"Certainly; that is well. Nothing is too rich and
sweet to be offered to your beauty," and Don José
made as if to fling his purse into her hands.

"No, no! my pedestal will hold me up too high. The
fall would be fatal—unbearable, since I should return
to the gutter."

"This is the right time to meet her," chuckled the
intriguer, speaking aloud with suave accents. "Once
on the pedestal you are entitled to, think that a ready
and mighty hand may sustain you if you become giddy
at the outset, when unaccustomed to the elevation!
My hand is ready if not mighty," added he, hypocritic-
ally, for his modesty was palpably false. "But do not
shrink. I am but the statuary who is content when his
statue is reared on its base. Let me only be allowed
to worship with the others!"

This was the first time that she had spoken with an
educated man who might comprehend her still vague
longings. For Don Cæsar, airy and restless, had never
inspired this kind of confidence. She forgot the place
and the time—everything—to outpour her host of trou-
blesome thoughts.

"Oh, you flatter me, but the street-singer and dancer
for the herd. She reckons her own worth closer; or, at

least, she knows what poor esteem is really given her. She covets gold."

"I see that!" and he said to himself: "That fills me with anticipation of molding you, my image."

"Gold; it will free from that hideous crew—from bondage, at which my soul spurns and which loathes it all."

"Ambitious! Good, good! Be ambitious! We are not all clods to smell eternally of the earth."

"I am like a felon in chains—no means to sever them, no strength to break them, but gold furnishes the fire which will in time melt them. Each gift, then, such as I owe to you, and the other gentlemen, and the populace, though in pence, all help to keep up the consuming flame. I shall yet be free!"

Don José smiled, and almost looked handsome in the glow. This was the heaven-sent instrument. The king in love with her; she aspiring to the highest degree; and he enamored, though he did not quite acknowledge this tender point.

"Sir, sir, have I not cause to dread the end?"

"Fudge! What end?"

"What comes to all my sisters in the family—the royal mark?"

She slapped her shoulder. José shuddered, for he could not contemplate even in fancy the possibility of this beautiful being burned on the shoulder by the hangman's brand.

"Never!" cried he, warmly. "It would be profanation! You intimate that you may not be a gypsy! By my halidom, we will produce the documents to prove that! If we find not some parents to own you, then it will be beyond the stretch of the—never mind! All things can be done to gratify beauty allied with wit! The royal mark, quotha! You will wear the royal marks, indeed, but they will be—all your wishes conceive! Your foreshadowings are not dark but light—rays from the lamp of the throne room! Zoons! when one has your gifts, presentiments are all magic! Your atmosphere is one of hope!"

"I grant that since the queen applauded me, and promised me her support in bettering my wild and uncultured mind, I cherished the thought that my ambition ceased to be criminal."

Don José rubbed his hands.

"Come, come," said he, fondly, in his most coaxing voice; "turn for turn, let me play the soothsayer. I have crossed your hand with gold—let me read upon it the golden future." He took her hand and caressed it with his other. It was like a serpent coiling around a dove. "Believe me, confide in this adorer, and by my hope of salvation, here and above, all, all you yearn for shall be fulfilled."

In the recess, his eyes burned like coals out of the inmost heat, again.

"Fulfilled? all? ah, you do not know how boundless are a maiden's yearnings."

"I have a failing—I do so like to help the young and meritorious in this world of impediments. I, luckily, have the power to solidify your dreams into realities."

"You!"

He let his mantle unfold, and the sumptuousness of his court attire, the gold ornaments, the badges and insignia impressed her, for the Egyptians had biased her mind toward tinsel and glitter. She was overcome, impressed, enchanted.

"Your wishes shall be laws for the princes and dukes."

She panted; it was like unexpectedly uncovering a table loaded with luxuries before a starveling.

"You need only quit those sordid environs, those scurvy associates, to link yourself longer with whom will drag you by the same chains to the cart-tail for a whipping, to the stocks for a forced rest, to the gallows for a suspension from all active life! Come to a life at the end of which is not the hole by the wayside, but a tomb in the vault of your ancestors! Wear no wreaths of humble flowers but a crown of gold and gems, no ragged skirt but a robe with velvet train and pages bearing up the weight! You have only to come to your first step toward that goal! You are now the darling of Madrid. With my aid you will be the glory of Spain!"

"No, no!" she gasped, but did not snatch away her hand from his warm and tightening grip.

"Pish! a woman's nay stands but for naught!" said he, drawing her out of the recess.

But instinct told her to shun this rock which might afford a short rest, but would dash her to pieces inevitably when its time came also to be thrown down into shivers.

At this instant, a flourish of trumpets was heard at the cathedral. The queen must have gone there for the ceremonies of Easter, for the *fanfare* indicated that one of the royal family was thus greeted on coming forth. There was a rush of the loungers on the plaza and the hundreds, gathering in lines behind the archers and halberdiers, raised a loud cheer of "Long life to the queen!"

"The queen!" re-echoed the gypsy dancer, "she is above mercenary impulse! She has been good to me! I repelled her offers to lift me out of my misery! Well, rather her to trust to than you, sir, without offense! I will appeal to her majesty."

Contrary to her apprehension, the courtier did not try to detain her. After all, the queen, having engaged him to be her confidant, this was an escape from one shark into the jaw of its mate!

He released her hand, muttered: "Ever I wish you

well!" and merrily blew a kiss after her in her flight, nimble as a fawn's.

Then he laughed deeply to himself, and thought that he had mastered more arduous problems than to manipulate the plastic nature of a girl to his purposes. His reasoning was clear. The king admired this witch of all Madrid. The piece of vanity whom impudent aspirations raised to the fellowship of royalty must be grateful to him who had furnished the carriage-steps.

"What about her origin? She seems much above her low degree. She is a fairy to be a gitana! Oh, we will forge a family record, as I promised her! The greater she is made, the greater will be the queen's animosity when she discovers it is Maritana, her rival! It is an unpardonable wrong for any woman to bear, and keenest in all in a queen. She will resent it! Oh, my guardian angel's day, this! I held back from presuming that so shortly all would come into my lap out of that thorny tree."

He was about to follow to where the queen was stepping into her carriage at the church entrance, when a violent commotion not only filled the Jewry outlet, but a surge of the human sea burst forth.

In a moment he was entangled in a host of men, citizens, gypsies, vagabonds and watchmen, trying in vain to suppress a tumult.

Making a sign by which his agents in the multitude would recognize the head of the royal police, José fortified himself with some twenty of these desperadoes and peered into the scuffle.

"Death of my life!" said he; "it is the partner of that gypsy dancer! It is—oh, my cousin, the dissipated Count of Garofa!"

CHAPTER IV.

It was only by a glimpse that Don José had recognized his college mate at the University of Salamanca, patronized by the nobility twenty years before.

This glimpse was temporarily afforded. For the man was set upon by several bullies and swashbucklers, who, unable to draw their preposterously long swords in a close combat, hung about the victim as bulldogs upon a baited bull.

The single fighter held his own, using his dagger by the hilt, so held as to beat like a maul; he pummeled, blow for blow, evaded the treacherous stabs by catching the points in his rolled-up cloak, as a true Spaniard and one inured to such encounters could alone do. Presently two or three of the hectors, who had enough of the struggle, one-sided though it was, stumbled and fell into the kennel, where their blood mingled with the garbage and mud. The others, grasped by the muffled arm, gasped that they were strangled, and implored relief for the love of the martrys, whose fate their own promised to equal. Lastly, a persistent antagonist, resorting to treachery worse than that already attempted without serious avail, dropped on all fours and sought to hamstring the brave and unconquerable hero.

Perceiving or divining this cowardly move, Don Cæsar lifted his stout Cordovan boot, which, while without spur, was dangerous with its massy heel. He dealt such a kick as a wild horse might alone imitate, and the wretch, his breath knocked out of his body, rolled twenty paces until brought to a stop against the first house door, over which hung one of those wooden crosses denoting that the plague-stricken lay there.

Dispensing with this final attacker, Bazan slowly released the pair, whom he had not ceased to hug. They staggered back, as if the bear of the Pyrenees had embraced them, opened their mouths without power to emit a cry, and fell doubled up.

The victor stood erect, looked round with a ferocious glare, as if seeking fresh foes, and uttered a "*Viva España* and the Garofas!" like a warcry.

"Don't you get up," said he sarcastically to the fallen scoundrels, sprawling and vainly trying to stand on their feet. "You asses are only in your natural position—on your hoofs!"

Then, as if he were before a mirror in a dressing-room of his ancestral mansion, he leisurely pulled his tatters into a show of decency.

The victory and this coolness deserved a better result than instantly befell it.

The watchmen, reinforced by their comrades coming over from the cathedral, where they were no longer required since the queen had departed, did not care to handle the beaten ruffians, besmeared with mire and blood. According to the best traditions of their profession, to make an arrest without much regard to the guilt of the party, and with as much respect for their own safety as possible, they moved in a mass upon the solitary man. They reasoned that, formidable though he had been to the bandits, he was now exhausted and must submit to the authorized apprehenders. Besides, it is regretable to say, but already the degraded Count of Garofa bore a bad name among the archers of the city watch from having turned over their sentry-boxes and set cords across the street to trip them up.

They surrounded Don Cæsar. It was a wise manœuvre, since their ranks separated him from the outcasts' quarter, seething with excitement at this furious hurly-burly.

He seemed to disregard them in his attention to his frayed toilet. The bystanders, after admiring him for his courage, now smiled at his reckless humor.

"The curs!" said he, loudly, like one who lived in popular breath, "they have spoiled my ruffles, veritable Brabant lace! But for it disgracing my sword, which came out of the armory of Vincenzo of the Rose-alley, Toledo, I should have spitted the whole six of them like larks for a breakfast! Zoons!" continued he with a pretended distress, which drew out a roar, "they have despoiled me of my gold-thread galloon, a yard good measure, worth three pistoles!"

The watchmen crept nearer and began to close in.

"See," said he, recognizing his old foes, with a merry nod, "I call upon you as witnesses that the cutpurses have carried away my purse—green silk with silver cord, woven for me by a pretty seamstress of the Santa Catharina quarter, and she would not accept a penny piece for it! My purse, my purse! Oh, frowning Fortune, cursed dame!" he sang, "and I had invited the aldermen of the Red Cross parish and the chief clerk of the corrector to supper at the Castle-and-Lion on a baked pig-of-the-waters with a pasty of venison to follow, which venison came from a royal buck, killed, between ourselves, when the king was not hunting!"

"We will provide for your supper," said the lieutenant of the watch, advancing with the thought that this irrepressible jester would be wasted on "the ruck" when he might amuse them in the guard-room. "I offer you lodgings in the casa of the public corrector!"

"Your old apartments!" added a waggish sergeant.

"Arrest me, the butt, the foil, the victim of this outrage!" cried the injured Don Cæsar, clapping his hand noisily to his sword. "I, to be lodged where those night-butterflies are entitled to the first pick of beds! I, confounded with those Knights of the Moon; I, indubitably Knight of San Jago, of the Fleece, and the Sepulchre! Gentlemen of the Watch, hie you to recover my property, which was taken by those highwaymen, and leave my presence!"

Two or three hands were held out to clutch his collar.

"Hold, did you not hear me—that the rogues had conveyed off my purse—now I know that I cannot slip through your fingers since I cannot grease the fist!"

The allusion to the guardians being corrupt filled their chief with indignation.

"My men," said he, in a hoarse voice, "bring that runagate along—his part is played, his song ended! I believe that he has given the quietus to one of those unfortunate fellows—see, he stirs not in the gutter!"

"Bah!" said Don Cæsar, "you ought to be better judge of a man in liquor! If he looks reddened, it is the splatter of wine—he broke a bottle of cherry brandy when I first smacked his chaps! Do you see," he went on to gain time, "that is a knave not to be pitied. An illiterate dog, and from the alien regions, too. I believe he is Dutch! Centes, no clerk! for, when he sat at the board to throw the bones with me, he hailed me as a countryman of Sir Vantess. Shade of the romancero! Cervantes, to be knighted, only—that should have been lifted to the peerage for his immortal novel! But this dullard, he no sooner heard I was a noble, than he asked me after the health of Don Quickshot! and Hanky Panky! Don Quixote and Sancho Pancho, thus transmogrified by a blundering Hollander! I would I had stabbed him for his ignorance, but you would say that I beat him with my superior sword-play because he beat me at dice-play!"

"Enough prating!" said the acting-captain of the watch, "bring the loiterer along at quick pace!"

By this time, the more daring of the beggarmen and the Bohemians had gathered in order to fall in a body upon the flank of their enemies, and it seemed that Don Cæsar would as easily escape the archers as he did the gamesters, but rather by assistance than by his single address.

"Hold!" broke in a voice not awaited, as the Marquis of Santarem, drawing back his cloak to show the badge of lieutenant-criminal, stepped up to the watchmen. "Let that man go. I myself saw most of the riot, and he was solely acting on self-defense. Drive home those spillings of the Jewry to swelter in their resorts and clear the square of saunterers, for it is too late for good men to be abroad."

As his agents also revealed their office and supported him in ordering the archers about, the chief of the watch sullenly obeyed.

Don Cæsar, left untouched, hesitating between re-joining his companions, who allowed themselves to be hustled into the purlieus of the rear of the cathedral, or to thank this befriender, saw the latter beckon to him.

He pressed on his sword hilt, which threw up behind him the frayed cloak into a burlesque martial draping, and boldly came up to the nobleman.

Some charitable hands proceeded to help the fallen rascals to limp away; and, indeed, none of them were seriously hurt, with their toughened skins and skill in avoiding stabs.

"As you announced your degree," began Don José, "I

cannot be mistaken in addressing you, my lord, as Don Cæsar de Bazan?"

"I am he."

"We are cousins, and we were in the class of theology at Salamanca, were we not?"

He tilted back his hat to show his face, at present irradiated with the inviting mien of one seeking an end by gentle means.

"Now, give me grace. It is Cousin José! Count——"

"I am the Marquis of Santarem. I suppose you have been out of sound of the court herald proclaiming changes of rank?"

"Yes, I have been among the Turks! Not that I notice the difference in the manners here. You will overlook my disordered costume, for those light-fingered gentry did not touch me lightly!"

"I suppose, coz, you were careless enough to drink with them. Well, no harm befalls the drunken!"

"I, drunk! Not in a hogshead of it, like that English prince drowned in Malmsey! If I am preserved while my hat is battered and my garments frayed, it is through the love of the angels (he saluted with his hat) for good men!"

José held out his hand. His old friend looked greedily at the ruff, it was of the costly Brabant lace with which he had affected to gird his own wrists. He sighed.

"Marquis, and so much of a grandee that the city watch bowed and allowed themselves to be called off their prey! Well, you have prospered!"

"And you? Still the same devil-may-care that had a good heart and a kind nature!"

"Ay—'a scholar is always in frolicsome mood!' as we sang at the university! And I am still a scholar, learning to—well, everything but drink—that came so early that I believe I was cradled in a puncheon!"

"You are still young yet; you look not old, but jaded!"

"My old playfellow, the heart is a coin with youth on one side and wisdom on the reverse! That applies to you, Senor Gravity, for I am the coin stamped out and imperfectly smoothed on the *recto*, where, the Lord only knows what word will be implanted. 'Disinherited,' I guess!"

"You drink deep?"

"To the dregs, and they are bitter——"

"Fond of good living?".

"I have a marrow bone for my back tooth!"

"Not fond of dress?"

"Poverty is a field of nettles—they card out one's fine linen and warm woolens! The scapegoat has a ragged vest! I am a free commoner now! higher than a count—a king! And my kingdom is those airy pastures—the air! the sweet, free air!"

"Is this all that is left of that noble name and princely fortune?"

"The princely fortune has left—the noble name is left —you look too much of the peacock making his wheel to require it to back a note, but it may serve you at a pinch!"

"No, I thank you," returned the marquis, proudly.

"I see you ride the high horse—now, I am chums with Poverty, and the poor have no shame!"

"I have reached up to great things—I had hoped that you would have secured the same, in some foreign land, where a good sword is valued to its utmost."

"I may not have done great things," replied Cæsar, laughing, "but I have done great men—Florentine merchants, Lombard money-princes, usurers of all races! And if I have not reached great prizes, I have over-reached those who enjoyed them. But all in honor! That is why I sleep between ease and honor, so rarely quiet bedfellows!"

"You may sleep in your own bed soon!" said José, fervently, with feigned cordiality.

"It will have to be redeemed from the pawnbrokers!"

"I thought that your sire left you a fortune!"

"True! But when I returned from Algiers they had let me loose without a stitch on me—it took all to renew my wardrobe and linen, my clothes, and—throat!"

"And my father paid all your debts once!"

"He did, and I shall be glad if his son puts me under the like obligation! I am frank, eh?"

"Devilish too much so!" muttered the marquis.

"The force of habit piled up fresh ones! They are not outlawed yet, unhappily!"

"Two or three fortunes! You would bankrupt the treasury of Peru! This is paying dearly for your dance-music!"

"That depends on the kind of dance and the partners!"

"Humph!" and José frowned, recalling the measure paced before the queen by this saucy speaker and Maritana.

"But I am not singing psalms of despair! I am now clean as a splinter! Necessity is a better teacher than any of the greybeards at the university! When one's purse is swept out like a chimney, one bears its being whisked off without a whimper. Besides, if a robber borrowed it, I may win it back, filled anew, over the card board. Not having money, I am not teased by poor relatives, which freedom you will appreciate unless you have changed your character, being—you will excuse me!—rather curmudgeonly! I have not an acre, so I have no grumbling tenantry to face when I stroll through the country. I have no laid-down road, so that I never swear at taking a wrong turning. All my paths, while with the gypsies, lead to Roam!—ha! ha! I have nothing to take care of

but my sword. The scabbard is out at elbows, like its
master, but the sight of the sharp steel peeping through
saves me from molestation as the spirit of a gentleman
peeping out of a ragged coat saves him from insult!"

During his levity, the more serious noble had been
studying his unfortunate kinsman.

"You were out of Spain once—you are the type of the
Corsair who becomes admiral of the free-seamen! Why
did you return?"

"Madrid lured me!" responded the rover with unexpected pathos—"the Manzaneres, where there is still
enough water to wash one's shirt and still enough sun-
shine to dry it. Madrid lured me with the hope that
whenever I should re-enter its hallowed walls I might
find no remembrances——"

"Of your follies?"

"Fie, moralist!—of my creditors! But I was out!
They are still in! Creditors die, but have heirs; their bills
are like the ravens—more and more sharp, and numer-
ous! Christian and heathen graces, they still remain
three; but credit is numberless! My creditors multiply
like the blessed, and my interest increases on their paper!
The children have grown up to look forward to my return home as for the fabulous wealthy uncle from the
golden Americas."

"Perfectly penniless, eh?" and José rubbed his hands
covertly.

"The only perfection I can boast!"

"That is sad! for Madrid is a city of pleasure—very
expensive!"

"One can still fuddle at the cost of those whom one
fuddled when he had means!"

"Wine will be more dear—the city has doubled the cess
at the gates!"

"I can gamble for farthing stakes——"

"There is a fresh edict against petty gaming!"

"Ah, you should know, for the police as well as the watch obeyed you, and let you balk them of their prey as if you were Keeper of the Lions and could rob them of their bones!"

"I occupy a certain position, true—and that is why I can assure you tippling, dicing, and even sauntering, are no longer healthy pursuits in the capital!"

"Well, you saw a specimen of what is diversion—the sport of kings on a small scale—fighting——"

He proudly looked round upon the late battlefield.

"Why, my poor friend, fortune is dead counter to you there."

"You do not say so! In what way? Fighting is born with man. To draw the sword comes as naturally to a gentleman as drawing breath."

"Yes; but, you pagan, you would not know among those gypsies, without law or religion, that Carnival week commences this very day; and the Royal Council are going to issue a proclamation that death shall be the penalty of crossing swords."

"Now, then, by St. Andrew's cross! this goes beyond endurance! Would our king ruin the swordsmiths? Death for not being killed in a duel! How the logical must laugh at that argument! The first monarch was a successful soldier, says the sage whom we were bored with at the college! And how the royals have degenerated to issue such a stupid pronunciamento! No duels! Is one to throw away money on the professional blood-letters? Unless I am bled regularly I should run amuck —like the Malays—and trace a bloody swath in the first concourse of Madrid!"

"Oh, you must restrain your arm for seven days—just

a little week while you fast, to cool your blood. You will
have the rest of the year to practice homicide."

"A sennight! This is hard for one. The Church bids
me fast and make my blood thin and cold! The State
bids me control my hot temper, with which I might be
comfortable! I must not draw wine or the sword! Well,
if you are one of the king's council who give him this
counsel, I do not congratulate you! By the way, you
have not defined yourself. Marquis, I know; but are you
of the State Council?"

"I? I am the last of whom the king would ask counsel
in his affairs—of the heart! I am nobody!"

"We are at evens! But I doubt," thought Cæsar, du-
biously, "a man who can call off the hounds of the police
—he is a great potentate and worth truckling to, if I
were a truckler. Bah! I want nothing of anybody—that
is, for poor me! But—ah! that girl!—Maritana, who
longs for freedom from the gypsies, from her gilded
trappings under which she capers for the pence of the
vulgar and the gold of the upstarts. Now, if I could induce my cousin to assist her in her commendable desire
to arise!"

"Well," said Don José, unable to suppress his jeer,
although he might require this sword, if not this head,
"plunge your blade and your poll, to cool them, in the
fountain—the municipality is generous of the ice-spring!"

He pointed laughingly to the public basin, a relic of
the Moorish rule and providence; a massive group of
Oriental lions spouted the clear liquid from their gaping
mouths and lashed the pool with their tufted tails.

"With no dwelling, I might as well drown myself!
Oh, for the week to be slept off in one nap, and a good,
stout quarreler to beard me!" cried Don Cæsar, mock-
ingly, as he joined his hands in this warlike prayer.

His fellow-student looked at him narrowly as he leaned on the marble circle and was reflected in the surface, the image of despair.

"Alackaday! We shall be burying him instead of the Carnival!" said he, with pretended grief.

A Paramount Picture.

MARITANA RETURNS THE JEWELS STOLEN FROM DON CAESAR.

The Spanish Dancer.

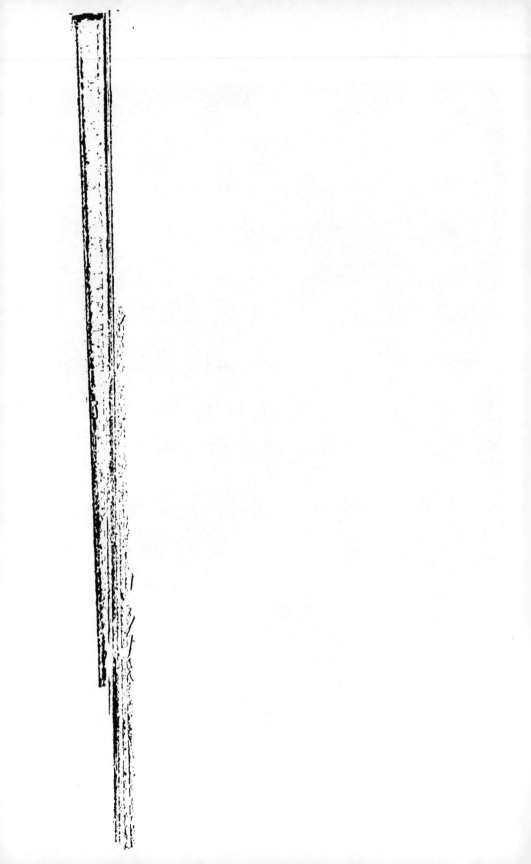

CHAPTER V

DON CÆSAR'S CHALLENGE.

There came to the water fount two persons, deep in their own troubles.

One of them was a youth, stalwart and dingy of complexion like a gunsmith's apprentice. He was struggling hard, as his quivering under lip showed, to keep back his tears.

His companion was one of those burly Galician peasants who come to town believing that the streets are paved with gold, but who trudge daily to and fro conveying water to the thirsty, but not without remuneration. On the contrary, the water carriers of Spanish cities—and such was Senor Pacolo—charge as much as they dare for the porterage, and more, when the heat augments and the tide runs low.

As his unfortunate companion needed not money, the worthy fellow was profuse with offers of sympathy and encouragement.

"Nay, nay, little Master Lazarillo," said he, "do not spurn graces—my free offices! I have learned to bear my burdens with quiet, but I uphold you in your rebellion against tyranny. For it is tyranny, since you are the armorer's 'prentice and not a soldier bound, to have that captain of the Royal Arquebusiers pitch on one so lowly!"

"Friend Pacolo," returned the youth, shaking his hand, "let this be our farewell. Sell my goods at your lodgings for what will bury me. Your poor comrade who came out of the same mountains as you will never lay his head under their pines! Bury me anywhere, but in the coun-

try if you can. I am not ungrateful to you for your
kindness, and you are sound as a priest in warning me
from self-murder—the most cowardly of murders! But
I have but one desire now—it is to die!"

He made a motion as if to mount the basin edge and
throw himself into the water.

"Refrain!" cried Don Cæsar, suddenly, on seeing the
shadow projected across the surface from the lamp at the
drinking-shop. "How do you know but that I, deprived
of wine, may stoop to drink of that water?"

"If you please, sir," intervened the water carrier, "this
lad wishes to make a hole in the water, which might be
filled by older and less promising men!"

"Why, it is a likely youth, and ought not to lag with
hanging bridle!" commented José. "If you have lost
your master's money box do not throw your life over as
the stake by which to win it back! Rather go into the
gypsy-ward yonder, where you will not have water
thrown at you any more than the petty pilfering! By our
Lady! you might better go for a sailor if you have a leaning toward the molten crystal over which Cortez and
Pizarro marched to empire!"

"If you please, sir, he is bent on dying!" repeated
Pacolo.

"Then let him straighten himself on living! Drowning
is not one of those courses to be taken in a hurry! Bah!
die before you are pricked by your beard coming, and long
before you can have felt those prickings of remorse!
Wait till you arrive at my age, and stand between taking
to water—as a drink!—and being burned with pent-up
courage—like those frontier towns, which, in Holland, if
taken by us, are burnt, and if the Dutch find they cannot
be maintained, are submerged in this vile fluid, water!"

"He is an armorer's apprentice, my master," continued
the carrier, hoping that time would cool the youth's ar-

dor; "and he ought to shoot himself—if there is anything in the saying, 'live by a trade, die in the same!'"

"No truth, friend—or the ropemakers would go up the hangman's ladder!"

"Your honor is right! Drown? Marry! are we frogs to think such a passage out of misery?"

"You, too, are wise. No, boy, do not drown, in preference to this stable, lovely and flowery earth, in that unstable and muddy element!" moralized Don Cæsar. "The thought has given me what we scholars call the ague, and my late companions, the wanderers, 'the shivery-shakes'— coarse, but convincing. You wish for death—you, a minor, who cannot be plagued with duns and creditors!"

"He is plagued with a cursed mean master," interrupted Pacolo, "who would not draw you out a pistole unless you drew out a pistol on him! This knave—but you tell the gentleman your story, for he might give you good advice——"

"It is all he can give at present. But out with it, my lad!" He sat on the basin edge and swung his legs. "If you have to do with instruments of war, I can be the judge, for, look ye, a gentleman-at-arms is necessarily a gentleman of arms. To it!"

"My name, sir, is Lazarillo. I am learning my trade of gunsmith, and my master, instead of instructing me in the craft, set me to keeping in order the firearms at the royal arsenal, which adjoins the prison, while the new arsenal is building."

"Very good—so far, no harm. To furbish up arms is part of a good soldier's duties."

"Well, sir, some one left a window open, and the dew, blowing in, the barrels were spotted with rust. The captain fell foul of my master in consequence, and he, to avoid the tongue-lashing, laid all the blame upon my

shoulders and consented that the old martinet should have
a dozen lashes laid on me!"

"He did! I should knock spots out of the old leop-
ard!" ejaculated Cæsar, not in the least judicially. "I
have not the pleasure of the acquaintance of your estim-
able employer, but I could give him a leathering!"

"So I ran out not to receive the lashes!"

"A dozen lashes, eh?" and the don's shoulders heaved
at the idea.

Since his wanderings with the gypsies he had seen
what flogging implied in those days for physical argu-
ments.

"Oh, it is not the number, sir," continued the boy, almost weeping because of having met sympathy in this
high quarter. "But I am a Spaniard, a mountaineer, and
though we can stand suffering, we will not put up with a
whiplash!"

"Bravo! my little Achilles!" cried Don Cæsar, forgetting all about the amateur judgeship, "this is a true son of
Spain!" He rose, and, going over to where Don José
had stood, apart, musing, he took his bent arm familiarly
and resumed: "Cousin, we two must intercede with this
military savage!"

"Alas, my own lieutenant and my master's wife joined
to plead for me, but the captain said that he would ply
the scourge with his own hand rather than have the little
blockhead escape! meaning by blockhead, yours to serve,
sir!" and Lazarillo clasped his hands to Bazan as assuredly he would not do to the miserable autocrat.

"Don't be uneasy. We will be your advocates, noble
advocates! José, you must tell him under his own nose
to desist—this is no way to drum up recruits by chastis-
ing the boys! You, who lord it over the police and the
watch, I warrant that, though nobody, you can cut the
comb of this chanticleer!"

"You will pardon me," said the marquis, withdrawing his arm with softness, like that oiling his voice, "but I cannot put captains of the Royal Arquebusiers in my pocket! Do not interfere—what are a few stripes more or less to the budding soldier!"

"It depends upon where they are placed," replied Don Cæsar, dryly, "for, on the arm, they make a corporal—on the back, an assassin!—captains have been shot in the back of the head for unjustly 'striping' a trooper!"

"Let him shoot him when the time comes. I mind my own business, and do not soil my fingers!" and José walked a little way off from the fountain.

"Ah! after your protestations of good-will, you fall away like this water!" Cæsar said this as he indignantly withdrew his hand from the basin in which he had plunged it, as though to wash off the contagion impregnated by the faithless friend's rich sleeve.

"You may be banished to the Azores Islands for revolt against the king's uniform," observed the criminal police chief, as a last word.

"I would prefer the Nutmeg Islands, so that I might spice my wine! but, banish me, if you will! let it be after I have remonstrated with this disgrace to this uniform if he persists in his inhumanity!"

As José retired to watch at a safe standing, there was a clink of arms and a smell of the fuses being lit, with which the hand guns were fired.

At this token of approaching combat, Don Cæsar's mien absolutely altered. Any traces of the enervating influences of the wine cup were blown away. He straightened himself, and, assuming a gallant attitude, with one hand on his tilted sword and the other on his hip, he waited for the comers.

"Get thee behind me, thou little Beelzebub," said he to

the refugee, "you little guess what a pickle you may have soused me in, before we are through with you!"

"It is they!" said the boy. "They have pursued me, but I will not be lashed like a dog!"

"Peace; and trust us. We are going to defend you!"

"We?" asked Lazarillo and his humble friend in a breath.

"Assuredly WE! Don Cæsar de Bazan and his Split-steel, his good blade!"

The plaza was deserted. The chains had been stretched across the street-heads, opening into the square, and the houses had become "blind" by shutters going up before the windows and the doors having even the wickets sealed. A few lights twinkled, generally in the garret windows. Shadows stole away across the space as a file of "hawkbushmen" tramped over toward the fountain. They were not the civic watch, not the armed police, but the royal men-at-arms. They wore buff breeches, thigh-plates and shin-plates, as well as cuirasses, which gleamed in the scattered beams. Across the steel plate barred the black leather bandolier, containing the cartridges for the guns, and each carried at the side a long coil of whitened rope, being the match for igniting the powder in the pans.

Their helmets were of almond shape, and bore a green plume along the crest. This plume denoted that they were on service.

They were headed by a grizzled veteran, whose short-cropped hair showed just under the steel cap, gilded to distinguish him from the subalterns. This was Captain Octavio Herreno, Viscount Aguastintas, who had fretted for twelve years at lack of promotion into the palace corps, where the regulations were light and the duties formalities.

Don José halloaed to his friend, and made a sign for him not to use his sword.

"Oh, hang the edict! Still, it is Carnival week—let us respect Mother Church, although I only know one prayer: 'Let me never be tired of the only life I have ever known.'"

So he reluctantly released his grip of his sword pommel and let his hands fall by his sides, where they flapped, however, with impatience, like a cock's wings when about to crow a challenge.

Pacolo shrewdly harbored himself with the fountain between, and, peering forth between two lions' heads, he stared, muttering:

"I much blunder if this Boabdil of a musketeer will not rue his plucking out little Lazarillo from that gentleman's ward, for, never forgive me! but he will receive such a drubbing as the Algerines gave the Emperor Karl!"

"Do not run again!" whispered Bazan to the trembling lad; "you wear my colors now! They may crush me as between Upper and Lower Andalusia, but till then do not budge!"

In spite of the gloom, the two or three figures over at the water pool were visible to the searchers. They marched straightway thither.

The captain, perked up with his post, did not dream of any opposition. He halted his men at the basin, and, pointing out the shrinking boy with his gloved hand, said, utterly ignoring the others by:

"Ho! so you dared not go among the gypsies for refuge, in spite of your knowing what I promised, and that I am a man of my word! It is your prisoner. Secure him!"

The roisterer, doffing his hat and flourishing its broken feather in a long-drawn bow, deferentially saluted with an air which advertised him as a finished cavalier, and said, in a voice to soften a stone effigy:

"You will excuse, Captain Don Octavio; I crave a moment. Allow me, that is, suffer your servant to intercede with prelude, oration and peroration, according to the humanities, for this trifling young delinquent."

Disregarding the eloquent suitor, the captain cried, angrily, to his arquebusiers:

"Are you deaf? I said, arrest!"

The troopers advanced, but their step was slow; they recognized in the solitary obstacle not the ex-courtier, but the madcap who had sunk to familiarity with the fag-ends of the town. His exploits had all reached the guardroom, not excepting this latest; indeed, his prowess in defeating the gang of gamesters had been recounted like a page out of Plutarch.

Lazarillo, more daunted by the fear that he had uselessly embroiled his gallant champion fell on his knees, which he might not have done on his own account.

"Mercy!" he cried in a sonorous voice, "mercy! Be a brave captain, and forgive!"

"My captain!" said Bazan, with the same suppressed tone, "are you in your turn grown dumb—for that springald is speaking to you—you, Don Octavio! The poor creature is suing for mercy, which a true soldier always listens to, if he cannot grant! Mark, I add my appeal to his supplication for pardon."

"Who the deuce are you, scarecrow, who has not even mended your tatters before entering a royal capital! But, sirrah, you go back to your duty! Resume the leather-cloth and shine up the armor! And no tears, they will only spot the steel, and they cannot soften my heart! As for this miserable mummer——" for Don Cæsar was rising in a somewhat threatening attitude, which had caused the soldiers to stop short

"That cursed decree!" muttered Bazan, recollecting. "Oh, blind mortality, which blusters when but a sheet of parchment is the buckler betwixt him and the itching sword! If it were not the blessed diabolical week when one must not carry out the dictates of humanity!" He became calm by a powerful effort. "Captain, my noble don, why object to your collecting the lamb into the fold! Pretty field where the flock are this kind of war wolf! But, let that pass! and let it pass that there shall be no ignominous blows, eh? no cuts of the cord, only fit for criminals who join the flagellating monks! That boy has the heart of a soldier and will make his mark yet! How glad you will be to have spared him!"

"Spared nothing—a flogged soldier takes care not to let the enemy see his back," returned the martinet, chuckling, like a rusty hinge, at his own stern joke.

"You should pardon!" He caught him by the cloak as he whirled around, contemptuously. "You must pardon my page!"

"Hands off! Do not infect me with the reek of the ghetto!" cried the other, testily, and facing the shuddering, cowering boy, who seemed to be praying.

"Remember the edict!" hissed Don José in his cousin's ear, as he glided toward him. "You must bear his taunts, too!"

Cæsar shook him off and took two steps, which placed him between soldiers and commander and their object of pursuit.

"You offended me, sir, by turning a deaf ear! You insult me by diverting your eye when I address you! You are a soldier and by rank a nobleman—so am I! I no longer throw my cloak over this boy as a pleader for the general assistance against a bully and a butcher, but as my page, since I have no doubt he will enter into my service! Now——"

"Your page? You who have not the wherewithal to clothe your back, keep a boy?"

"Nay, I can keep my back from being scored by a sword cut and my page's from your stirrup strap! I have pledged my honor to protect this lad, mind you, and I am now imploring or suing for you to forgive and release!"

"What on earth are you going to do?"

"What I solicit in vain, it is my regular course to compel!" was the forlorn gentleman's curt and tranquil answer.

"There will certainly be a thrashing for the hawk-busher!" muttered Pacolo, in his retreat.

"You are mightily insolent, consort of the banned and exorcised!"

"Bandy no more words. The decree against dueling does not include my correcting a brutal dog who presumes upon wearing the royal collar! In spite of all, with death my portion, you must, if truly Don Octavio Herreno, make me the honorable amends!"

"Defiance from a beggar!"

"Who would not ask the alms of his life from you. It is I who beggar your nobility of a year! I am a grandee of Spain, and my blade will ennoble yours by its touch. I am Don Cæsar de Bazan——"

"It is a name trailed in the gutter," returned the captain, although sobered.

"I am, moreover, head of the Counts of Garofa." He put on his hat with so lofty an air that it became the newest shape in the finest felt and the feather repaired its crack and its curl, and he appeared like a favorite of the king.

The Garofas had the signal privilege of wearing their hats in the royal presence—that is, were the equal of kings. A Garofa used to say: "I and the king!"

"It was I who stooped in suing to you, merely a viscount of purchased creation, and by forcing me to apply my sword to you in correction is due the misdemeanor of infringing the royal decree!"

"A challenge to a king's officer at the front of his men?" faltered the old soldier, almost frothing with rage.

"In front of your men, accept, or retire with them in shame!"

"Oh, it is not meet that even you should doubt the mettle of the king's officers. If you will follow me where we will not have the cathedral walls to shadow us, or holy ground to be defiled, I will prove that my manhood is not of yesterday if my letters of nobility are."

Confident that the Count of Garofa, however degraded by association with the lees of the capital, would not flinch thus committed, he cried to his men:

"File! By single file, march!" and the troop disappeared in the court to the south of the great religious edifice and were absorbed to the last glitter of steel in the intense gloom.

"Oh, no, you must not waste your life for such as me!" cried the cause of this strife. "I would rather return to my master and let this browbeating captain wreak his spite to the full!"

"Oh, no, not since you will be my page! You might, if you prefer no change of service, run to that lieutenant who would have spared you the shame of a whipping— and let him know that there will be a vacancy for his promotion before morning!"

Then nodding to Pacolo, who softly came out of his shelter, he confided the youth to him, and, whistling a marching tune, he plunged into the same mass of murkiness which seemed the entrance to the pit of darkness.

At the same time he saw at the other end of this

passage, where it debouched upon a little square edged
with young trees, a spread of ruddy light.

"That is not the moon," said he, striding on, and shiv-
ering, for his clothes were like lacework and the wind
was chill, "but the glare of the hearth of the Next Sovereign! What an excellent idea, since the loser can pass
away, with a good glass of wine to start him on the long
journey, and the winner can drink without fear that he is
taking his last drop! Dash that edict! 'the last drop!'
I jest too truly, perchance!"

He quickened his gait and soon arrived at the famous
dueling ground.

The Minor Cathedral square, called familiarly "the
Dandiprats' walk," was the favorite stalking-ground of
the "bucks and the deer." It was full of shops, or rather
booths, since the building of solid structures was prohibited on church land, where it would have recalled the
traffic in the Temple, and citizens and courtiers mingled
with the odd serenity born of implacable classification.

As coaches could not get into the inclosure, all were
on foot and the red heel was knocked against by the
clumsy bark sandal of the peasant and the trooper's heavy
high boot.

But at night, especially if the moon shone with the fullness of lustre known in that sunny clime, it was the site
of encounters to decide by force of arms current ques-
tions. Under the hardened eyes of the persons up at
the house windows, gallants died as coolly for a ribbon,
a political question or a family feud. By the police closing the eye in the Minor plaza, this was the only safe
place where one could, without interruption, hazard the
life on a sword point.

Sometimes the idlers would see all the ladies of fame
by day on this field of honor, which was also a court of
beauty; at night the same lookers-on might see all the

gallants watching a duel, not always single but of two or three pairs.

As a military man, Captain Octavio was well acquainted with the spot.

It was even said that he did not lose in the purse by choosing this rendezvous, since it was a relative of his, and an old wardog, too, who had served in the French campaigns under his flag, who kept the eating-house with the singular title.

But it was not unreasonable; it was witty, as wit was judged then.

This hostel, where there were no beds, since its busiest time was after dark and its gamblers and carousers came not there to sleep, was illumined handsomely; out of all small windows poured the light, and out of the ground-floor doorway, large enough to admit a coach, shone the tremendous glare from a furnace and an open fire, before which the spit revolved.

All this brightness shot across the square, where the promenaders wore off the grass, and enabled one to use a knife and fork or a sword, as one feasted or fought, without wishing for the day.

The old soldier, having learned to cook the provisions stolen by the foragers, since armies were miserably provisioned, had all the arts at his spoon-end. He had sauces which tickled the jaded palate, pies which delighted the epicures, and, lastly, wines which never paid the city dues, but were, they say, brought back in the empty bier every time there was a military funeral out of the garrison and palace.

To be sure, the rumor being circulated that the king had more strictly than heretofore prohibited settlement of differences between sword wearers with their side companion, a gloom should have fallen on the Next Sovereign, but she did not lessen by a jot the triumphant smile with which she was depicted on the signboard.

This board did not swing on a rod at a post, for the wind came down furiously from the north sometimes, and mine host would have bitterly regretted a three-bottle guest being flattened by the sign.

It was set in the front over the door of lozenge shape, like a funeral panel of a great house.

"The Next Sovereign," as we should have explained, was simply a portrait of a beauty, not identifiable, but woman in the general. Considering that whenever there is a king there is a woman in the background, if not by his side, and that to her are attributed all the acts from the throne which incur comment, the sarcasm in presenting her as the ruler *in posse* was good enough to laugh at.

But then, those who feasted at the Sovereign were easily made to laugh. Always omitting the duelist, who never left the ground to enter the tavern.

As the challenger had surmised, here was where he found his antagonist awaiting him; he had consoled himself for losing the apprentice gunsmith by exhausting the flagon of wine brought out. He had dismissed his troop, we know, but retained a sub-officer and pressed into service as a second a civilian acquaintance upon the ground, who thanked him for the diversion.

"Capital site!" said Don Cæsar, critically, as if he had not known the spot before. "Over there is a leather-bottle maker's stall. It has been found so handy to sew up a slash when a bungler has been at work, and did not kill his man neatly!"

This was not very encouraging, but the Captain of Arquebusiers was tough. The host nodded to the tattered nobleman as if he knew him of old, and without sending a waiter to get his order, went on his fat legs to bring out a bottle of Tetuan wine, which, growing on soil impregnated with magnetic iron, was reckoned to suit fighting men.

"It is the fortifier, my lord," said he. "You will pink your man in the first bout, if you drink one glass! You will pierce him in the second, if you drink two; and if you finish the flask, you will finish him!"

"Halloa!" cried the errant knight, astounded, "he is your own officer, and set you up here! You astonish me as much as if you presented your bill."

"Oh, I do not mind the score! You will have your rights soon, and your steward will settle your long account! A gypsy foretold that!"

"But," went on Don Cæsar, drinking and approving, "this does not explain why you should desire me to be the better in crossing steel with your old captain?"

"Well, he owes me considerable, and I understand that he will pay tavern bills while he lives!"

"Oh, the family have his estate under their control, poor infant!" sighed the broken noble. "After all, he may be set free by my boring him in the midriff!"

Between proven swordsmen, the preliminaries were brief.

A sort of ring was formed of the spectators. The seconds planted their men, for Cæsar's reputation had promptly produced two adherents, especially as the landlord promised to regale them, and the blades were soon grating in that first testing which precedes all scientific combats.

The Arquebusier Captain was redoubtable and famous in the capital and all his garrison towns for his feats.

But varied as had been his experiences, they were as an A B C book to the lexicon of private warfare in which our hero was as proficient. Consider that it is given to few in a short lifetime to have been conspicuous at court, prisoner with the Algerine corsairs, and participant in

' those medleys when gypsies, smugglers, bandits and the scum of the cities intermingled and employed without any rules weapons so diverse as the dagger, the knife and the stiletto. It may be stated that almost every province of Spain boasted a brand of knife, and each knife had its school of fence proper to it. In all of these, by actual encounter, Don Cæsar had learned lessons. While not fitting him for handling the gentleman's arm, it gave him suppleness of wrist, quickness in defense, and rapidity of the thought to direct the thrust which sadly nonpulsed the arquebusier.

In the first bout, his sword was detached from his grasp by a trick more familiar to wielders of the scimetar than the long sword, but it succeeded. The captain protested a mishap, alleging that he had slipped in the "maybutter," a playful name for a flowering plant; he was allowed to repeat the charge. This time Don Cæsar received him with a ward and a reply lunge out of the old French school, when victory was attained by poking as with a spear. The blade entered the upper sword-arm, and would have penetrated the chest to boot, but the don was not persistent; he called out "blood!" and the seconds agreed that he ought to cease then, as their man was unable to continue the conflict. But the obstinate captain, desiring to continue with a change of hand, Don Cæsar laughingly assented, saying that he was ambidexter, and that his antagonist would lose nothing.

But the seconds would not assent. They nobly regarded honor as satisfied, and threatened to charge the captain if he did not put up his blade.

It was then inquired, according to usage, if anything in the course of the sword play—pretty play!—had offended "the witnesses." It was perfectly in the rules for them to carry on the quarrel. But the odor from the roasts was so appetizing that they were nearly drowned by the

A Paramount Picture.

THE GYPSY GIRL DANCES AMID HER MINSTRELS

The Spanish Dancer.

water in their mouths, and there was no blood in their eyes.

There was more than a little doubt that they would have supper, as in duty bound, out of either the principals, but the host solved that by pointing to a table spread by the doorway, where the waiters began to bring dishes, platters and vessels, proclaiming a hearty festival.

"In carnival?" said Cæsar, as if he had qualms.

"Did you pick up the tenets in the gypsy quarter?" ventured the host. "Know that I have received three wounds in the wars with the Turks—so that I am a tried and true Christian. You shall have fish, and eggs, and herbs, and the wine is water of the river Jordan!"

Unfortunately, there was not given time to verify the host's assertion of not sinning against the ecclesiastical mandates, for, just as the party were seated comfortably, the only blot to the jollity being the arquebusier's bandaged arm, a pale-faced neighbor of the Next Sovereign rushing up to the host, in his nightcap and bed-wrapper, stuttering in alarm:

"My racketty boy, who did not come in before we locked the door, climbed in at my window and said that there is an edict against dueling!"

"So there is," said the landlord, with an innocent face. "I had the proclamation on a printed sheet to be stuck up on my door lintel—an edict, bless my soul!"

"Forbidding it, with the capital penalty!"

"A fig!" cried the captain, whose first glass of wi—that is, Jordan water—had restored the vitality lost through his cut. "I am authorized to bear arms, in and out of Carnival! The king's officer can fight at all seasons, that is what he is sworn in to do!"

"But, Don Cæsar!" said the host, "he is not the king's officer!"

"Ensign of the Devil's Own, rather!"

"And you, gentlemen, the seconds, what the law calls aids and no-betters! Oh, haste into the church for sanctuary!"

"All the sooner, as I hear the patrol! See their torches by the church!"

There was great confusion; all rose.

Half an hour afterward, when Don José, afraid bitherto to pass down in the dark to the still-lighted square, reached it at the heels of the watch, he hastened to inquire about his cousin.

The tale was straight.

At the close of the duel, when the parties were washing away the stain of defeat on one side, and toasting the glory on the other, the edict was called to mind. The captain allowed his friends to take him into the hospital adjacent to the cathedral, which was thus a refuge not to be invaded by the civic and military arms. As for the friend of the outcasts, who had proven to be an accomplished swordsman and a noble of the realm, he had forbidden his friends to interfere, and had let himself be conveyed into the city tower, where he would probably remain until led out for execution. Trial was not necessary for an infraction of the royal mandates.

"Oh, I knew," muttered the plotter, "that he would not fall by the sword; he is such an adept! But to be snatched away when I might make use of him? Condemned to death—ah, I think I see my way to rise, or, at least, to raise my puppet by the rope which hangs him!"

Joyously he resisted the host's entreaty for him to taste his blessed water from the Jordan, and hurried away from the square.

CHAPTER VI.

ON ANOTHER'S MISSION.

Don José left the one bright spot in slumberous Madrid and returned to the great square.

He stood in a corner, and perceived a solitary figure crossing the plaza. He noted that when accosted by his men in ambush the stranger replied with a potent password, for they let him pass as readily as they had their superior.

Pricked by this mystery, a little jealous that another had his might, he came forth and threw himself in the way.

A light strayed from a flickering lamp at a devotional post.

"The mischief! It is our old friend, the Marquis of Castello-Rotondo! Why, Master of the Lapdogs, what do you out of doors at this untimely hour? You will catch your death of cold, and we shall have to go into half-mourning!"

"Oh, my dear Don José! believe me that I am not prowling the filthy streets by my own prompting! It is, between ourselves, our good queen's orders."

"I know that the king's writ runs day and night, but the queen's wishes?—since when have they had the proviso: 'Posthaste and no stoppages?'"

"Since she has gone crazy—save the mark!—over this gypsy witch who has cozened her into second childhood! She wakes up and sends a token to her that she is to be by her side early in the morning."

"Oh, not Maritana?"

"There is none other! Surely, she is incomparable!

But the queen ought not to have the failings of uncrowned mortals."

"I must always agree with your lordship's sense. But why seek such a wild girl as a gypsy in a city ditch by night? As well hunt a black rabbit with a ferret having no lantern round its neck."

"Oh, I can find her," replied the old nobleman, with a fatuous smile; "I am free of the ghetto."

"The devil you are! Impossible! Why, you know my rank and its power over the unruly—but I would not venture down into that sink of iniquity with my badge of office. No, the scum would throttle me and run away with the collar to pledge it!"

"Oh, I dare say they are capable of it; but, I repeat, I am free of the family!"

"Is it purchasable with money, friend?"

"I took the first steps thereby. . I have been a very good friend to the Bohemian, first on my own estate in the province of Murcia, where they are allowed to camp, cut wood for firing and poach a little."

"Well, for the rarity of such leniency, I do not doubt that they might be grateful danglers on your excellency's kindness."

"It was a good recommendation when I came to town, too!"

"It saved your pocket from being picked?"

"My throat from being cut!—for these Zingari are no sticklers!"

"But apart from the natural softness of your head—I mean your heart—marquis," continued the police head, thinking that even in this stupid sycophant there might be reason for chatting with him, "how do you bind these masterless rogues to be decorous?"

"I pay several annuities to prosecute some searches of mine!"

"Oho! You do not interfere with the police prerogative of restoring stolen property, do you? It would go hard with me to have to arrest your excellency!"

"Tut, tut! The property I seek is live stock. In a word, I have been seeking for over fifteen weary years a child."

"A child! Oh, my poor friend!"

"As a father!"

"I excuse your blushes——"

"Blushes, sir?—tears!" and the old man wiped his eyes showily. "You may know that when I was young I was a testy, choleric tomfool!"

"I could guess that!"

"Besides my ancestral estate there was a large sum in gold, derived from trading with the East, which was to accrue to me if I became father of an heir."

"Oh, a son?"

"Exactly. And we had a daughter!"

"What a slip!"

"Yes, a fair slip of a girl—hang my ill-fortune and hers! for I was so enraged, wanting money terribly at the nick to advance me at court, that I put the deceptive imp from us!"

"Unnatural parent! Ugolino!" and he tapped him on the shoulder as if arresting him.

The dotard cackled.

"Or rather, I talked of putting the child out of the world!"

"Horrible!"

"This alarmed my wife, who thought that I was maddened beyond control! She conferred with her confidential maid, and the two formed a counter plot. They hired some vagabonds to take the child out over the balcony and across the moat in the midnight!"

"But, being a make-believe——"

"Unfortunately, the rogues did their task completely.

They carried away the babe, and did it so cleverly that their traces were entirely lost!"

"This is harrowing!"

"All we learned was that my blundering lady had entrusted our darling to gypsies—things of no country—who are here to-day and——"

"In the jail to-morrow!"

"At all events, there is no line which we could follow. At last my wife was advised to apply to the Duke of Egypt——"

"The pretended king of these homeless wanderers, just so!"

"He offered his aid and charged so much for his acolytes! It has cost me a pretty penny, especially when I fail to be advanced lucratively at court——"

"Oh, that may be mended!"

"Thank you, my lord—I would you had the power to mend my lacerated heart!"

"Our lady! lacerated, when you proposed the suppression of the heiress because she was not the heir!"

"Oh, that was my joke—it is the kidnapers who took it too deeply in earnest! But they are nearing the goal!"

"How—tell me! How do you feel so much eagerness to recover what was a detriment years ago?"

"Because the dolt of an attorney to whom was confided the papers of my relative, did not inform me till he died, a few years ago, that a second testament amended the former and left the vast sum to my offspring whatever the sex!"

"So, now I understand the revival of affection! I wish you success with your hirelings."

"Then, if you will let me pass——"

"But you said that you visited them by order of the queen?"

"I am trying to kill—that is, catch two birds with the same lure!"

"Let me see; the queen is the patroness of that dancer—pride of their tribe?"

"She begs her to come live in the palace beside her!"

"She refused! She is a stone! But to penetrate tne accursed ward—you must be furnished with a more powerful open-sesame than the queen's name!"

"It is true; this scarf makes all doors open and all windows turn! The gypsies sleep in the open air, but you understand the figure!"

"Let me see that scarf!" The old marquis drew a curious Indian fabric from his bosom, and the other examined it as well as he could in the poor light. It was embroidered with Arabic letters, perhaps a prayer, but it looked what they called "magical." Don José shivered a little, and, without letting the noble perceive it, kissed the muslin.

"It is Maritana's," he said.

"Yes, and that is why I can, under its shelter, pierce to the King of the Gitanos' presence. Poor king—his throne an empty wine-cask, his sceptre a seaman's pipe, and his cup a pewter pot."

"Listen," said José, gravely, retaining the scarf. "My police inform me that there has been uncommon agitation in this region of blackness since a fight of gamesters over their spoil. The flame of riot spreads, and there has been another 'ruffling,' from which a captain of the guards lies bleeding in the hospital; so, as your life is precious to your lost child—and the royal lapdogs— I would beg to relieve you of your mission this time. Let one of my men replace you!"

"Well, this is kind, but——"

"Hie home and resume your broken rest. In the morning tell the queen that you fearlessly executed your errand, and that Maritana, notified of her wish, will have the honor to present herself at the appointed hour!"

"Good; but if she should not come?"

"What is that to your lordship? It will be another of her tantrums! But I believe you may confidently asseverate that she will be at the queen's feet a suppliant for some favor——"

"Which her majesty will be only too glad to meet. I never saw one woman more fond of another."

"Go! If my police accost you, say 'Josephus'—that will pass!"

The instant that the plotter was left alone, he set to laughing, noiselessly, and crushed up the scarf in his hands against his beating breast.

"Why, Fortune is surely my friend!" said he. "It is I who will venture into the lair of his grace of Egypt. The knowledge I gain of their mode of life may be useful to the police minister, as the interview with Maritana will advantage the future prime minister."

At the ingress to the forbidden region he wavered. It was fairly quiet now, since the wassailers had been stupefied by their potions and were wearied by their long tramps for bread and filching during the day.

There was no artificial lights, only the starlight and the vague lustre of a rising moon. The long and narrow court which was the ghetto's main street, was encumbered with peddlers' packs, fishmongers' carts and fruit stalls, while the owners, strewn about as if overthrown by a gale, reposed at random. The repose was fitful, and there was a continual murmur mingled with the snoring.

Don José would have refrained from risking himself among the slumberers, who would perhaps spring up and knife him before he could explain how he came to step upon them, but he spied several figures stealing about in the mass, like watchers.

Emboldened a little, he thrust himself into the squalid passage and groped his way. He did not stoop or skulk, but designedly made himself prominent. Immediately one of the wakeful came toward him and brandished a cudgel.

He hastened to display the scarf and utter the watch-word of the marquis:

"Castillo-Rotondo—from the queen to Maritana!"

Both acted like a charm; not only did the challenger bow, but silently offered his escort. Thus he was piloted unimpeded to the middle of the alley, where the razed foundation of a once-noble mansion afforded shelter to the vagrants in case of a thunderstorm.

As there was no ceiling to the large basement, the gypsies had made tents of old sailcloth and those tarred sheets used by farmers to preserve cut grass until carted into mows.

In one of these tents, occupied by herself alone, the visitor was glad to see the object of his quest.

On his waving the scarf, Maritana rose from sitting on a stool, and advanced to receive him. But, perceiving that he, in the prime of life, bore no resemblance to the old noble, she stopped and exclaimed:

"From her gracious majesty? No, you are not the usual messenger!"

"I am as good," returned Don José, confidently and breathing more freely at noticing that nobody questioned his presence or, indeed, intruded on the girl's privacy. "You remember me, of course? Yet, I think that I cooled a warmth on your cheeks—checked the flow of pleasant thoughts which prevented you sleeping—perhaps they were as delightful as any dreams which might have arisen during your rest!"

"The name of the queen brings smiles to my cheek, sir."

"Yes, you may consider yourself rich in her favor. Rely on her—confide in me, whom she honors with her trust, and ere long the most dazzling of the court beauties will be eclipsed by your splendor."

Her eyes flashed, but instantly repelling the picture his words conjured up, she firmly said:

"I am not going to listen to such 'flummery!' I dare not! My brothers here would stab me to the death if they thought I was to be allured from their midst—my sisters would rend me to shreds if they saw me forsaking them to live in your palace! I do not dispute that my longings are for an easier, a less worrying life, but I was born to it; I have lived it and I must, I suppose, die in it!"

"Never! Does the pearl pray not to be drawn up out of the mud; the diamond that it shall evermore remain in the casing of worthless rock? Trust to your aspirations —to the queen—to him who beseeches you to rise—to try your wings."

"They will not carry me far or high in golden bands! Oh, you cannot deceive me with glozing speech! My roving life has taught me truths above my years! These, my eyes, have seen the plaything of the munificent become the broken doll in the dust next day! No, no, I should be a poor fortune-teller if I did not foresee my destiny!"

"You do not believe your own prophecies!" declared the marquis, energetically. "You may gull the fools who bribe you to promise them the boons they do not deserve, but you know that you are——" he lowered his voice, for one must not fling at the hosts on their own hearth, "you are cheats! Now, I will show you that I learned the black arts as well as the spotless ones at my,

university—the Moors left their hidden lore there, my
gentle maid. That tells me that you fail to tell the truth
because you are not a daughter of the stars——"

"Ah!"

"I will show my skill—unerring, studied, to be depended upon. Give me your hand."

She obeyed him, somewhat impressed by his gravity
and fervency.

He dandled it adoringly. He smoothed it, pretended
to examine the palm, and cried, as if inspired:

"It is clear! You will rise out of the fog and miasma
of this bog; from among these lepers and toads, to be
among the wearers of crowns—or, at least, the coronet!"

"Crowns—coronets!" she murmured, and he felt her
hand start with a bounding of her heart.

"You will become a peeress of the realm!" said he,
earnestly, watching the effect of his pledge.

"A peeress?"

"Countess, marchioness—some such rank!"

She shook her head; she withdrew her hand, which
turned cold.

"You mislead as we do; a gypsy, a peeress? a pagan, a
disbeliever, blessed by the bishops as a countess? You
are a dreamer or a deceiver! The queen did not send
you to play such tricks!"

"The queen sent me to buoy up your soul, to feed your
flame, to encourage you in your hopes!" said the tempter,
energetically, to back his own falsity. "She would not
hold out to you a mockery, but an honorable elevation.
Become a Christian by the rites, and you will be a countess with the Church's benediction!"

"The queen could do this, no doubt!" said Maritana,
faltering.

"And I!" proudly added the noble. "You see you do
not guess my position or you would not doubt that here

speaks a potent friend. Yea, I can realize all the ex-pectations you harbor and which I have multiplied. What is wanted to make you a countess?"

"Too many needs! First, I should require noble birth!"

"Oh, we will arrange that!" said he, lightly. "I hinted at that!"

"My parents, found as you say, would have to be prince and princess, I suppose?"

"We will provide the aristocratic parents," returned the marquis, confidently.

"Or I should be raised to the dignity by marriage——"

"That is a good way!" approved José, smiling paternally.

"To find a count?" said she, meditating.

"Do not look afar when you have one under your hand!"

"You! you are a count?"

"Oh, better than that, but—hold! how happy! One would not seek in a gypsy camp for a true peer of Spain, but poverty, waste and recklessness makes a man fellow with the lowest!"

"Oh, you speak of Don Cæsar de Bazan—poor gallant!"

"Poor? A man with his title cannot be poor if he brings his hand to the right market! With that hand he can lift any of his present companions to his level! A ruined spendthrift, his losses can be repaired—his noble lineage will replace him in his seat!"

"I should like him to be restored, sir," said the girl, sympathetically, "for he is indeed noble—he has saved me from insults worse than death! I owe him much! He has taught me what a gentleman is like!"

"He shall place you where you shall learn what a lady

does! In a word, I am not only messenger of our queen, but intermediary of my cousin, Cæsar! He loves you!"

"Don Cæsar loves me?"

José shuddered: he saw that he had-chanced on a fact which went beyond his wishes. This girl loved the wildling, and he was espousing the cousin whom he detested at heart, to the woman who had enthralled him more than he cared to avow.

"It is he who loves me! it is for me that he has dwelt with us, liars, thieves, blood-spillers? Ah, he must love, to suffer their lazar-house, as you see it, for his abode, their infectious company for society, their fate, peradventure, to become his own! I see, I see! It is not misery which dragged him down and held him in the kennel— it is love—love for me!"

"I see that you make it an easy task for his advocate!"

"His advocate?"

"Oh, my cousin is so timid—in matters of love! I am sure that, married to the woman of his choice, he will no longer rove—that the family will be content with him, thus happily settled down, and as they restore him the sway over his fettered estates, I will restore him his place at court!"

"How good you are! Have you the power?"

"My lady the countess *in futuro!* you are doing the honor to confer with Don José de Santarem, marquis and police minister to the king, his favorite minister! and on passing good terms likewise with the queen, your patroness!"

Maritana bowed her head: the moon shone into the dirty passage and a stray reflected ray encircled her fair brow with an aureole.

"Look!" said the police chief, holding up a coquettish Venetian handglass which dangled from her girdle, "the

countess is crowned! Dream no more! you have not
leaned on phantoms!"

"No, no! his proud family will not love me because
he does. They will not welcome me any more than the
court! not even king and queen—not your might, however enviable, can introduce the daughter of nothing—
who will be a countess but by the count's grace!"

"You forget half my promise—you shall have noble
parents to answer for you! They might not have stood
sponsors at your christening—though much may be said
on that head!—but they will reply for you at the bridal
altar!"

Maritana's face shone with bliss.

"Can you leave here as freely as I was admitted to
you?" he questioned in a guarded voice.

"Certainly! who would dare detain me? We are free,
we gypsies!"

"Well, freedom's daughter," said he, gayly, holding out
his hand as if to lead her into the dance, "let me conduct you to wear fetters of gold and silk—but they will
set light—brought to you, by lover, king and queen!"

The girl caught up a mantle, draped herself while taking the first step, and accompanied her guide out of the
vile suburb, believing that she would never enter it again.

Light was her heart, though filled with happiness, but
it was not so light as her companion's. He was already
tasting a triumph.

CHAPTER VII.

AWAITING THE GALLOWS.

The city authorities, too often reproached for letting the Jewry be the eyesore of Madrid, saw in the prisoner, Don Cæsar, a type of the spendthrifts who presented a bad example and fortified the rabble by their having a noble among them, would no doubt have dealt harshly with their catch. Unfortunately for their zeal, a special order from the council removed the Count of Garofa from their jurisdiction on the ground that he could appeal to a tribunal of his peers, and he was transferred from the city prison to the House of Correction, one of a castellated group of buildings, together with which was the semi-private residence of the police lieutenant.

But the hapless adventurer had gained nothing much by the removal. A court of high justices, with whose degree the reduced peer could find no fault, heard the deposition by the midnight oil and, conferring merely for form's sake, decided that the king's decree was exclusive of mercy. Don Cæsar de Bazan, Count of Garofa, etc., was returned to his cell, condemned to die the death of felons, all within an hour.

"To a fast liver, a fast death, all in the Fast time!" cried the incorrigible jester.

Alas! the jailers were dull clods, the rust and dust had stopped up their ears; they were such stiff and stern audience that the gallant, accustomed to bad society rather than none, was rejoiced no little by a visitor who came to stay a lifetime—his!

"Lazarillo?" cried he.

"It is I, my lord."

"A fellow-prisoner?"

"You forget—I was appointed your page, my lord! In that capacity I sued the corregidor to let me share your last hour——"

"You are exact as a clock—it is an hour! I thank the corregidor, since he permitted this boon!"

"Yes, he said that you might require me, since I could write."

"A sorry accomplishment! If, when I was implored to set my name to the back of a 'kite'—that is, a note which flies so high that it goes out of sight—I had been able to say: I cannot write, I should have saved ten *per centum* of my loose cash! You are grateful and the prison governor is kind!"

"Perhaps not so kind," said Lazarillo, roguishly.

"How is that?"

"He hinted that if I could inspire such confidence in you that you would tell where you had buried your share of the plunder which your friends, the gypsies, must have gained over the usual haul by your skillful planning and leadership in their pillaging, cloak-snatching and purse-cutting, why, he would go bail for me for quitting my prenticeship and give me a tithe of the sums recovered."

"So, so, it was time that I quitted this scurrilous world! To believe that a Garofa drinks with thieves only to thieve with them, when he wants the cup replenished! And I signed the petition in my heyday for that rascal to become corregidor! If ever I have a day to spare, I would call on him with a cane and correct the corrector!"

"A day to spare," repeated the boy, looking out of the window at the great clock in the courtyard gilded by the rising sun. "It is less than two of the twenty-four that you can call your own, poor master!"

"Almost two hours," yawned Don Cæsar, sinking back in the armless wooden chair, "I shall cheat the hangman by dying bored to death in ten of such minutes. How do those life prisoners beguile the time?"

"No experience, sir," said Lazarillo, making the tour of the apartment, which was tolerable and the best that they could give a peer.

"Boy, if you were a man and you had scant two hours to while away, how would you wear them out?—heigho!"

"Ay de mi!" responded Lazarillo, piously, "if I were your lordship, I would pass them in turning over the errors of my misspent career!"

"You would! 'Out of the mouths of babes comes wisdom!' Recall my errors in a couple of hours! Balderdash! You are forgiven for being ignorant of my career! Sum up my past errors—no, youth; no, there is not sufficient time to head the chapters! Let me see, as you boast of your clerkship—suppose I let you draw up my will! Oh, you need not ring for a ream of paper and a quart of ink, to say nothing of a sheaf of quills— my estate will not take more than a line! No, that would not take up the two hours!"

Lazarillo was cut to the heart by the thoughtlessness and jocularity. He fell on his knee to the speaker and took his hand, saying, piteously:

"Good, my master; make peace with the Church!"

"Oh, I am easy on the point of the steeple! Never did I eat of a stolen porker but I dropped a coin in the begging-box for St. Anthony, because it was his pig, and to St. Matthew because he was a publican!"

"My lord," sobbed the boy, "I am the cause of this clipping of your wings—you are going to give up your life for poor little me! Tell me, is there no deed in my capacity by which I can testify to my regret and my thankfulness?"

In his excitement, he caught the other by the dingy, raveled ruffle.

"Why, yes, you can oblige me extremely—by showing a little more regard for my Mechlin lace! See! you have torn it so that the dainty deathsman, rejecting it as his perquisite, will scornfully cast it aside to his assistant!"

"What a mishap! Have you, a noble of the realm, no one to intercede for you? no one who can speak face to face with our lord the king? Are all to act like heirs— who wish you out of their way?"

"Don't harrow me by talking of heirs! If I had heirs, and being thirsty, they went down into my castle cellar, by Silenus! they would have to suck the staves, for sorry a drop have I left in one of them!" He smacked his lips like cracking a coach-whip.

"Will no one plead for you?"

"Wait—only it would be too late! But perhaps already, the movement in my favor is being made!"

"What movement?"

"Oh, I see—on the mental mirror, of course—a long and multitudinous procession, venerable old men, with tears in their gummy eyes, with scrips full of protested paper, with bills a yard long, hastening out to the palace, throwing themselves, like Orientals, in the path of the royal coach and crying out in voices to crack the panels:

" 'Sire, mercy! Life for Don Cæsar, Count of Garofa!' "

"Oh, you have a few friends who will do this?"

"Hum! I do not say yea to 'friends,' but creditors! creditors! my boy, who see, with my kicking away the ladder, the last tie removed which attached me to their files and ledgers!"

"But you have noble friends, exalted companions?"

"The last of my friends was that host of the Next Sovereign, who chalked up the cost of the supper with which I treated the associates in my last duel! And my last knightly companions were the Caballeros of the Hempen Collar of St. Nick! I do not malign them—I dare say they

would like to call, but there are reasons, which delicate
susceptibilities will appreciate, preventing them knocking
at a prison door. They might be recognized, they might,
dear little Lazarillo, as still owing a part of a term of
residence herein! I forgive them! Friends—friends?"

He sang lustily, without a sad note:

"King Pandion is dead, dead, dead!
All his friends are lapped in lead!"

"To die alone!" sobbed the boy, muffling his face in his
flowing sleeve.

"Oh, we are a family of sensitiveness, the Garofas.
When my ancestors rode over the battlefield they used to
exterminate the Moors—they could not bear to see them
linger in pain! They were caused such infinite dolor when
they were sued to pay a dollar that they put off the payment to the Judgment Day! They could not bear to see
me in these dumps—so they stay away, out of pure tenderness!"

The door had been opened during this pathetic lament.
A man was ushered in ceremoniously by a head warder,
and he and the turnkey saluted as they withdrew. The
visitor wore a short cloak, and on lifting up the front of
his wide hat he disclosed well-known features.

"You forget me, who does not stay away!" said this
newcomer.

Cæsar had heard the door close and the lock again grating under the key. He rose and returned the salute.

"If it is not my cousin, then I am in a vision!" said he,
with insulting surprise.

The page retired, unnoticed, into the recess where the
bed stood amid hangings. He knelt and prayed.

"You wrong me, cousin, by this amaze!" said José, reproachfully. "Have I not always been your friend? You
do not know that since I became chief of his majesty's

police I removed the official records which would **have** paraded the disgrace of the Garofas to posterity! Come, do I not prove my sincerity by coming to you when you have committed a crime in the teeth of the royal mandates?"

"If you had called on me at the city prison and got them to treat me as became my rank, it would be a point in your favor!"

"I was doing better than that. I obtained your transfer to this jail—a state's prison, and imposing no stigma!"

"By the black goat of my friends, the Gitanos! This is a boon! Why, the other, rotten, dilapidated, could have been stormed by the vagabonds and I rescued, while this old fort, where a regiment is in barracks, is stout enough to be irresistible! I thank you for nothing, cousin!"

"There must be something I can do?"

"Well, let your sympathy be manifested by hurrying on my execution!"

"Hurrying it on!" ejaculated José, astounded, while a broken-hearted sob came from the praying boy.

"To be sure! That cursed cider at the city lockup gave me a toothache, and there is no such sovereign specific to stop a jumping pang as the tightening of a halter."

"Ah, it is there that I may be in time to serve you."

He looked at his huge box of a watch and shook his head.

"Our clock says one and a quarter hours!" said the profligate, coolly. "You see that the reproach was undeserved that I was a thief of time! I like to be exact when life is so short!"

"It may be lengthened in your case, so that we may understand each other."

He took a stool which the boy had used and faced his relative calmly, though he felt that the negotiation would be arduous with such a flippant debater.

"My time, my lord, is all my own—and hence, all your own!" observed Cæsar, with excruciating politeness. "You will overlook my offering no whet over this possibly dry talk, for, in fact, the steward has gone away with the cupboard key—in short, we are at the beck of the servants here. There is too much care—lock and key!"

"Don Cæsar, what would be your dying request, provided that I had in my power to grant it?"

"Don José, my dying request would logically be to live longer!"

"After the royal decision that the king will listen to no plea for mercy for controvening his express injunction, that I cannot engage. But I swear, as the king's premier ——"

"Hallo! have you got your leg up? Whew! what an honor to the Santarems, who are, after all, subsidiary Garofas! But, mark you! the premiership is a skittish horse to ride. Mind you do not get thrown in putting it through the preliminary canter!"

"Let me alone for that; I am not so weak a jockey. But as the prime minister, and as your friend and kinsman, you may have anything you state, always excepting the life."

"A Santarem a premier! Oh, that I had accepted the proposal of my friend the king of the Egyptians to be his right-hand man! Two prime ministers in our families! What honors!"

"Your desire!"

"How awkward, for I do not want anything so much as what I am about to lose—my life!"

"Nothing else—no acquaintance, no little light-of-love" —earnestly—"no dependent——"

A blubbering from the alcove reminded Don Cæsar of his volunteer page.

"By the dog which died, recognizing the old Ulysses!"

cried he; "you hit it! There is an *attaché* who clings to me like the cat following a sprig of catmint! I should like to do something for my footboy, who is likely to be the world's football unless he is coated with leather!"

"That boy? It was owing to him that you are in the present quandary. You owe him—little."

"As he had served without pay, it is meet that I should leave him a pension—out of your estate!"

"Cousin, this is a trifle. I will provide for the youth."

"So kind of you!" and Cæsar bowed low. "I pay you beforehand with a thousand thanks!"

There fell an irksome pause, during which they heard the low sobbing of the boy—whose note turned, however, from sadness of one kind to a sad gladness of another.

"Nothing more?"

"Lord, no! I think that is all."

José looked perplexed, for the silence about Maritana augured ill for his plot.

"Life is a jest, and one should quit when it pleases best!" said the lively one.

José feared that he could not engage him in his project for so trifling a return.

"Oh," said he, abruptly, "you jest without considering the manner of your leap off this earth!"

"There is something in that! You are no friend to dangle a rope before me! A rope—faugh!"

"By the royal favor, a silk rope has been substituted for the hempen one!" remarked Don José, in an irritating, bitter tone.

"Why, death ought to come to a gentleman by a sword-point of scimetar edge! How lonely I should have felt in paradise at being dispatched there direct for killing the infidel, and so making sure of glory! And the fire that slays out of a hand-gun mouth is not to be sneezed at!

But a beastly dog's leash! Yes, my lord, I find I have one request!"

"Name it, my dear!"

"I will leave the gallows to my creditors and the rope to be used first hand on the keeper of the city prison who offered me, a peer, hard cider! But let me be shot offhand by soldiers! This page of mine tells me that they have served out to the guards some very fine arquebuses, fresh from the Parisian smithies, and quick, clean and sure! I will embrace the honor of their first fruits! Who cannot brave death from brave men? Let me be shot, and meanwhile, let me treat to drink the bold fellows!"

"Drink with your executioners?"

"Don Cæsar has drunk with the sheriff who served him with an eviction! I have sipped with sinners, gulped with gypsies, and clanked the cannikin with coach-strippers! A carouse with jailers and marksmen will not sully the Count of Garofa!"

"You shall enjoy your wish," said the minister, nodding.

"No deception to a dying man?"

"On the name of the Santarem!"

"We will toast each other! It is rather unfair, for while I can sincerely wish them long life, theirs to the like will be hollow—hollow as this earth!"

"My dear, there shall be such a banquet as will recall the love-feasts of the ancients!" cried José, enthusiastically—"our revels at the college and yours among the wreckers of your argosy!"

"Good! The best eating is when another foots the bill!" said the other, like a judge. "My gullet will enjoy this feast, for it began to ache at the fear that the rope would be greased by vulgar tallow!"

"You are an odd fish!" said the minister, laughing in

spite of himself. "There is nothing else but to present my condition!"

"Ah, I might know there would be the P. S.—'Please settle while the tapster is in the room!'"

When they were solemnly seated again, their seats drawn up closely, so that the page should not overhear their dialogue, Cæsar asked what was required of him.

"Not much for a man who might have lost his head. Your hand, Don Cæsar!"

"My hand—with absolutely nothing in it?"

"Oh, it will be full! I simply desire that you should marry!"

"Marry? I am over young! No? Over poor? No! Well, I see no use in this! Is all I can bequeath to the Garofas a widow—a wife for an hour and a half?" said he, looking out at the clock.

"Why, this is under the seal!" returned José, mysteriously.

"I call it the same! It cannot be for my fortune, because the poor relict would have nothing but my debts and my title—no title deeds! Still, the name of Garofa may have its value! Ah, in your late experience of the world watched by the police, you met a woman who wished to become a lady—a countess—I see!"

"It might be so!"

"Well, she shall have it! Anything to oblige a lady!" said the gallant, puffing his words out like so many feathers.

"I thought so," muttered the other; "poverty may not be baseness, but it is a branch of knavery!" He rubbed his hands again as if his palms were itching.

"A name! My name! It is nothing to me and the sooner it decks a wedding certificate as my memorial tomb, the better for the survivor, widow, and the gravestone-graver! Besides, I wanted to fill up my time!

Marriage is something to do—something which I have not done—and one way to kill the Old Fellow with the grass-cutter and the egg-boiler is as good as another! Another philosophical reflection, if my coming out as a Plato does not startle you, José, in so short a honeymoon we cannot have any long tiffs!"

"Let us see; you agree to confer the title of Countess of Garofa on my selection——"

"As we give a name to a flower, let her be as covered with charms as her late lamented was with debts! Oh, there goes with it all my claims, rights and interests in the lands of Garofa, if you can set foot on anything worth my setting my hand and seal unto. Well, I did not lose it in the law courts, anyway—only fools and stubborn-heads fatten lawyers! By the bye, what is the lady's name—her pedigree?"

"Seek not a good woman's pedigree!" retorted his cousin, sententiously.

"A good woman! That is something new—a saint in the Garofas at length! Is she young?"

"Do not ask a woman's age."

"I understand your delicacy, and I smile with you. I wager my life—no, that is hardly mine! My name—no, that will soon be another's—the halter which I re-nounce, that the dame is over fifty!"

"No matter."

"Not in the least; the bargain is struck! I am going to marry—take a wife, as I used, as a boy, to take physic —with my eyes shut."

"You need not do that. The lady, with the modesty of her sex in general and of our race in particular, will wear the orthodox veil, but thick as a Moslem would prescribe, and that will effectually shut out your seeing her attrac-tions."

"Thanks for the delicate consideration shown the

Count of Garofa; as for that to be paid the countess, can
you not double the veil, that she shall not see the bridegroom's groom-of-the-stable-like condition?"

"Faith, you are in your traveling-dress, and the affrays
—first with the arquebusier captain, and then with the
alguazils—have rent it sorely!"

"The legs of the breeches do not match—you see that?
Well, it came about that the tailor I last employed, on
saying that he would not drive a needle unless paid in
advance, and, having half sent on account, laid before me
only one-half the breeches! It is a breach of common
decency between tailor and customer—but, better half a
leg than none. I cobbled it up with the other half of an
old pair!"

"Do not deplore! You shall have a costume becoming
the Count of Garofa! The other cell has been turned
into a dressing-room, as the soldiers' messroom has been
into a banqueting-hall! You see, you are served in all
your suits excellently!"

"If I hear a bad word against your excellency in the
country whither I go, for you may have sent a slanderer
there already, count on my cramming his calumny down
his throat! Now, have with me as you will! Deck me
as the fatted calf! Crown me with rosy-posies as the
pole of May, and lead me to the altar! Epitaph upon the
Last and Best Count of Garofa, *alias* 'the Gay Rover!'
who departed this life in his nine-and-twentieth year,
regretting it was not by so many reverses changed into
ninety-and-two of them!

> "All through his life, he gayly spurned
>   Those common bonds which tie men;
>   Yet freely freedom sacrificed
>   To be the slave of Hymen"

"Boy," said Don José, to the lad coming respectfully

and with some warmth of eye out of his covert, "you are in my service henceforth. This way, cousin, dear!"

Cæsar lagged a little. After the gush of fervor had come second thought, and he muttered under his easy smile:

"What suit does he prosecute for this suit he gives me? Oh, he offers a sausage to secure a whole pig! He is marrying off an old frump of a housekeeper so as to utilize my death!"

CHAPTER VIII.

PREPARING TO DIE.

Don José went into the governor's own rooms, which had been handed over to him during his stay.

He refreshed him with wine and felicitated himself on his astute management. Ordinary diplomatists let men be hanged and make no use of them. His superior tact had converted the useless Don Cæsar into a lever to raise his fortunes.

"He will be married and give my peerless Maritana a title in which she will be resplendent, while he trailed it in the mire. Without wishing it or guessing it, he has assisted in the attainment of my highest desires!"

The varlet awaiting his orders was given such as would have the feast for the soldiery got ready, as well as all the preparations for the drumhead wedding in the castle chapel.

After the removal of the barrier to further progress in Don Cæsar's execution, Maritana would be titled, and the king might advance his suit without censure at stooping too low. "Garofa" would hide the gypsy brand. The plotter only trembled lest he might be blamed by the queen for using her name in bending the dancing-girl to his course. But he believed that she would in time close her eyes to anything perpetrated against her rival. The only thing was that he must not fan her resentment, or he should lose in the girl his only hold on the jellyfish with a crown known as Carlos, "the royal imbecile."

The clock was on the stroke of six when a courier came to the gates seeking the police minister, who had not yet been proclaimed minister-in-chief of state, though placed so in the court chronicles.

José broke open the packet with some trepidation; such waders in troubled waters are ever apprehensive lest they stumble into the deep and meet some sharp which would maim them in their enterprise.

It was the royal pardon, spite of precedent, and the royal word that, this time, forgiveness was debarred.

The truth was that Cæsar's family, learning that the king had waived the letter of the decree and allowed the bullet to be substituted for the halter, had taken a step further and so besought, pleaded and bewailed that Don Carlos had relented altogether.

"Cæsar is pardoned!" growled the minister. "Luckily this reaches my hand, and not the corregidor's. Poor, weak Charles! But it is well that he should do an occasional kind act in order that his ministers should get applauded now and then! All know the course! A subject is doomed to death—well! but the good king is appealed to and his melting heart is reached—well! Of course, the blowpipe ministerial did the fusion, and the pardon is written by the minister and signed by the king, who gets but part the praise. It is sad, but one of those inexplicable counter-tides set in, which will run in the best-governed kingdom: the pardon arrived too late! It is like the doctor's boy, stopping to play leapfrog and bringing the phial of panacea in time to sprinkle it on the coffin! What a mournful mishap!" and he wiped his eyes after wiping his lips. "My poor coz! He was to be turned off to the musket-practice at seven and this pardon will not arrive until eight!"

He buttoned the paper up securely in his inner pocket.

"But you will see that the king and his new prime minister will be blessed for the exercise of the crown's

finest prerogative, which, I believe, is also Messire St.
Peter's!"

While finishing the wine and feeling the diverted pardon press on his usually petrified heart, he heard the
soldiers in the yard.   Rejoiced by the feast which was to
be given to overcome that dread and dismal mood evolved
from a military execution, they were singing, as they
polished their arms to look their best in the culprit's
honor :

> "With measured step and gloomy brow,
>   Behold the dreadful choice platoon:
> Where solemnly dead masses flow
>   To one whose corse will fall eftsoon!
>   But what recks he who meets that call
>   When, like a soldier, still, he'll fall?
>
> With jocund cheek and lightsome gait,
>   Behold return they who have slain;
> No dismal chants intimidate
>   The one who's finished life's campaign.
>   Oh, what shall reck who meets that call
>   And, like a soldier brave, will fall?"

José started with a shock, for in the person who entered he saw not the man already dead in his eyes, but
a perfect renewal of all that had made the mad-headed
Count of Garofa the idol of the court.

Cæsar was attired with the most scrupulous care in
the truly magnificent costume which his cousin had furnished.   Nothing could be in more extreme contrast to
the miserable, faded, frayed and tousled finery which he
had discarded.   Here was all the sumptuousness which the
gloomy monarchs of semi-monastical Spain had vainly
sought to blot out.   Satin, silk, gold and beaded lace,
plumes, silk hose, and regalia of the orders of chivalry to
which he was entitled—he was a mannikin for a cos-
tumer's window but for the manner of his bearing it off.

It was that of the born aristocrat, used to such pomp from infancy.

It was the bridegroom's dress, true; but he resembled more, from a slight seriousness on his brow, that warrior who was wont to don his finest suit when he went into action.

"Ah, coz, the phœnix rises out of the ash heap!" cried he, with overflowing gayety. "Are velvet and gold thrown away upon your kinsman? Do you see, I the more sincerely thank you for this compliment, as who knows but that I may meet St. Michael, king of the warrior angels, and I wish to do credit to my corps!"

"St. Michael! Where you are going, I doubt he was ever!"

"Oh, you are behindhand with your Scripture! Did not the sword-bearing archangel chase the fiends into Tophet?"

"You will be the figurehead at the banquet, that is positive," continued the prime minister. "I have had everything prepared as becomes a marriage of a grandee. Look into the other hall!"

Cæsar peeped, and started back from the gorgeous spread. When this prison-house was a Moorish palace, never had its board been loaded with such dainties.

"Wine in flagons of parcel-gilt! This is setting silver apples in basins of gold! I would wish you could create my guests noble, so that they would not be outranked by that Westphalian boar, that right royal buck's haunch, that imperial swan, roasted in its tail! Wine, wine!"

"Then there is nothing lacking?"

"Yes, one thing—one savor, one adornment, one tidbit! Woman, lovely woman! But why did I say woman? It reminds me of my coming disaster—my marriage!"

"It is true! I will immediately present to you the Countess de Bazan!"

With these words he quitted the apartment, and, allured by the table, Don Cæsar passed into the armory hall.

It was hastily, but passably, decorated for the extraordinary ceremony within those gray walls, streaked with the rust of chains. But the soldiers of the firing-file, together with their comrades, gave but a fleeting glance to the man they were about to slay, on beholding the bounteous display.

"The Germans," said the shining host, "have a morality; that all good things go in threes. I must say that here we have three good things, indeed," taking his place at the head of the board, "good welcome!"

"All hail Don Cæsar de Bazan!"

"Good entertainment!"

A murmur of approval, as from bees at the edge of honey cups.

"And good-sped to the departing host!"

There was a protest in a deep voice at this untimely reminder.

"They all three make good company, the best company! Comrades, for I was an ensign in the Royal Guards, fall to!"

There was a great scuffling as the men dropped into their seats and proceeded to demolish the pies and pasties, which were only made to increase their thirst.

"The sole regret I feel—but do not let it be a damper— is my being compelled to limit our regale! I have an appointment of some moment—very few moments, egad!"

He stood up, the others at ease, all having fully-charged bumpers.

"Aha, Oporto, I hail thee, old and early friend—also, my latest one! 'Tis long since we met, and I have been palmed off with pretenders, who claimed kin with thee,

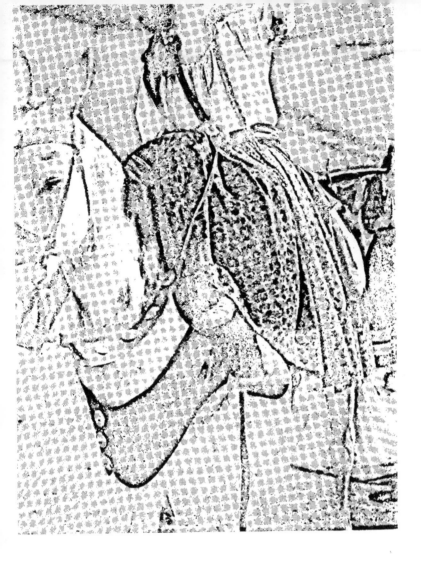

POLA NEGRI IN HERBERT BRENON'S

without foundation of a grape! True descendant of the vine, tempter of Father Noah, who would not have taken to the boats if you had been the chief component of the flood! Offspring of our sister Portugal, me seems, you have a Moorish smack! Fill up again, boys! Now, to one who is not yet entitled to grace my board—to the lady of my house! to the health of the Countess of Bazan and Garofa!"

Rising, the troopers shouted the toast till the rafters of the old Alcazar threatened to be down about their ruddy ears.

"Gentlemen of the Arquebuse," said the host, rising for the last time, "it is proper and of good usage for the traveler starting on a vague journey, the knight pricking forth on his errand, the mariner adventuring to sea, to preach a moral to those who wish him well! Listen to mine, which has the brevity of wit and a novelty which may recommend it!" With an unshaken voice, mellow with the wine, he trolled:

"No doubt there's a lay—(for the rhymer spares none)
To the bride of a day, wed in name—still a nun!
To no end may you browse, among verse, sweet or sour!
There's no line to the Spouse who was wed for an hour!

Oh, soldiers, we're sheep, whose time ne'er's our own,
We let others reap where hast'ly we've sown;
We're roused from the plank; we're marched from the bower,
No rest but where sank the Spouse of an Hour!

Did Methusalem wed? If so, early and once?
Living nine hundred years! Fie! who'd vie with that dunce?
Far happier Jove, when his dread golden shower
Divorced from his love that great Spouse of an Hour!"

He turned amid the somewhat sad applause to the window, which gave a limited view of Madrid's scores of steeples, spires and towers, and said, with false emotion:

"Farewell, my natal city! I have yearned to hang

upon your neck, and you came precious near to hanging
me on your gibbet! Farewell, the seventy churches
which I have never intruded upon, and the ten thousand
taverns, wineshops and popular resorts, where I have
run up many a flight of stairs and longer bills! Farewell, blessed bells, which will about the same time ring
in my wedding and my funeral! Farewell, squares and
gardens, where I have laid my drunken pate! Farewell,
the palace grand entrance, into which I have been mar-
shaled with the grandees' honors, and the Fuencanal
Arch, out of which I have been expelled with my vagrant
friends by the beadle of St. Espirito's. Farewell, Hall of
Battles in the Escurial, where my ancestors' doughty
deeds are depicted, and petty hall of battles in the Next
Sovereign ding-house, where my feats are dented in the
wall with empty wine pots and knife points which missed
my ear! Farewell!"

The clock struck half-past six. The morning was
ablaze in the east, and the city glistened in every passage
open to the god of day.

There was a flourish of trumpets.

A man clad in black opened the door and shed dullness over the festive chamber by his suit and demeanor.

It was the usher of the prison director. He announced
all unpleasant matters, as a stage manager has to apologize for disappointing the audience.

"My lord," said he in a lugubrious croak like a bit-
tern's; "the judge desires a hearing!"

"What, my old acquaintance, the justice of the Insol-
vent Debtors' Court!" cried the gentleman in the white
satin, advancing briskly.

"No, my lord," replied the usher, reproachfully. "The
Chief Justiciary!"

"Really? They do the Count of Garofa too much
honor! Let him come!"

CHAPTER IX.

WEDDED BEHIND PRISON BARS.

There was an impressive show. The judge was accompanied by two juniors, several secretaries, registers, clerks, what not, with a special guard of halberdiers. Don Cæsar, in his brightness, seemed a butterfly among bloated black spiders. He bowed to the judge, lowly it was true, but perhaps his bow was even more respectful to the Chief Alguazil, next to the Minister of Police in his estimation.

A tribunal was improvised for the legal dignitary by placing a chair on a platform, whence the wine butt was drawn, and the judge, flourishing a parchment, intoned in a Jeremiah's voice as follows:

"In the name of the king, Don Carlos, etc.

"His majesty graciously accords to Don Cæsar of Bazan, the Count of Garofa, etc., his royal grace! The count will not suffer the death designated to offenders in this degree at the hands of the common executioner, nor yet of the royal headsman, but, by our royal pleasure, will be conducted from the hold of his present prison to the barrack-yard of the Royal Arquebusiers, under their escort, and be shot by a file of the commander's selection."

"It may be to the royal pleasure," murmured the culprit, "but I will be hanged, that is, will be shot! if it is to mine!"

This was not heard by the judge, who darted at him a lingering glance, like one who was losing a prey, and folding up the order, which his clerk took, he solemnly bowed to the unfortunate man and retired.

At the door he paused and remarked grumblingly to his secretary:

"What mountebank's trick is this? He is tricked out like the gypsy dancers, only that the material is genuine. Is he. allowed to put all the plunder out of goldsmiths, drapers and bootmakers upon his back?"

"I think, my lord," said the writer, "that, as the condemned leaves all his attire to the deathsmen, he, having been of the guards, in his younger and better days, wants to remunerate them well for shooting him with fatal aim!"

It was a quarter to seven—Don Cæsar resumed his stand at the table head, as if they had not been interrupted.

"You will tell me," said he genially, "if a poet's infatuation for his children leads him to surfeit you, but I have just time to enchant you with another couplet of my composition! Little did I think, when I wrote out the rough draft, years ago, in the camp before Tarbes, that this little impromptu should give so much amelioration to the sharpest of pangs!"

They could not do more, for such a host, than fall into "attention," and assume such stolidity as characterizes the military hearing "orders of the day."

"You will pardon me, my lord," said the usher, who had dropped out of the ranks of the sinister cortege, and taken a drink out of a flagon without being asked. "But they are going to smother up this case so that your name may go down to posterity unsmirched."

"You don't say that?" said the host. "They are not going to burn me, that I shall say nothing?"

"But they will burn all the papers!"

"Then they should burn the judges and accessories as well, for that justice is a blab—I can tell that by the mouth on him! Never mind, if my verse is spared, that

will be enough to immortalize the Count of Garofa! Not
many counts of my house have done so little guiltily as
murder—the grammar of his time! To my last verse,
gentlemen!"

And as fluently as before he recited:

"So envy the Jack, whose wedlock was curt!
If one's snatched off the rack, the less depth to one's hurt.
He may mock at the cloud full of storms—let them lour;
What of lightning can shroud the blest Spouse of an Hour?"

The recitation was a little marred by an organ in the
chapel, tuning up mournfully, and soon the monks were
heard practicing a hymneal pæon so dolefully that "the
Jubilate" might as well have been "the Misericordium."

"Hark! she comes! Gentlemen, decorum—here comes
my wife!"

Lazarillo appeared at the door and sang out lustily:

"Way for the Countess of Garofa and Bazan!"

Behind a veiled figure, robed in rich white, Don José
showed himself. He wore a vizard, which concealed his
identity from few. Several enigmatical persons, his
agents, or the prison governor's servants, brought up the
rear. After the sedate judge's cohort, this was tame.

The soldiers had saluted the lady, but embarrassed by
the indelicacy of their confronting the spouse of the man
they were about to convert into a human sieve, they le-
vanted with celerity. Lazarillo, struck with a sudden
thought as he noticed that the wine had got into even
their hardened skulls, fleetly followed them, and was
eager to make friends with them by proving that he had
not forgotten, in becoming a page, the art of loading the
firearms.

The marquis whispered to his cousin:

"Bear your promise in mind. Not a word! Not a
peep!"

Don Cæsar shook his head; the veil was impenetrable.

"The bride awaits the bridegroom's hand," said the master over this unwonted ceremony.

The count took the hand presented with curiosity; it was soft and yet not wholly that of a court lady, bathed in a glove of unguent by night and embalmed by day. There was no jewel on it by which a patrician could tell the wearer. It was quite a small hand to belong to that tall figure. It had not a wrinkle; but, then, all the wrinkles might be on the head. He stared in vain, for never had a woman in Christendom been so muffled up before.

He was interrupted in his fruitless scrutiny by Don José significantly indicating the time on his watch.

He had ten minutes more.

He gallantly lifted the hand to his lips and imprinted a kiss upon it, while he said:

"My Dulcina, to you I devote the remainder of my existence!"

A servant took up her train, and the two went out by a door leading into the passage for the chapel.

At every turn and nook there was a warder.

"Verily," observed Don Cæsar, "the governor thinks I might take French leave. But if this, by any chance, is one of those to whom I promised eternal love, he might guess that she would never let me escape between this and the altar."

He could not well beat a retreat, for the prime minister followed closely behind them.

"He has no faith in me," muttered the Benedict; "now I hold that it will be fair to thwart him in this detestable scheme."

The marquis' varlet had been left behind; he ceased in a testing of the dregs in the wine cups on hearing steps at the main doorway. A servant of the corregidor, delighted at being able to spoil his sport, uttered in a sonorous voice:

"Their lordship and ladyship, the Marquis of Castello-Rotondo and the Marchioness of Ditto," and, in a lower voice: "Comrade, you are to show them to Don José, your master, as soon as the function is over in the chapel."

The domestic looked with amusement on the old gentleman and his lady, another wrinkled dame relic of the previous reign, who had plastered out the creases without canceling them, and rouged without the irritation becoming a blush, and blackened around her sunken eyes without bringing them anew to the front.

"Where on earth can they have brought us, by the marquis' wish?" inquired the old noble, disdaining to question the menial.

"Is it a prison?" counter-queried the lady, scanning the vault and barred windows with awe.

Her lord had made the round of the table and examined with a lens set in his canehead, the residue of the more substantial part of the feast.

"This cannot be a prison, though attached to the house of correction, for this never was prison fare, a dish of ortolans prepared in sauce after the imperial mode, such as can emanate solely from the first cuisine of Madrid; venison, teal, mountain pigeons; no prison fare."

"Is it a monastery?"

"Up aloft it does look monastic—but here on our level some wine is left, and it is choice. Now, in a monastery refectory there is no good wine, and if there were, they would not have left a drop. No, my darling angel, this is not a monastery!"

"What place can it be, then, into which to drag such blue-blooded beings as our select selves?"

"My seraphic one, it does not amount to a fly-speck where we are. Suffice it, that we have done precisely what the eminent Don José has laid down; and who thinks to censure a prime minister? He sent a coach for us, quite up to our style——"

"The coach-and-four was quite good enough, and I know my rights."

"The driver said he was ordered to take us somewhere, and put us down there. Why have we been set down somewhere? If the delay is to be long before an elucidation, I shall bend to consoling myself," and he proceeded to lift a bottle to his parched lips.

"Armeric! desist! there is a waiter in the room!" shrieked the marchioness.

"That is only Don José's man—who has, I warrant, seen his master drink out of the pail when it was summer-heat. If he eyes me sourly, it is because he had his hand on this bottle for himself."

"This is all very well, in obedience to the king's first minister, but as regards Don José, who is only of your own rank, why should you consent to be his mere puppet?"

"I am not a puppet! the Castello-Rotondos——"

"Yes, I have had their exploits at the time when the Cid was their armor-bearer drummed into me. It seems to me that you can do nothing without him. All you possess seems at his nod and beck."

"All but my adored wife."

"Pooh, pooh," but she was flattered.

"A rash hand—a rough word to her, and out flies the sword of my forefathers——"

"So far, that you would not recover it in time to transfix the insulter."

"Subtility of fence! You ladies would know nothing about such manly matters. I am afraid, like all dames of the court, nest of ingrates, that you despise that sacred

sentiment which goes by the euphonious name of gratitude!"

"Gratitude? I find that the art of ingratiating thrives
best with one in the palace."

"What were we before we were taken up by this rising
politician?"

"Happy."

"Happy, perhaps, but nobodies—vegetables in the
rural districts. I bore a proud old title; the Castello-
Rotondos were known like the two Castles of Castile,
but I was in a corner, cobwebbed over. You were radi-
ant with loveliness, but your charms were like a rich
flower's lost among weeds. My merits were going to
seed—your beauty was unseen. Was it not Don José of
Santarem who, running against me at a hunt in my
grounds of the Round-Tower, accepted my apology for
being nearly unhorsed, and assured me that he would die
if I did not come to court?"

"He certainly remembered you when you went up to
town with me."

"Yes, he included you in the invitation. He said that
the queen was not the mirthfulest of monarchs' consorts;
that she required cheering up, and that you, with your
bright sallies, would stir up as my ancestors did the
enemy in making upon them their sallies from the
Round-Tower."

"He gave you a court appointment," said the marchioness, smiling.

"A sinecure; to keep the maps in order in the Escurial
library. I was the royal cartularist and chartographer
honorary. That is a link on a chain which lengthens it
out and made my neighbors glare with envy when they
saw the badge on my right shoulder. A golden compass
stuck on a map of the world, with Madrid the center."

"Then it was the marquis who gave you a higher step," said the lady, with the same flattering smirk.

"Yes, I am now, still thanks to Santarem, chief keeper of the regal hennery—I mean, pheasantry—the aviarist royal."

"But why should your talents be restricted to raising Indian fowl?"

"My lady, I do not raise them—I eat them. I confess that I never had so many friends as since I had the excess of golden pheasants to bestow among my acquaintances."

"But to hatch turkeys."

"Madam, do not speak with inconsiderateness of incubation. For these honors, which my brother peer has kindly showered upon me, I have vowed to devote myself to forwarding his wishes, and I may say that never would he have been police minister without my strenuous exertions, and not premier but for my trumpeting his claim for the exalted post."

"Then," said the lady, pouting, "he might at least create you keeper of the seals instead of the Indian gamecocks——"

"Bless us and save us, the lord chancellor does not keep seals of the ocean—they are, the Lord conserve your girlish guilelessness; they are wax stamps of quite another kidney. So I meet his wishes and comply with them all, however incomprehensible they are to us."

"Well, he certainly acted a kind part in finding for us our long-lost darling, Maria."

"That is so—he had great daring to go in among the gypsies to wrench from the Duke of Egypt the final answer, which they had fobbed me off from for years. But there is no refusing anything to a minister of police. The criminals may well be fearful of the lieutenant-criminal."

"Only, we have but his word for it—suppose not that he, a noble, would deceive a brother noble, but that those necromancers have deceived him. This girl suddenly produced from the shadowy world of vagabondage might be a changeling palmed off on us by the sons of Ananias."

The old marquis shuddered, but quickly replied:

"Well, I am so eager to see our darling again that I would be easily cheated—I admit so much, but you, the mother! ah, the mother's instinct is not to be deluded. You will recognize your Maria, or I will go in eternal exile to the Holy Land!"

"Without me? What would I and your daughter be, with no mind so clever as yours, no sword so keen and ready to defend us in case we were insulted?"

"Your honor menaced!" cried Castello-Rotondos. "Let a breath attack your honor, or my child's, and this good blade, made at Fuentes by the celebrated sword-smith, the cross-eyed Leon, would leap out of its case! You do not tell me that any one has lampooned my own, my beauteous?"

"Well, not yet, but I foresee that, in accepting this stray child, educated in the hedge-school and finished in the thieves' kitchen of the Bohemians, we are laying ourselves open to many a slur at our being easily gulled. Against me, who can raise a whisper, but this waif, this foundling, who becomes our fondling so mysteriously and suddenly—I am afraid, my own, that you will want to defend with both short and long sword."

"Tush! You will be the best defender of our pet! You, who have with your virtue, repelled those fulsome tongues which for thirty years have merely treasured the hope to speak to you of your attractions. Time himself treads on your cheek without leaving a footprint; your features are unalterable; your beauty is still the base for the deepest-drunk toast at our table, where the wine of my own vintage supplements the culls out of the royal pheasantry!"

"You may kiss me for that sentiment!—but on the hand, pray, for the horrid gnats out of the river-pools have specked my cheek. I have had to inundate it with balm, in spite of my aversion for toilet devices."

"Yes, you would detest artifice. But, hark!"

"There is somebody coming——"

"With a torch!"

"That will enlighten us!"

"Enlighten!—torch? What a fine wit she has! Well," chuckled the old beau, "I wedded that woman because she chaffed me into the union, and I believe that I shall go off to the blest mansions all the gayer because she will let slip some brilliancy at my deathbed!"

"Now," said she, smoothing her laces as a hen strokes down her ruffled feathers, "we shall discover where we are, and perhaps meet this errant daughter of ours!"

"Indeed, it is Don José, and he is not alone!"

"He has a young woman with him!"

"But she is in bridal costume!" cried the marchioness as the Marquis of Santarem appeared, preceded by two pages bearing flambeaus, cermoniously escorting Maritana, still veiled as when united in matrimony to the happy-unhappy Don Cæsar.

"I wish you joy," said the lord of Santarem, presenting Maritana, who made a courtesy as finished as the old lady's, though less stiffly and with the elegance of a trained dancer. "The king, at my instance, has added to your posts that of Master of the Warrens!"

"The head warrener? I am to have the royal rabbits under my charge. Oh, my!" and Castello-Rotondo clasped his hands in rapture.

"As well make him keeper of the whole menagerie at

once!" grumbled the lady, who saw that the stranger was uncommonly handsome and very young.

"Lady fair," continued the marquis, bowing to her and smiling as if she had spoken the most pleasant remark, "the king has not forgotten your exemplary conduct, which keeps the maids of honor in due trim. He begs your acceptance of the late hunting-box at *Las Delices,* with servants, equipment, all in full order, where he further beseeches you to make it pleasant for your daughter, the Donna Maria of Castello-Rotondo——"

"Daughter!" exclaimed the couple in a breath.

Maritana unveiled, for the good nature under the senile silliness was clear to her piercing eyes. Her surpassing brightness and winsomeness completed the capture. The marquis thrilled all over, and his wife melted. Their countenances beamed with smiles.

"Good!" Don José spoke to himself. "A thousand ducats on it my fiction is the truth! The Duke of Egypt did kidnap the old fool's child, and this is the one. I could have sworn from the outset that Maritana was no plebeian. Good! good! I wanted a lady by birth to rule the king, and by so ruling let me rule! I am not the first premier who used the petticoat as a shield and overcame all opposition by a woman's fan! The sword is for brutes; the pen for bookmen; but the fan, it is the instrument for which Archimedes of the court alone wish. It moves the world of fashion and politics, and there is no other!"

Still the two women, insensibly nearing, did not come to contact. It was like two feathers on the pond—they were attracted, but yet something repelled.

"Don José de Santarem declines any thanks for this blessed reunion," said he, loftily. "It is to the persistent researches of the marquis that the recovery of your daughter is due. At the last moment I gave a final impulse which pushes the dear Maritana into her mother's arms.

I hold all the proofs, which the marquis can verify. But I am overzealous—I should have relied on the heaven which has relented in its spite! The voice of nature stirs that bosom—that heart of a thousand! Mother, embrace your child! Father, thank Heaven for this restoration!"

Maritana forgot all but that she had yearned many and many a year for a mother! She opened her arms and sank swooning with joy upon the old marchioness' scraggy neck. The skinny arms met behind her back, and the Marquis of Castello-Rotondo trotted around the pair like a tailor admiring a new suit on a beau, weeping and uttering little cries of delight like a hen which had found a swan's egg and flattered herself that she had laid it.

"Our child!" they both muttered.

"How fair—the image of her maternal progenitress at that age!" exclaimed the courtier.

"I see myself in her!" added the lady.

"Capital!" muttered the minister. "I have made many grin with a skillful lie, but this time, I believe with truth, I have filled that trio with happiness! This will bring a blessing upon the rest of my plan!"

The clock struck seven in the prison yard and the reverberations entered the hall.

"You will therefore take yourself with your new-found child to the hunting pavilion, with which the king favors you! It is convenient to the court, where, as soon as she has rubbed off the asperities gained in conventional life, the Lady Maritana, Countess of Garofa, will assume her place!"

"The Countess of Garofa?"

"Undoubtedly countess! for I was present as best man at her happy wedding with my cousin. You see, I have nothing to win thanks upon—I was only acting for the gain of the family!"

"Then we become relatives?"

"Marquis, we are brothers!" and José shook the other's hand demonstratively.

"I see, I see! The king bestows the hunting-box upon my daughter for the sake of her husband—his favorite, as his father was the last monarch's?"

"Well, no! Out of respect for his memory!"

"His memory?"

"Exactly; for——" he held his hand up to beg attention.

The silence was broken by a volley of firearms, which sent dull echoes through the thick prison air.

"Great heavens! Musketry!"

"A salvo of joy!" corrected José, with a reassuring smile. "In honor of the marriage."

"But are we not to see our happy son-in-law?"

"Not yet—marquis; he has gone on the king's service to another world!"

"Oh, the New World, where all brave Spaniards go?"

"Precisely—the new world to him! Take your daughter to your new residence. I will notify you when you may present your thanks to his majesty."

He placed them in charge of his footmen to be conducted to the carriage-and-four still waiting. Then, going to the window, he peered out between the curtains at the prostrate form on the parade-ground, with two penitent friars crouching over it and unrolling the cere cloth.

"Good-night, Cousin Cæsar!" said he, waving his hand.

CHAPTER X.

THE HUSBAND OF PSYCHE.

When the sovereigns of Spain became enervated and, instead of risking their lives in battles, lost only time in petty pursuits, such as the shooting of small birds, since falconry was too exacting a pastime, the gunsmiths contrived lighter and surer firearms. The princes first to carry fowling-pieces worthy the title were of Spain.

This led to the hunting-boxes, in which were held nightly revels after the slaying of big game, becoming shooting pavilions. Here the mild sportsmen discussed, on the table, the woodcock, snipe and hares, which had superseded the wolf, boar and roebuck.

Such a shooting shelter, magnified with luxuries, adorned with decorations by Italian artists and paintings by Velasquez and his disciples, received the Countess of Garofa, under the tutelage of her suddenly-provided father and mother.

It is one of the redeeming features of the court, which has few, to let nothing disturb its surface, for, if you accept a proclaimed event as settled, argument ceases, and consequently there cannot arise the acrimony of debate.

As every family pretending to antiquity had its legend of a stolen heir, sometimes abducted by eagles, sometimes by those human birds of prey, the gypsies, the tale of Maritana being rescued from the everlasting wanderers was to be endured. The story was embellished by mystery of the midnight marriage, followed by an unaccountable fusillade in the Corregidor's courtyard; this was claimed by one tale-teller to have been fatal to the bridegroom, and by another to have so little injured him

that he was very palpably living, but was journeying to Gibraltar and thence voyaging in Africa along the coast.

This abrupt self-banishment on the part of a penniless adventurer was a daily occurrence in that era of fortunes made by adventurers in the still productive East. Besides, Don Cæsar was known to have been in the Algerian service, a polite way of putting the fact that, as a slave, he had rowed in the pirates' galleys.

This disappearance of the husband, blotting out his commonplace life among the vagrants and her short but bright career as a mountebank, songstress and dancer, was sufficiently striking as to furnish the *débutante* with the halo of attraction, which brought all eyes to bear upon her.

Then, again, the family of Castello-Rotondo, whose head was continually favored with proofs of the royal esteem, took up the daggers for Maritana, and it was as much as one's life was worth to hint—simply to hint— that her restoration was more than a passing step from the nunnery to the parlor.

If some still questioned the gypsy abducting and argued that the cunning rogues had offered the first sharp and pretty girl at hand for the position of daughter of one marquis, *protégée* of another, and wife of a count, the ready reply was that none but a creature born of the *sangre-azul* and educated according to the school of gentility, could so stand the inquisition of social arbitresses.

But all fell to the ground and "kowtowed" when, after having given the hunting-pavilion to the Castello-Rotondos, the king announced that he would celebrate the union of the Two Crowns' anniversary by a *battue* in that park and be the guest of honor at a gala in the evening.

Maritana, Countess of Garofa, was "accepted." There was not a word to say.

The day had been delightful; the game had come like

docile lambs to the range of the royal sportsman, who had bags full enough to feast all the patients in all the hospitals of Madrid; at dusk the fireworks began to sparkle and blaze. The lanterns shone like glowworms and fireflies. The spaces at the crossroads had each their little entertainments, masquerades, burlettas, clowns and, columbines, musical scenas, and balls on the lawn.

There were hopes that the hereditary sulks of the kings would die out in Carlos, who had never reached this height of lightheartedness.

The hosts were in the seventh heavens. Relying on the favor from both sovereign and his premier, the parasites fastened themselves upon the marquis and his dame. They could not well felicitate their daughter, as she relegated to the background until the existence of her husband was authoritatively declared by the police minister. He was inquiring the more rigidly and closely as his own relative was the vanished grandee.

She could see a little of the shooting party, perhaps, through the bars of her windows, the jalousies or Venetian blinds borrowed from the Orientals by the Italians and the Spanish. But of the banquet she was not to have a peep. She hoped that if the news of Don Cæsar having in some way escaped the doom which had befallen him in spite of the royal pardon should arrive, she might be allowed in at the "wine and nuts" period.

But Don José, whether or not he had spurred on his "familiars," as they were called, to ascertain the truth in the popular report that his cousin, having sinned against the goodness of justice as much as against social canons by his escapades, had been carried away by the Prince of Evil, came with a smooth countenance to join the choice assembly in the boudoir of the marchioness. Here were merely members of the families of Castello-Rotondo and the marchioness.

Don José joined them with a saddened visage, but under his breath he whispered to the host and the guest, without letting the bereaved one hear:

"We shall have a consoling visit before the night is out!"

Therefore, with a good heart, those who were as prepared to mourn as encourage began to broaden their faces and wag the tongue merrily.

Two or three continued assiduous court to the old dame.

Others lauded the marquis and besought remembrance as he mounted the gilded steps.

"Never," said the young Knight of Xarragona, flaunting in a Parisian suit, for he was fresh from the French court, accompanying an envoy, to negotiate another of those treaties which were called "piecrust" (pâté) because they were so short and easily broken, "never in my experience" (he was about three-and-twenty), "never did I see a woman look so charming as your lady. I have not the honor to have seen the daughter of the house priorily, but I can aver that no one would assume that they were other than sisters!"

"Elder sister, if you please," interrupted the marchioness, with a simper.

"Now, I protest!"

"And I," said his companion, an Italian stripling who had reached Madrid to learn the language.

The marquis strutted and thought that in unanimity must be truth.

"My young friends," said he, puffing out like a pigeon, "you must come again and see my gallery—I have appended to it—append is good, for they are not on the panels but 'hung'—depended, see!—several masterpieces by our own artists, for I detest the skinny saints of your old Italians and the blue-eyed crockery madonnas of the

Dutch! You show so much taste in other matters that I am sure you are first-rate judges of paintings——"

"At the present rage for cosmetics and tints," said the pert youth, "one who can judge paintings can judge feminine beauty!"

The premier was studying the captive saved from the Egyptians steadfastly. Her abstraction seemed to him founded on ambition, and this chimed in with his key-note:

"All goes well. This musing shows intellect. She will be a ruler for Spain, under my tuition!"

There was a glow of the fireworks without and bursts of all kinds of music.

Castello-Rotondo went up to his patron, who was so enrapt.

"Have you been sated with the *fête,* in which I see your hand? Our dark women must look lovely under the artificial lights. Your magic has caused the stern hidalgos to throw off their usual taciturnity and they are prattling light nonsense in the bowers like pages! I see, though, that you regard most fixedly my daughter—does she not bear her trying new station well?"

"She is a princess!" said José, with unguarded enthusiasm. "Blood will tell! She has merely stepped upon the pedestal destined for her!"

"May it be but a stepping-stone to a higher position! Under your auspices, who knows how high her husband may arise! For it is undoubted—I had it from the writer for the Royal Signet—that the king, with his unfaltering support of the old nobility, did grant a full pardon to the luckless Don Cæsar."

"I—I think that we may presume that, if he were shot down, it was not fatally!"

"That will fill my poor child with hope!"

"Only he must have fainted from loss of blood. That

is how two or three penitent friars, conveying the body
away as if it were a dead rag cast off by all mankind, deposited it in some catacomb of the mountains, and to
cover their stupid error, relate all sorts of insensate
stories."

"Do you hope for his return——"

"Wounded and weak, perhaps; but able to bear his re-
placement in society. What is your opinion?"

"Oh, the reformed rake is known to become a steady
pillar of the state. Ah, you and he, cousins that are like
brothers, you might, indeed, be the two pillars of the
state—our twin columns of Hercules, incomparable, un-
surpassable—'*Ne plus ultra!*'"

"I see that your opinion is mine—you are unrivaled as
a courtier. You will get on in the palace, my lord."

"With your aid, my lord."

"Your tact is so fine—your obedience so utter."

"*Quita!* have done!" and the old noble attempted to
blush.

"By the way, how are the royal birds, under your care,
coming on?"

"They are coming off excellently. I am happy to say
that there is not a bishop in all Spain superior to them in
plumpness."

"I suppose you are not wedded for life to the establishment of poulterer royal?"

"I—I—prefer horses and dogs, of course, as a nobleman."

"You have met the fairy godfather—at least, you may
have one of your wishes while awaiting the other to be
fulfilled."

"Would you overwhelm me?"

"It is rumored to me that Don Canino Barcahunda,
whose absence from the hunt to-day was attributed to a
fall off his horse, was bitten by one of his charges, on

whose tail he had incautiously stepped. If he should retire on a pension on account of this wound received in
service, why——"

"Oh, he is master of the royal lapdogs, descended
unbroken from the Chow-chows sent hither by the Great
Cham to Pope Clement, who sent a pair to our King
Philip! Master of the lapdogs! I—catch me lest I
lose my footing! Oh, I never aspired to that dignity!
Canino had it by right of succession and taste, for he
loves pugs! His nose verifies that taste! But I—am I
worthy of such a distinction, dear Don José?"

"You have peculiar parts which entitle you to be set
foremost on the list of applicants!"

"My lord, if I secure that post, count on all the ladies
of your preference having the choice of the litters!"

"Yes, but see how those fops are pestering your lady!
I think such coxcombs should be taught a lesson! Get
your hand in by breaking those puppies, ha, ha!"

Trying to assume the air of a jealous Ottoman, the
old dotard hurried over to where the gallants were amus-
ing themselves at the dowager's expense.

This left the plotter to center his attention upon Maritana. He spoke to her and she started as if she had forgotten the surroundings.

"You are traveling in a voyage to the moon!" said he,
softly, "but how can you be pleased with a festival seen
through the windowpane. But soon, I engage, you will
be able to participate in such rejoicings. There is all
at your disposition which wealth and taste can bring—
nothing is wanting but——" he paused for her to sup-
ply the omission.

Maritana heaved a sigh as if the gems on her bodice
weighed upon her.

"Mother of mercy!" said she at length, with much
melancholy, "nothing is wanting but one whose absence

left a void here, and this yearning for a companion makes me loathe the glitter and the perfumes and the melody which grate on my senses!"

A footman glided skillfully among the guests and went up to the minister, to whom he said, in a carefully-modulated voice:

"Please your lordship, the personage expected has come into the little red room."

José smiled with relief. He beckoned to the marquis and remarked like one who could not be refused:

"I wish to hold a private confabulation with a friend here. Could you kindly manage to clear the floor of these flutterings?"

This was somewhat unceremonious and quite opposite to the old routinist's conduct, but it had to be done, he did not doubt.

"Oh, it will not be difficult," returned he quickly to hide his surprise if not his chagrin as host. "I will induce my rich cousins to go out into the Moorish divan, where I open the flasks of wine from the royal cellars, and I will turn out my poor cousins on the balcony over the patio, where they shall have the wine that was in the cellars here for the hard-drinking huntsmen. If that does not rid us of them, do not count me more your deliverer from nuisances!"

But after he had stiltedly shown out the antonished guests, he and his wife were called back by the self-appointed director.

"I should like the dear countess to stay with her daughter," observed he like a command. "And you will also oblige me by lingering."

"Oh, it is we who are obliged," said the lady.

"I know I am—for I am going to the dogs!" chuckled the marquis.

Don José went up to the brooding Maritana and uttered wheedlingly in her ear:

"This merrymaking shall be perfect, for it is going to have 'the presence here of one whose absence left a void in your bosom and yearning for a companion!'"

Then, without waiting to mark the effect of her words thus emphatically repeated, he quitted the room by the side door used by the messenger who had stated that a visitor was waiting for him.

Maritana turned bewildered to her father, saying:

"Did you hear those last words, father? You are the host and invited all the party! Will another present himself whom I have not seen in our family circle?"

"I dare say so!"

"Who?"

"Oh, that is the mystery—the crowning surprise!" replied the old lord. "I did not catch what Don José was driving at—or rather, driving in upon us, nolly-volly; but I think it is my duty to echo everything he says!"

"Father!" cried Maritana, "what does all this mean? Why this continued mystery? I am told that the marriage ceremony through which I went as meekly as a captive slave, was the wish of my benefactress, the queen. But the queen—she does not accompany her mate to this holiday—and I am told, on begging to be allowed to see her, that I must wait!"

Her blue eyes burned as if to emit sparks to consume those who impeded her.

"Here I am, perplexed, racked about my husband of an hour! All sorts of stories pester me like ephemeræ! They sting and they rankle! I am told that he has been exiled; that he was shot and has died; that the very soul of him was carried away by the Enemy of all!" She crossed herself devoutly, showing that either her earliest training had come back or that, in a few hours, she had absorbed the manners of her regained degree.

"Wait, wait! but I am not used to waiting! The poor wanderer would not wait—I do not see that the rich girl, daughter of an old imperious house, and wife of a noble, should be told to wait! Tell me, dear mother, dearest father—is Don José deceiving us—is he trifling with me!" Her eyes expressed no good will to him who made a jest of her.

"But, my dear, you must have seen your husband when you stood beside him?"

"It was because I stood beside him, and not before him, that I saw next to nothing of him," replied Maritana, crossly. "I was stifling in a provokingly thick veil, and he seemed bound not to draw it aside! I could have wished that the priest would have insisted on bestowing upon me the kiss of benediction, but in order that my husband might have seen, I trust, that he was not drawing a blank, as the gypsies say, in the lottery of love! But, no I did not see him then—he did not see me and I—I—that is, he—he! we have not seen one another since!" and she began to sob in her handkerchief.

"This," said the marquis, "this is the downright blindness of love! To marry and not see the man! There could be nothing to admire!"

"You are mistaken, sir!" rebuked Maritana, "for it was his generosity in lifting out of the straw the poor wanderer, the dancer and singer who lived on the alms of the liberal! He defended me when I most lacked a defender, fate having deprived me of those naturally my shield and buckler!"

"You are her shield, I am her buckler! well said, my dear!" said the marquis, clapping his bony hands.

"For my sake—for I believe he remained with the band merely to enjoy my coquettish company! I was cruel to him—I made him my butt, my music-holder, my accompanyist, my—my——"

"Well, all comes right! He is a count; you a marquis' child! Hope on—I will, once fixed in the royal favor, have this matter set right despite a dozen Don Josés!"

"Hist, he returns!" whispered the marchioness.

Her husband wilted as if a sirocco had bounded over the sea and blasted him.

"I will demand," said Maritana, "yes, demand of this Don José when I shall see the queen and the king, if I must have resort to the highest tribunals for justice and enlightenment!"

"Hush, he is here!" stammered the marquis, as the person in question re-entered the apartment.

He wore a joyous, contented mien. He advanced without trepidation to Maritana, who had taken a step toward him also unflinchingly.

"Sir, my lord, when am I to see my husband?"

"I am glad to be in the nick to answer that question," responded he without hesitation as if he had full satisfaction ready. "You are to see your mate this day."

"That is direct—this day?"

"This evening, then."

The marquis turned to the speaker with an inquiring, puzzled eye.

"Then he is not dead, and his soul——"

José made a crushing sign for him to be silent.

"Surely, sir, I have misunderstood the facts all along," faltered Maritana, with pain at her relief being at the cost of too hastily reprimanding one still her friend.

"Pray be calm," said the minister, with cold suavity. "I have hurried hither with the good news."

The marquis clasped his wife's arm and drew her toward the pair.

"Now we shall learn something at last," said he.

Unfortunately, José heard him, and, wheeling round and taking him by the hand, as he was holding the marchioness', drew him up to the nearest doorway, saying imperatively:

"Leave me with your daughter, my cousin's wife, which authorizes the breach of decorum! Besides, your guests are clamoring for you."

The old couple withdrew with disappointment clouding their brows.

Maritana faced round as the noble returned, and firmly said:

"Now that we are at last alone, let me hear all—best or worst! Where is my husband?"

"He is at hand!"

A cloaked figure, indeed, crept out from behind the tapestry screening a secret door, and stood like an actor waiting for the cue to discover himself, his glowing eyes, however, fastened rather upon the woman than the man.

"At hand?" muttered Maritana, without comprising all the room in her hasty glance.

"Remember that he has made his peace with his king, but not with the Church, whose offices he spurned, and with whose born enemies the gypsies, he too long ran his course! He is under the ban and must keep himself close lest he sleep in the dungeons of the Holy Inquisition!"

His hearer shivered, for the dread of the Holy Brotherhood was more poignant in a gitana than in any other, even the Jew. The Jew sometimes became a convert; a Bohemian never!

"But you say he is here?"

"Yes, for your sake he has ventured!"

"Oh, my cousin, you shall be my brother for this! Let us find a place of security for him, between us! Let me flee with him if there is no harbor in Spain! Let me—oh, where is he? Do you not see I am dying a hundred deaths? Where is my beloved?"

"Here!" answered José, dramatically, as he beckoned the mantled man to approach, confident that he had leveled the path.

CHAPTER XI.

When the cloak was thrown aside from the form of the cavalier who stepped into the place from which José respectfully retired, Maritana shrank, but it was purely with surprise, not with repugnance.

She was gazing upon a somewhat remarkable man.

Don Carlos was handsome after the Bourbon pattern; he was generous of money as a Medici, frank in speech as a descendant of King Henry of Navarre and France. He was very winsome, after an acquaintance. When he was forced by the united powers of Spain, France and Austria to give way as to the Duchy of Tuscany in favor of this youth, Jean-Gaston received him with tears, but when, later, this displacer was called away, he bade him farewell with tears of regret.

He saluted her with the courtesy of a royal cavalier.

"The Lady Maria del Castello-Rotondo," said he, with sad reproach, "do you not remember me?"

"Ye-es; I have seen you before." She still shrank back and whispered to Don José: "This is not the man I was married to!"

"It is the man beside whom you stood at the altar!" said the liar, stoutly. "You gave your hand to that hand —that hand was clasped in yours!"

The Father of Lies could not have articulated more distinctly or used a more sincere tone.

"But that was Don Cæsar de Bazan!"

"Oh, this is Don Cæsar! Am I to be cheated in my own cousin? The Don Cæsar whom you knew among those dogs of Mahound was but a byblow of our family—he assumed the name to draw it in the dust! It is he on whom all the ill-odor should fall and cling! This is my honored cousin—your favored husband!"

"No," said Maritana to herself, laying her hand on her bosom, where responded not a flutter. "This is not my Don Cæsar—not my love, not my mate!"

"Come, come," interrupted the king, disconcerted by this odd check to the usual current of royal whims, and too enrapt to show his vexation, "is this the reception meet for one whose eyes followed you in many of your erratic strolls, whose servants watched you when the hotbloods would have carried you off as the Romans bore away the Sabines; who was charmed, when the gross populace turned, disgusted, away by the poesy in your songs falling into the melancholy strain!"

"I do not forget how generous you were to me! It is a further recompense for a songstress to meet with a sympathetic admirer, but I trembled while I accepted your bounty."

"You trembled—good! for it is the tremor of love that the bards ever tell of; the current shooting from one breast to another, the circulation of love which Ovid related long before the surgeons found it out to be imitated by the blood! My happiness was centered in you as your fortunes in me! I determined to raise you, pearl in the slime, to the diadem where you instinctively aspired. Resolving that I should share my passion with you, I resolved that you should share my wealth!"

"That is," suggested Don José, "wealth when it was restored to you, for, as Don Cæsar, under a cloud you had but your title!"

"But now we meet both under happier auspices! You are elevated to your place of birth, I am promised restoration of all I forfeited by my rebellion against social laws and the king's edicts. Now, you have but to give me one smile, one word of love, and you will be my sovereign mistress! I live for you again, and for you alone!"

Don José rubbed his hands and nodded like a stage-instructor, proud of his pupil.

"Not so loud, Don Cæsar!" said he, but with such mild reproof; "the menials might hear!"

"Lovely one," continued the king, believing her silence was in his favor, and pursuing a course cut-and-dried between him and his accomplice, "my return must not be known until I am formally declared free from apprehension, moral and physical. But my danger should not separate you from me——"

"Danger," broke in the unctuous, sermonizing voice of the chorus, "ought to more closely unite husband and wife!"

"What is the world to us? We can be happy remote! Let us dwell in a nook of Arcady together!"

"Together!" repeated Maritana, confounded like a wild bird between two of those dogs which hunt together, one chasing until the prey is exhausted, whereupon the other springs upon it the more securely.

"A few miles from town is a blessed hermitage for lovers."

"Lovers," added the prompter in this duet, "on whose plight Mother Church has smiled!"

"If we meet there——" pursued the royal courtier.

"Pray, my cousin, do not delay! The guests will be inquiring for you," whispered Don José.

"My lord, I cannot leave my parents thus suddenly," said Maritana, who had time to consider over her part.

"Leave her to me," suggested the intriguer to the king. "The guests are returning indoors, methinks. Sir, the countess is right. It would not be seemly to have her leave her home in the midst of the joviality without explanation. She might be followed by some of those hotspurs, and you might be followed, also! Come away—I guarantee that she will keep the tryst!"

"Some one is coming!" snarled the king, wild with indignation that his privacy was intruded upon, and about to draw his dagger, if not his sword. He had forgotten that he was pretending to be less than sovereign.

"Oh, to let go my grip——"

The king's face was suffused with angry blood; his eyes had the yellow tint of tiger's, taunted with a withdrawn bone.

"Quick, quick!" cried his sycophant, throwing the cloak over him and clasping it. "This is the safest way. Into the gardens and begone!"

Maritana saw the exit managed with skill and expedition. She looked sorrowfully at her trinkets and resplendent dresses.

She thought that she had sold herself to a keener misery than she had previously known, and at what a cost. Wife of a man who daunted her without her knowing why—one whose wealth, which his air proclaimed, attracted her less than Don Cæsar's poverty.

It was the marchioness whose stiff petticoats had rustled loudly in the corridor. She looked amazed at seeing Maritana in tears. Don José made her a sign to conduct her daughter out and condole with her.

He remained there, smiling, as if tears always caused him joy.

"The king is a schoolboy at love-making," sneered he. "But the wildered dove must be put in the cage alone, and then all the obstacles which still baffle me will be brushed away like motes that temporarily obscure the sunbeam."

He prepared to excuse himself to the host, and make him have a coach got ready and place his daughter in it for a departure which political reasons connected with

her husband, commanded. He was on the doorsill when he felt a hand pluck him humbly by the sleeve.

He turned quickly and angrily. A bent form, clad in a monk's greasy and threadbare russet robe, presented a blot on the thick Tunisian rug and against the Bruges arras.

"Who are you? What want you?" said he, brutally, thinking it was one of his agents in disguise.

"Alms," was the doleful reply, "for a poor man who has lost his name and his wife!"

"A monk lose his wife?" repeated Don José, mute in consternation at so bad a jest under this holy surface. "What devil of a monk is this?"

"That ever-merry devil, your cousin!"

The cowl was tossed back with a reckless turn of the head, and the saucy face with its unquenchable eyes looked serenely into his own.

"Don Cæsar!"

"In search of his wife!"

CHAPTER XII.

FACING THE FIRING LINE.

On the bridegroom being placed for execution before the corporal's file, he requested only one thing, to wit: that he should not be blindfolded.

"In boarding a ship, when I was fighting the Algerine Corsairs," he explained, "I often had to rush along the slippery deck into the gaping mouth of a pivot-gun, and to face the hand guns, that small change of cannon. I cannot bear being hoodwinked."

Without anything but his careless courage prompting him, he had, in waiving that common acquiescence in human weakness, done the finest act toward his saving. For at the instant of the soldiers taking slow aim with the improved French inventions, which were still sufficiently clumsy, he caught a glimpse of Lazarillo covertly making impressive signs to him.

When a man's life is suspended on a word of command, all his senses become sharpened. He believed that the pantomime of the intelligent youngster implied that he had in some way juggled with the muskets. Considering that he was an armorer in the bud, this was significant.

So he took the hint in the most probable manner.

As soon as he saw that each lighted match, attached to a lever, was about to drop upon the pan filled with powder, he shut his eyes, and at the fizz—not the flash, which was a shade later—he dropped and was floundering on the ground as the smoke, impelled in his direction, momentarily hid his body.

He shut his eyes and set his teeth.

But as the detonation still ran along within the walled

inclosure, he was sure that he had not been touched by any projectile.

"Dash me! but that little imp has in some way rendered those firearms innocuous!"

So he curled himself up, kicked out as with the last spasm, and the *rigor mortis* seemed to spread over him as he became stiff as a ramrod.

He had not long to wait for the natural sequel.

Three or four men, not military, came deliberately toward him from a buttress, where they had been sheltered from the shots, if any went astray.

One was the surgeon attached to the prison, the other two monks; at least, they were clad in the long robe, with hood coming to a point, slit with eyeholes, which denoted they were no doubt of the Penitential Fraternity. These usually dealt with the remains of those executed persons who had no friends to obtain the grace of interring the body in their guise.

"Unless my wife has determined to add my earthly casing to the row in the family vault," thought he, "I doubt that these good fathers will be emissaries of my cousin— who might prefer that all traces of me should be lost in the paupers' pit!"

These charitable brethren carried a large sheet of tanned canvas which was the winding-sheet of their "customers."

They were also supplied with prayer-books, chained to their waist-girdle of rope, with beads, blessed candle and a box of unguent. They knelt down, and Don Cæsar heard at his two ears a hash of Dog Latin which, perhaps, was not meant to be comprehended by the vulgar or learned.

"I suppose that is a prayer for the dead," said he to himself, very dubious.

In the meantime the surgeon took out with daintiness,

for he was a fop in his way—what they called in the town where he was a favorite, "the ladies' doctor"—a notebook, with a silver-point used as a writing implement. He proceeded to take notes, which must have been exceedingly valuable, since he kept his distance.

"What are the wounds?" asked he as soon as he believed he had given good measure to the prayers.

Luckily the fine doublet of Don Cæsar had been torn open at the breast, and his underclothes had more than one hole and slit and were stained with grease and probably blood as well. So one of the monks answered with natural impulse founded on this misleading aspect:

"Why, doctor," snuffling, "the poor fellow is riddled like a folio with bookworms! there are at least two round holes here!" and he held his fat hand over the bosom, which did not rise and fall in the least.

"Ah, wound in the super-auricular region," said the delicate son of Galen, "and another in the intercostal section! You will accept my thanks, for I am going to a supper in the town, and this fellow, over whom was merely thrown those spruce habiliments, came out of the Jewry and, lastly, out of the cells where I lost several patients through jail fever!"

Whereupon, shutting his book with a snap and sniffing at a handkerchief dipped in aromatic vinegar, he nodded "good-by" to the subject so briefly dismissed, and trotted off to where the governor would receive his official statement that the dead prisoner was duly removed from his charge.

"Was it likely," observed the fatter monk of the pair to his companion, across the body, "that I would, if possible, let him cut and snip with his scissors this lovely satin? I have a buyer for it, Omfrio, d'ye see!"

"A buyer!" thought the pretended corpse, "Lord between us! suppose they have a buyer for my flesh-and-bones as well!"

Unfortunately, he could not indulge even in the mild relief of a shudder. But the monks, with a celerity born of practice, proceeded to roll him up in the sheet so that he could imagine what the mummies of his friends, the Egyptians, must have felt, presuming there is *post-mortem* sensation.

While working, they continued their dialogue, coolly professional, in a tone and with a frankness altogether too elucidatory to warm the blood of their patient.

Never was dialogue more calculated to enchain the subject, and he did not lose a syllable.

"So, so," crackled one voice, "we are again to deprive the common pit of the corpse? Is it to go into the catacomb of Our Good Works Church?"

"My dear old Anselmo, this hapless mortal is to stay, like the body of Mahomet, whose name be cursed thrice, seven times and even nine, by the way, as a misleading prophet! in suspense?"

"Do you mean we are to hang it up?"

"Metaphorically, my brother! But what a blessing—this time, we can take away the body openly and above-board."

"Yes, Omfrio, we have the pass verified. I suppose it was obtained through the insistance of his relatives, for this is no common wastrel——"

"He is a scion, by the side of some noble house, who assumed the family name only to disgrace it! This is seen every day, considering that families put all the good members in the Church and cast the others into the army, or to loiter through life in bad company!"

"Oh, I am not the lawful heir to Garofa? Ah! this is a story set afloat by that hanged Don José!" thought the "Dead One."

"And the family have redeemed the excrescence?"

"They want to do so. But there are other claimants!"

"Hallioa'" thought the subject under discussion, wincing mentally, "I am more in request dead than alive!"

"Where do we take him, then? I heard that his patrimonial estates were dissipated into thin air!"

"*Selah!* it is so!" spoke Cæsar, so low under his breath that he did not hear the sound himself.

"They are buried under an avalanche of mortgages, *post-obits*, repudiated notes of hand, protests *et ceterae!*"

A soldier who stood a little way off, to guard the dead until out of the prison yard, crossed himself at this scrap of Latin which, in his innocence, he took for a pious adjuration.

"Go on," said he apologetically. "I do not follow you —I scarce know my *Credo!*"

"Anselmo," continued the monk, but so as not to be overheard by the sentinel, "we have but to convey it to the chapel of our convent——"

"The Good Works?"

"Where he is to rest *pro-tempore,* until his destination is settled upon. Mark, his cousin is no less than the Marquis of Santarem, raised to the premiership yesterday, and he will for the name's sake have him fitly disposed of!"

"He shall be handled tenderly, for he has become more precious since he cast off his mortal integuments than ever before!"

"Amen! Ah, what a leap-frog game life is! Down goes one cousin, making a back, and over goes the other with a skip, and rises into the foremost office of the kingdom! A clod, here—there, a diamond out of its shell!"

"Fine old family!" reflectively pursued the monk, who was securing the sheet by its frayed edges supplying the thread. "I was, when 'rusticated' once, down among the Garofas! It was said, whenever a Barefoot stubbed his toe on a stone, that the stone was not there when the Garofas first were lords!"

"Holy brother, we know sometimes where we were born, but seldom where we will die and be buried This Garofa, granting he is Garofa, may never rest beneath his ancestral stones."

"No, not with his cousin so powerful as to draw his corse from the pauper grave?"

"I intimated, dull pate that you are! that there was another bidder?"

"So you did!"

"You forget that, though it is forbidden to mutilate the casket of the soul, even to discover secrets useful to the race, the 'prentice 'sawbones' of the university, as well of Salamanca as of Saragossa, or of Segovia, which is only a step over the sierra, and, consequently, nearer home, give its weight in copper for that human pasty which they like to carve up in the dissecting-room."

"I believe at last in the ghouls and the vampires!" thought Don Cæsar.

"It would not be the first time," said Omfrio, frankly, "that I have heard of bodies being diverted from the crypt to that haunt of deservation!"

"And, still, there is another bidder."

"Well, I admire this treasure!" said Omfrio, playfully patting the cased packet, luckily not where it was sensitive. "It is like the country we live in—three contestants for it—kaiser, French prince and our own Don Carlos!"

"Between the three, I am likely to be quartered," moaned Cæsar, inaudibly.

"Yes, his boon companions——"

"Not the cadgers, the lepers, the gypsies——"

"The gypsies, through their king, not a bad fellow."

"An excellent old scoundrel! He had forced me to drink with him when I lost my way and strayed into the ward under ban."

"Forced you to drink?" incredulously.

"Well, the rogue held up a horn with one dirty paw and brandished an ugly, crooked, saw-edged poniard in the other similarly dirty, and saying that it was 'tears,' which I was vowed to drink. I was compelled to gulp it down. Happily," and he smacked his pendent lips, "it was the wine called irreverently 'lachrymae," and I was well out of it. Then he added insult to the ignominy! He gave to me, who was seeking to bestow alms on these vermin, a bag of coppers, saying it was for my Christian poor."

"Well, it is this merry Duke of Egypt who will, I doubt not, offer a bag of silver, not of gold, to our abbot for this adopted brother of theirs."

"Adopted brother?"

"Without doubt. Have you not seen him dance with the pretty girl, the prettiest of them all, who has set the courtiers dreaming? Well, the foresworn knight learned those steps on their witches' Sabbath. Dressed only in a smear of hog's fat, they dance around Behemoth, or Levi Nathan, one of their infernal deities."

"It would ill become the abbot to lodge the poor wretch in those excommunicated hands."

"Oh, that he will not, unless the bribe is overtopping."

"Still, it is a horror—profanity in person," and the monk rattled his rosary, and, in his excitement, lashed the body a little smartly with it.

"I honor your words," thought the body, "but I owe you one for your frantic gestures."

"But have you done? Here comes old Pedro, with his mule. It is good for him to bring his strongest beast, for the dead weigh heavy."

"I only wish I could fall on you with all my weight, heartless monster," thought Cæsar; "ay, I would drop out of my lot in paradise to execute that judgment, you fat lump."

"With two panniers," said Anselmo; "are we to cut the body in half?"

"Cannibal—no! I shall occupy the other basket to counterbalance him."

"Heaven make it light for him!'

"His punishment?"

"No, the mule's burden—the two of ye."

"Yes, you can lead! We will exchange when we get half-way!"

The soldier looked on as the two lifted the bound body and set to placing it in one of the panniers.

"By the holy lance!" cried he, "I congratulate you, master friar, on your nerve. It is steel of the first forging. I have been soldiering, youth and man, these fourteen years, and not in the city garrisons either, and I would not, to be the constable of all the Spains, and stand with my sword of state before the king, ride cheek by cheek with only a wicker hedge betwixt, with a dead scapegrace, on a dark, rough road, infested with goblins and slain travelers."

"Oh, we are proof to Satan," rejoined Omfrio, carelessly.

After feeling the sensation of a log rolled several times, Don Cæsar felt that of being taken up and inserted, luckily head up, like a candle is put in its socket, in the basket most convenient. Pedro held the mule by the head, for it twitched with its hind legs and slightly whinnied a protest. The girth squeaked, and the weight depressed the filled basket.

"Thank my patron saint—if any of the Cæsars were made saints," thought he—"that they knew, in my shrouding one end from the other, and stood the human bottle neck upward. A pretty headache I should have had if they had pitched me in this wickerwork with my heels as the Antipodeans walk!"

The mule was shaken as by a blow from a battering-ram. It was Omfrio being hoisted between his brother and the muleteer into the other basket. This operation was performed much as the famous corpulent Cardinal Aldobrandino, "the eighth hill of Rome," was insinuated into his pantaloons—by letting him gradually descend by his own gravity.

"By Jimenez!" exclaimed the mule-driver, half alarmed about his beast having a broken back, and half proud at its being able to resist this weight, "the mule might well be born with a cross on its back! It has crosses to bear worse than humanity."

Nevertheless, the brute, bred and reared in the dale of Andorra to walk under loads which would have brought Samson to his knees, sustained the double cargo with fortitude, and slowly, but steadily, trudged over to the outer gate. Here the chief monk showed a pass, to which the gateman nodded, and the little party emerged into the street.

This led tortuously to the Escurial palace gate, whence they took the road over the ruggedness toward the hills along the Alberche River.

Pedro, whose journeys often took him to the seacoast, lit a short pipe, such as seamen called "nose-warmers," and silently smoked.

The monk, on foot, walking on the side of Don Cæsar, steadied the ghastly, sheeted head as the mule slipped and lurched.

"What are you moping over, Anselmo?" asked the one riding, half lulled by the movement, which had become fairly regular.

"Oh, you have awaked, eh? I was just regretting that this, our load of sin, was not still more in the market?"

"In what end?"

"Instead of carrying him so far as our convent, we might, if a fourth bidder—even the Prince of Darkness— appeared, strike a bargain with him——"

"Useless; he will have him any way!"

"Oh, he will, will he?" murmured Cæsar. "Not if I can spite him; but if he did come at the nick, I believe he would sweep all the dice into his cap. You are as deserving a niche in his oven as poor me, and as for this pagan of a mule-thrasher, by the oaths he uses in profusion, I pronounce that he has cast away his last hope of salvation."

"Did he not die penitent?" asked the walking monk.

"He died as he lived, flirting with women. The priest of the Corregidor, who ought to have known better, used up all his wind in the marriage service over this profligate in lieu of the burial one."

"Married and shot? it was a hasty snuffing of that candle called a man!"

"They just gave him time to swallow a drop of wine at the wedding feast. Oh, it was one of those formal weddings to give some harridan who had passed seventy years without an offer, reasons to bear the name of Countess of Garofa for a couple of years, when she will take the same road as he!"

"I hope the road will be impassable!" muttered Cæsar.

"I doubt that every woman, young or old, had gypsy, family and surgeon, contending for her legitimate prey!"

"Pedro, Pedro, you are plunging into the defile by El Molino del Rey—do you think we want to grind this poor scrag's bones at the king's mills?"

"Scrag, in your teeth!" muttered Don Cæsar, put out of his usual equable temper by the jolting and jerking, and having to play the dumb man for so long a time. "I may not weigh as much as this paunch in the other scale, but I would it were that of justice if I do not carry more flesh than you, you splinter!"

"We take it," replied the thin friar, "not to embarrass Brother Gregorio, who is on the south road, in his negotiation with the gypsy king——"

"Relics of Compostella! I learned in my studies that man has two souls, the good and the bad, but granting two geniuses, from what volume of the fathers do you draw that he has two bodies, unless he is twins?"

"He is hoaxing you," said the muleteer, filling his pipe again and stopping to light it from a tinder-box.

"Not at all, not my brother!" said Omfrio, indignantly. "It is meet to deceive those arch-deceivers, the sons of the Nile and Niger. They want to redeem their Joseph out of the pit? Well, we sell them a pig in a poke! At the carriers' halt, at Yniesta, the messengers of this wiseacre, the Duke of Egypt—I may say, the dupe! await the body of their dear Cæsar to be passed over to them for incineration, according to their belief, they should anticipate their papa, the unmentionable, for the consideration of forty or fifty pillar-dollars!"

"Forty? For selling an impenitent Christian's remains to the infidels! I never would consent to that! Fifty, or he should be wasted in his own family-vault!"

"It is the abbot who thought to beguile the brownskins. They will not see the substitution till daylight, and they may do what they like with the pauper carcass which died in the homeless ward of the Hospital of the Queen's Bounty!"

"How timely to enable the Gitanos to be duped!" laughed the friar.

"It is to be borne in mind," continued Omfrio, who decidedly saw the humorous side of things, "that the outlaws will not apply to the minister of police to have the fraud rectified."

"Omfrio, I thought to die of a surfeit of anchovy, which is my sole frailty, but you will be the death of me by laughing!"

Omfrio settled down again, and, what was more, pillowed his head upon the almost dislocated neck of Don Cæsar, cut in twain by the edge of the basket coming up to his armpits.

If Don Cæsar could have written his adventures, being of the nature which formed the "picaroon" novels of the mode, he would have set this one as the most singular of the collection.

From a wedding feast, to be trussed, enwrapped, used as a bolster, drawn along between two body-snatchers— for he did not believe them true, holy men—it was too abrupt a transition.

He would—at another and highly different time—perhaps smile at the double play upon his friend, the Duke of Egypt, but no tide of laughter set in as he was borne to he did not dare to guess what culmination.

If they had been genuine priests, he might have raised his voice in entreaty, but as it was it was not wise even to raise his aching shoulders in disgust.

"The bad point is," mused he, flattened under the dozing friar, "that this hideous proximity crushes out of me all my religion! What kind of mock monks are these which furnish their abbot!—Abbot of misrule! with stock in trade to sell to Gitanos, surgeons and weeping relatives?"

CHAPTER XIII.

TRICKING A TRICKSTER.

In the eagerness to arrive at the goal, the halt was short at the wayside cross, three uprights to commemorate a triple murder by footpads. The cavalier, packed like a ham, was tormented by what tantalizing stimulus was in the gurgling of a huge leather bottle from which the muleteer and the monks drank to the peace of the immolated three.

His throat was so dry that the smoke from the muledriver's pipe irritated it till refraining from coughing was a herculean task.

To him they had been journeying an age, but three hours might cover the distance, when a fair stop came.

The beast of burden gave a profound grunt of relief as the fat friar was helped out of the basket by the summary process of the girth being unbuckled and the panniers spilt on the grass. He set to stamping his feet, before a humble inn door. Don Cæsar could wish that he was free to leap out and lay about him with the muleteer's whip, but he was so cramped that he had no feeling below the neck.

A gleam of light and a whiff of hot air came out. The host, a squat man like a gnome of the mountain mines, waddled forth, bearing a bag at a time, of which he deposited three next the mule.

"These are sorted, fathers," said he. "Those two are fit to sell at the Rocsalinas mart, and the other for your abbot's own table! The much broken victuals I have kept for my larder. But halloa! what are you smuggling in the other pannier? Wine, again? or game out of the king's hunt, for I heard Senor Don Carlos was out with the gun. You are surely more clever than the Indians who, I have been told, weight t'other side of a wheelbarrow with a huge stone when their load is onesided.

"That," replied Omfric, who had dis-benumbed his legs, "that is a small wax taper, of one hundred and thirty pounds' weight, given by the devout worshipers of our St. Francis, to burn for his glorification in his own chapel in our monastery!"

The host laughed, and playfully buffeted the enwrapped head of the prisoner.

"Without setting fire to your taper," said he, "I stake my money box, which is empty at the moment, that its wick is human hair, and such as the wicked Roman emperor set up to light his garden withal, which is painted to the life on the wall of your cloisters."

All laughed and the mule, refreshed slightly by cropping a delicious clump of burrs, added a short guffaw-like bray to the mirthful burst.

Hyænas in a graveyard would not, to Don Cæsar's judgment, probably prejudiced, have had more blood-curdling notes.

The fresh filling of the void basket failed to counter-balance him, and he was fated to be kept awake by the stones which jutted out of the goat's path, striking the basket bottom now and then. The ascent was notice-able and the pace was slow. The fat monk puffed and panted and if the results he visited the boughs with, which lashed his sweating cheeks had come to pass, their way would have been marked by withered bushes.

Anselmo, lagging behind him, every little while grabbed at the mule's tail to give him a tug, and each time the mule gave a jerk, which almost drove Cæsar's heart and liver into one.

"If I was allotted only one prayer for fulfillment," thought the latter, "it should be that this asinine Christopher should dash out that villain's brains with a lash out of both hoofs."

Sooner than he hoped, they reached the final pause.

A heavy gate was clumsily banged open and the mule, though no stranger, was so tired as to blunder up against the oak and iron. The off-pannier was nearly smashed against the panel.

"A murrain on the beast!" vociferated Omfrio, "do you want to make a pancake of the comestibles! might you not as well have borne to the other side, lout, and bruised the carrion, not the wholesome meats!"

Not at all gently, but sourly and violently, the fatigued two unloaded the mule which Pedro had to hold, since it at last revolted, and they laid Don Cæsar on a paved courtyard.

Except that the stages of his hegira had been marked by too vivid impressions, he might conceive that he was still prostrate on the Correction House pavement.

The shock of his fall did not penetrate the thick coat of insensibility pervading his body, and nothing like a groan could be forced out of his sealed mouth. He fell like a pig of lead.

"Put the 'cold meat' in the buttery," commanded the porter, authoritatively. "It is the directions."

"Oh, you will learn what is the best offer in the day?" asked Omfrio.

"Yes; they do not have counts and grandees for sale every midday of the week!" answered the porter, closing the gate.

By each end, Don Cæsar felt a pair of hands lift him and he was carried with the utmost disrespect into a small room, as he calculated by its quick return of the sounds the shuffling feet made, odoriferous with cheese,

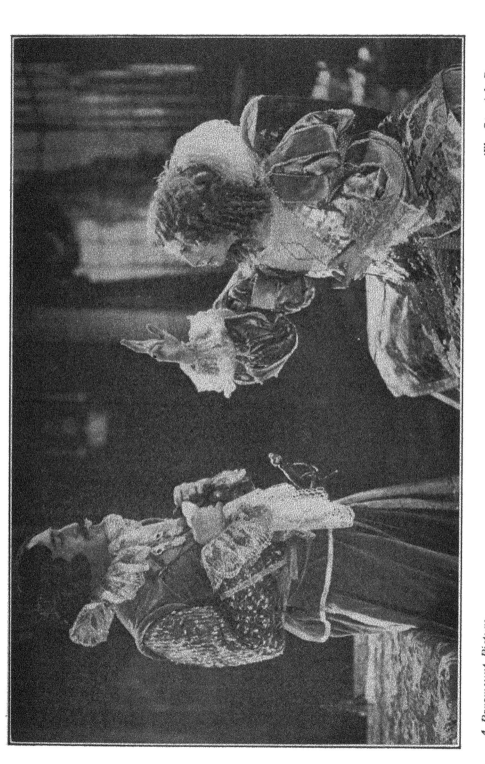

A Paramount Picture.   *The Spanish Dancer.*

QUEEN ISABEL INSTRUCTS SALLUSTE TO WATCH THE KING'S MOVEMENTS.

salt fish, smoked meats and the pitch with which wine-flasks were sealed. He was let drop upon bags which might, from their unpleasant feeling, contain nuts, and a door closing with a slap, all was dark and silent around him.

It was the instant when he should have exhaled a long breath, in evanescent relief, but he had lost the art of respiration.

The reek of the edibles brought the water chokingly to his lips, as it had come when the selfish monks regaled at the inn. This tortured him so that, had he been re-leased, he would have bitten into the first wine skin grasped at, or the first bottle would have had its neck wrung and been drained in spite of the strict table eti-quette which the noble had been taught by his tutor.

Another spell of anguish ensued, for he doubted very reasonably that such monks inhabited a monastery of succor to the afflicted.

"If ever," he muttered, "if ever I make the acquaint-ance of our holy father, the Pope, I will certainly beseech him to strike this imposition off the list of abbeys deserv-ing a place on the records for hospitality. I shall also desire him to have Father Anselmo hanged at the heels as a bob to that pendulum; Omfrio, both of whom I should suspend from the belfry hereto, at which a most dismal bell is now tolling, I surmise. It cannot be for masses on my head, for they will begrudge that!"

Emboldened by the renewed quiet, rats and mice be-gan to attack the holes they were boring, and the two or three which had already made mines, trotted gayly over the sacks and held councils on his body, with a view of determining if this new bag of stores contained a more desirable dainty.

"I read, somewhere, in the tomes whose titles I have forgotten," observed he, ruefully, "of a captive, much like me, who ingeniously anointed his bonds with tallow so that the vermin in his prison chewed the ropes asunder and he stood up, a free man. It is to my crossing that I cannot get sufficiently free to grease my bag, though, were that much vouchsafed me, I should make the exit without my friends', the rats', assistance."

Suddenly the rats scuttled out by the ways they had come. They had heard before the dull man the approach of some one. Indeed, a wicket in the wall, just an airhole, was quietly opened. Now it was not a cat, since few cats can draw a bolt, even to get at mice.

"A man! Not that I expect that these friars are not all of a tribe." His frigid heart stirred none the less. "I should say by his not using the regular ingress, that he is a thief. But I doubt that I am so valuable that I am sought to be stolen away from my good friend, this double—nay, treble-dealing abbot."

Thief or honest, this newcomer was assuredly not his acquaintance Omfrio, for he contrived to squeeze through the ventilator, planned small to prevent such overhauling the stores without due warrant. He did it with practised skill, crawled head down till his hands met a barrel, and then he dragged the rest of his figure through the aperture.

Sliding down upon the encumbered floor, he righted himself, squatted so that his head was on the level of the captive's and proceeded to whet a knife, till then carried between his teeth, on a cleared spot of the cemented floor.

Cæsar, whose views were formed entirely on conjecture upon what he heard, did not need this always nerve-exasperating sound to perch him on the ragged edge of ire.

"If this is a dumb man and deaf, I may die without his knowing who killed me in the dark," moaned he.

But the man had a tongue, and, as inevitably happens to a member of a community where silence is impressed on the inferiors, he made up with galloping garrulity when loneliness put the bit in his teeth.

He chuckled to himself as he felt the blade. It was more silly than cruel or hearty, this hilarity.

"This is an idiot," resolved the prisoner, not prone, lately, to be gentle in his judgments. "If he pleases me by his acts as much as he is pleased with his own sharpness, we shall be well out of it."

"That mutton-head, Omfrio, was so dead-beaten and sluggish after supper, which he hogged down," said this unexpected visitor, "that he is asleep and will not hark back to this dead."

"It is our dear boy Anselmo!" thought Don Cæsar. "Ah, to give him one fisticuff for every letter of his name! I could wish he had been christened as long as Asclepiodorusianus!"

He began to play his muscles by opening and closing his hands, as wrestlers do before seizing.

"He did not answer fully to the abbot, and so I ceased to be on tenterhooks lest he blabbed out that we had brought the dead away before the soldiers thought to strip him of his wedding garments."

"Upon my word," thought the prey of these vultures, "after the coat, the skin! I shall finally be buried, if ever, flayed to the core."

"His doublet was little stained with blood—and it will fetch ten or more crowns if I can find a Jew with an inch-wide patch of conscience at the South Barrier, by the Segovia Gate. Then, there are the breeches, with a gold galloon stripe which would trim a hat; the boots of the best Cordovan horsehide, with the spur-straps inlaid by fine Moorish art; the—eh? Oh, it is the rats! And the pearls were of a good size. All this means money, which

is not going to our common treasury. I will strip him,
add the duds to my pack, and, hey! over the mountains
in the morning!"

"I wish we could change places, brother, if that is your
plan of campaign. I feel a sore desire to rob these de-
spoilers, compared to whom my poor, maligned friends,
the gypses, are unblemished saints."

"How tough this duck is!" grumbled the monk. who
plied his keen whittle along the sack to cut the twine and
sunder all the envelope of the don.

"Ay, loose me, and you will find this duck confusedly
tough, if out of my net!" thought Cæsar, whose misery
was enhanced by his having to vent his choler silently.

If the steel had slipped and scratched him, he was determined not to have let a cry slip him. For he was re-
viving himself for a mortal struggle. Only once had he
known such a grim resolution. After a sortie, at the
siege of Pampeluna, being pinned down by his dead
horse, he was compelled to wait until the camp-followers,
stripping the dead and finishing the wounded, approached him so nearly that his last pistol shot should not
fail.

This deathlike quiet completely befogged the lay-
brother. With skill, considering the gloom, he had
ripped all the stitches right down the canvas where it was
joined, and sundered the cord which had come off his
waist at the inn, to secure the prize.

It was possible for Don Cæsar to spring up quite un-
fettered, like a snake bursting out of his old hide. He
did so.

But it was instantly to embrace the knife-bearer, and so
tightly that his ribs cracked, and he could not relax the
muscles containing the knife-haft.

"A sound, and I shall fasten my teeth in your throat!"
hissed he, with the concentrated fury of one so agonized

during four or five hours. "A move, and I will crush your ribs into your heart!"

Terror at the supposed reanimation of the dead had converted the man into that semblance of death which the victor was rapidly casting off. He let himself be disarmed as if he were petrified.

This captive was supine, as if his bones had been melted.

"I doubt your holiness, but I will give you a few minutes to say your prayers! Then I must kill you, to repay you for your cruelty on the road!"

"It was not I ground my weight into your marrow!" protested Anselmo. "It was that fat wight! I should say 'great weight!'"

"Why, I don't dislike this knave!" exclaimed Don Cæsar. "I do not rate your worthy of my—that is, your steel! But you are not lacking wit. Be useful, and I may lengthen the grace!"

"As I am not a holy man, I shall require five years' full measure and brimming to make my peace with Heaven! Oh, merciful sir, let me make the same with your excellent lordship first!"

"Gammon! and I am sick of gammon all the rest of my life from lying on this flitch! Why do you suppose I can be merciful?"

"On your wedding night, my lord—any boon should be granted!"

"Still witty; but jest less and tell me what kind of friars are you?"

"We are White Friars, sir, so called by a paradox, because we are gowned in black!"

"Still that vein—I must keep you on its edge, fellow, if—— You are of all colors?"

"White, gray and black! After the sun goes down and before the moon comes up, seen on the roads, you might take us for *contrabandistas*, smugglers, by your leave, dealers in varied goods——"

"Venders of dead bodies—augh! I thought myself in the Pit of Acheron in the gypsies' camp, but it appears that the Cordelers of the Cardarqua Range have in their monastery a deeper and blacker pool!"

"If you will spare me, my lord, and let us save ourselves from this pit?"

"Spare one who would not give the preference to one's own true friends in disposing of his corpse! how, now?"

"It was only flattering to hold your honor for the very highest bid!"

"Deuce take your trafficking! Did you look to Don José? If his soul were at stake, he would haggle to redeem it cheaper!"

"The abbot will take the biggest purse—it is his custom!"

"Surgeon, gypsy, my cousin—three furies who would rend me among them!"

"In your well-founded indignation, sir, you graze me with that knife! Steady hand means hale mind, my lord!"

"Excuses—I only should kill you with it!"

"What for? you are not dead yet! I ought to be rewarded for getting you out of the House of Correction! It is not so easy in a prisoner of your rank, believe me, count!"

"These rogues have been assisting prisoners of the state to evade their doom all along!"

"But your knife is inflaming the scratch it already established in the sub-clavian section!"

"Blood and wounds! have we the illustrious Dr. Torrerosi here, from Padua, who will locate a bullet buried out of sight with the magic lantern ray!"

"My good lord, it was while waiting for my money for

stiff-ones at the backstairs of the Medical Academy, that I picked up a little surgical lore!"

"Mind your own anatomy! Disclose! is this abbot more sanctified than you and your brothers?"

"He was, but he was defrocked for tipsiness. That caused them to appoint him director of our works."

"I would hear of his good works—carnal rather than spiritual, for a hundred!"

"Your honor is wrong—for we are spirituous above all! Abbot Scampedro is the guiding spirit, he directs, measures, compounds, presides over the brew——"

"What is your diabolical brew?"

"Why, sir! you who have a liquorish tooth, or common fame belies you, must have heard, if not tasted, no doubt, of the famous cordial of the Franciscans? That is how it comes the irreverent jesters call this 'the habitation of the cordial-heroes,' instead of the Cordilleroes, which meaneth the whipped of St. Prauk!"

"Oh, this monastery is the cordial distillery?" cried Don Cæsar, aghast. "By all that is delicious, I thought I was dreaming in Elysium, but there did come to me in the yard, an appetizing whiff of—out of the Persian rose gardens!"

"That is our brew! it will soften the savage! May it melt your lordship's obdurate bosom!"

CHAPTER XIV.

THE FUGITIVE'S FLIGHT.

"I could do with a quart of it," observed the recent captive, beginning to believe that he was near the end of this strait. "If it were not straining your cordiality too much, I would fain sample your concoctions!"

"My lord, it is hard to get at," replied the distillers' man, taking him in earnest, "for it is made for the Pope and the Princes of the Church, who—sworn not to partake of it, give it away to the hard-drinking kings and potentates!"

"That is why, not being vended, the Crown does not skim your vats?"

"Quite right, sir—no duty on us!"

"Does no preventive officer come noising about?"

"Nor nosing! This monastery, which has become a distillery, is advantageously situated: one half is church property, where the Crown officers have no footing, and the other half is Peculiar——"

"I should think so! a pest on it!"

"In ecclesiastical phrase, a Peculiar Establishment is one over whose foundation the Episcopacy has no jurisdiction!"

"Fine, this arrangement! I am sorry in the murk that you cannot see the smile of approval this arrangement brings out on my face! I see, when the excise gaugers come here. if they ever come, you move the goods upon the sacred land; when the prelate sends an investigator, shocked at the worldly manufacture, you shift them on the mundane side. My brother, your abbot will reach a high dignity! Pontiffs have been elected who were not half as ingenious as he!"

"He is pretty sharp!"

"I engage that he allows no leakage. For example, the drink you shared with your brother at the little inn, that would not be your invention?"

"Oh, I do not say there is no spoil—no spirits slightly off color or scorched! That excess avoids any *cess* by— but it is a mystery!"

"No doubt, when you are despatching a consignment to Rome, a barrel or two never gets mislaid on the road!"

"The muleteers, like that rascally Pedro, may execute little vagaries of that sort!"

"I am edified! I doubt not that France and Holland know the Cordial by—reputation! I see my duty to my king quite clearly," went on Don Cæsar, with a strong voice, quite himself with warmth at this wrongful exclusion of the public of topers from the quintessence. "I shall travel post-haste to my sovereign, who sorely prays for cash to prosecute the war a-foot with Germany and, eke, France, and I shall acquaint his majesty with the interesting fact that a call of his treasurer at the Monastery of Good Works will line his bags with the wherewithal to raise and equip a regiment——"

"More, too! And a train of artillery in supplement!"

"Of course, our pious monarch would not heed me if the Mother Church made this milk with her own hands for her own babes and sucklings, but as it is made by lay hands——"

"Fie! You would not do this, my lord!"

"The devil I would not! It is not you who can stay me!"

"I am a lamb in your hands, yet——"

"I distrust lambs who have steel teeth six or seven inches long—but, master lamb, I am a wolf—we have a traditional man-wolf in the Garofa family, like all genuine old families!"

"It is because you are a Garofa, a peer, a knight, that it ill beseems you to play the revealer—the informer— there, the despicable word is out!"

"There is something in that! I am poor, but I do not hanker after head-money!"

"Ah, my lord but I do!"

"Oho, you would, by the little I see—that is, know of you——"

"Pledge me——"

"Nothing but my word to pledge!"

"That suffices; let me receive the informer's pay, and I will not only assist you to escape, but guide you to the gentlemen of the Royal Excise Board, and, as you make a clean breast of mine by kindly removing your knee from it, I will do the same by the king!"

"But your friends, your dear brothers, would be troubled for this illicit distilling—some would be whipped with their own cords, some burnt in the hand, some ear-cropped! And the true monks would be exiled into the Indies or China!"

"They would deserve their doom, sir! It is heinous to cheat the good, trustful king, when he wants to defend the realm; it would be letting in the foreigner by with-holding the taxes on spirits! I see that if I was not pricked by remorse for my error, I ought to denounce out of pure patriotism!"

"But for the dark I should see this glory of a con-summate patriotic knave! We will see about terms when you show some loyalty to me, at present the arbiter of your fate. Rise, and come on—I mean, take the lead out of this rats' run!"

He pricked him between the shoulders with the knife.

"But it is because this is a rats' run that I cannot lead!

It was as much as I could do to pinch in at that airhole. You cannot follow, with your trunks bombasted in the fashion!"

"Then there is a wider outlet! For while you often slip in there, thin and long as a sausage-skin, you go out like the same stuffed!"

"You are an incontrovertible logician, my admirable lord! Sometimes, in order to comfort a brother, who has been put on short rations, I have taken out a little sack of delicacies!"

He removed, with the familiarity which dispensed with light, a large corn-chest in one angle and disclosed a considerable gap.

The two left the buttery by this hole, compelled to assume the ignoble attitude of reptiles; but, soon, they could stand up without the head brushing the ceiling or the elbows knocking the sides, in a tunnel, mostly earth, but protected by stonework where there might be a caving-in.

"This is a work of art!" said Cæsar, "the name of you rats is legion!"

"Yes, I had the help of other starvelings! They pushed me in to collect the material for a meal, since I am the thinnest of the brotherhood."

"Where are we now?"

"Under our chapel, lord! To our right, beyond that grating, black on the faint gray, is the old great hall. It is now our main stillhouse. There is no danger for we are laying on our oars, that is, awaiting the distillation to arrive at the point to run it off. We have an order for export, to Barcelona——"

"For the bishop in the infidel parts?" queried the ex-prisoner, maliciously.

He pushed the guide before him up to the high iron frame, where he saw, on the other side, by the glow of a furnace and a cobbler's candle, that is, with a double wick, an enormous vaulted room, scarcely passable from the complications of spiral pipes, vats, butts, tanks and distillery apparatus; from all exuded a smell of fermentation and vinous flavors, with delightful whiffs of aromatic herbs.

"That is it—that is what I smelt!" cried Cæsar, "this is a breath of Araby the Blessed! Nevertheless, I beg to know how we get out into the ordinary mountain air?"

"Nothing more simple! Going through the hall, for nothing is locked up, where nothing is to steal! we step out into the gardens. We cross and climb up over the wall, where a good sprawling fig tree offers a ladder which Omfrio can mount. Jumping down, we enter the first cottage or the first cabin of the charcoal-burners, and hire a mule or two. Thus, in the dawn, we may be knocking at the door of his majesty's commissioners of excise!"

"You may—but I—I must knock at my own door!"

"Your mansion-door! Oh, my lord, that you had a mansion!"

"Well, my wife's—the countess must dwell somewhere!"

"I should think she does. She is now, as far as I know, under the roof of the Marquis of Castello-Rotondo!"

"The—that old beau! Why, what the mischief does she there?"

"Where would it be more proper for a wife, bereaved of her husband on the wedding night, than to be harbored by her own father?"

"Her fath—Marit—her father—the old marquis!"

"My lord, along the road all news drifts, and the landlords repeat it. I heard from good authority that the Duke of Egypt had at last restored to the Marquis of Castello-Rotondo, from whom he has derived many years' income with his lies, his missing daughter who, I believe, was known as 'Maritana!' "

"Husband and parents found for her, all in one night! This is too much, too much!"

"If the joyful news commends poor Anselmo to your lordship, I shall not be too proud to remind you when you are again able to recompense the bearer properly!"

"Maritana, a Castello-Rotondo! my head is spinning!"

They were on the other side of the iron barrier by this.

"That is not joy—that is the fumes! To a novice, it is as good as a week's *debosh* to inhale the reek here!"

Cæsar followed him as in a dream. All was hushed. There was certainly a sonorous murmur somewhere in the hall, but perhaps a gurgling from a fissure in a pipe. They came to a door which gave, through a barred peep-hole, a glimpse of the gardens, and cold, blue sky. Suddenly, the sonorous sobbing ceased with a snort of surprise, and a dark mass, which had been taken for a heap of such tow as is wrapped about tubes to keep in the heat, revolved itself into a human form.

It was a burly man who bade them stand, in a voice broken by his being not half awake.

He did not look at the gowned man, but at Don Cæsar, who was in his conspicuous white wedding-suit, and certainly did not resemble the usual inhabitants of this monastic distillery.

He carried an Arabian matchlock, but the barrel had been cut down so that it resembled an *escopeta*, that is, a blunderbuss for firing stone balls. It was capable of pouring a half peck of slugs into a hippopotamus at thirty paces which would stagger him.

To the consternation of the escaping captive, who was going to employ his guide as a bulwark, this treacherous fellow dropped and at the same time yelled:

"Fire, Nunez! it is a spy!"

But once gun-shy, ever gun-shy! Don Cæsar had so re. cently learned that to stand to be shot at is worse than a crime—it is a fault! He accordingly imitated the falling of the lay-brother so accurately and rapidly that the shower of slugs whizzed over his head without any hurt, and he thumped the deceiver, on whom he landed with irresistible force.

The detonation was terrific in that somewhat encumbered, if not confined, space. The recoil of the ponderous firearm, meant to be fired from a rest, broke the wretch's shoulder and sent him against the edge of a tank, which, losing its cover, allowed him to topple over and back into the scalding contents.

Nunez added his screams to the cries arising throughout the convent, as he appeared with his head dripping with syrup and his hands glued to the tank sides.

Cæsar spurned Anselmo and sprang toward the door in the wall.

Simultaneously, the dark interior became alternatively somber and bright, like the old masters' "Resurrection-day," where the flames and the shadows chase each other till finally the former prevail.

The slugs had split and perforated the pipes—spirit shot forth and caught fire in long crescents in the air. The receptacles began to explode and boil over—the sparks fell from the woodwork and the tongues of fire wound around the worms. Those monks who had rushed to the scene recoiled at the several doors, for the draft turned toward them and scorched their frightened visages.

The hall was full of thin smoke and thick flame; on the floor writhed Anselmo, half-stunned, trying to rise from the warm bath of alcohol.

Cæsar had, without intending it, been entangled in his robe, with which he reached the opening; instinctively, on feeling the frigid night air, he dragged this envelope up to his shoulders and covered his compromising attire as he fled.

The starlight showed the wall cornice, with the fig twisting its boughs on the ledge.

With the agility which he could not have suspected in one so tried and long fasting, he clambered up, and, without pausing on the top, where he afforded too good a mark for a gunshot, he dropped over.

The ground was soft where he landed, and he had just sense enough to leap over the ditch.

Then, seized with a panic, as an immense chorus in alarm and horror of the false monks rent the air, for the hall was consuming like a bonfire drenched with turpentine, he fled at all speed.

He had been seen, for he heard as the last intelligible cry:

"There goes the Evil Spirit—he has fled with the souls of Nunez and Anselmo!"

There must have been two or three guards on the outside, for without looking back, he was conscious that he was followed.

He had the presence of mind to cry out:

"Look to the house! The preventive servants are upon you!"

The desire to save himself was supplemented by that to regain his beloved, and thwart the villainy which he conceived to be rife.

His cramps and palsies vanished. His head was as clear as his limbs were supple.

A deafening explosion sounded like an earthquake in the mountains. It was sparsely populated, yet seemed fairly alive from every dweller having been brought to his door.

He saw something speeding toward him, and stood to sell his repurchased freedom dearly, knife in hand. But it was only a horse, broken loose in the stable at the flash of fire and the explosion. He was too accomplished a cavalier not to know how to catch it by the trailing halter. He mounted agilely, and was immediately galloping toward the Madrid road.

Thus it was that may be read: Report of Don Senor Agapetto, Alcalde of Valsierra, confirmed by sworn depositions of worthy witnesses: It is established that the apparition which enkindled the serious conflagration in the Good Works Monastery, and bore away the souls of two of its lay-brothers, was the same unearthly horseman which carried off the body of the Count of Garofa, awaiting in pious hands interment, at the expense of his friends, at the said convent.

Don Cæsar foundered the borrowed steed, and was left exhausted under the wall of hunting-grounds, where he might have perished with cold and faintness but for a carriage coming up, drawn by four fine mules.

This carriage, with a good deal of secrecy, was placed by a postern in the wall, while the servants opened the same and stood on the wait.

The fugitive mustered the courage to ask alms, and, the domestics being good fellows, shared with the supposed runaway monk their flask of wine and bread and sausages. Thus refreshed, he listened while lolling with his appetite gratified, to their chat of the Madrid news.

Suddenly he started. He was galvanized.

This carriage was newly decorated, and on the panels glittered the arms of Garofa and Bazan.

This house within the walls was the Marquis of Castello-Rotondo's, a hunting-box presented to his dear master of the pheasantry by the king, and the carriage was to transport his daughter, lately made Countess of Garofa, on a little trip.

It was thus that, under the hood, the resuscitated Don Cæsar begged charity of his startled cousin.

CHAPTER XV.

CÆSAR AT AUCTION.

José was stupefied at confronting "Don Cæsar in search of his wife," as he plumply announced himself.

It was not until after a pause that he faltered, while his visitor contemplated himself in the tall Venetian mirrors:

"You; is it you—not dead?"

"I am bearing into your presence the vital part of myself."

"But how was your life saved?"

"A string of miracles."

"But who?"

"Oh, I owe all to you, for saving me from the gibbet."

"But you were still under the fire of the soldiers?"

"Yes, I was under their fire, which still smells in my, nostrils—that is quite true."

"I saw you led out to execution."

"I was led out martially and deferentially even."

"And I heard the guns go off."

"I heard them, too," added the other, complacently, "and at still closer hearing than your lordship."

He patted his body tenderly.

"I have the bullets somewhere."

"Extracted from your person by a skillful surgeon?"

"No, extracted by a—a person in my confidence——"

"But you fell?"

"Like the dead, for I could not hurt the soldiers' feelings by showing that no one had hit the mark at such close range!"

"Have I been cheated?"

"The Old Harry has. I can imagine him blotting out
the too-hasty entry of Garofa, Count Cæsar, and ap-
pending: 'A little later!' The illusion was perfect—it
took in several good judges, including a dandy of a doctor and two or three penitent friars. For a space, I was
as good—that is, as bad as dead, and thought that it
was all up with my creditors, unless you paid them out
of my scraps of fortune!"

Don José frowned. He was reflecting on who could
have betrayed him. It was clear, from his brow not
lightening, that he did not fix his suspicions on any one
in particular. Lazarillo was not in the least under the
ban.

Cæsar, having scrutinized the room, took an easy-
chair and began to nurse one of his feet, like a gouty
alderman.

"There seems to be a junketing here? Music, flowers,
fireworks, though where I came through I had a surfeit
of fireworks."

Don José shuddered and sniffed brimstone.

"There is a festival, at which you are out of place. Do
you not know you are in danger?"

"I am inured to dangers. I believe it suits my con-
stitution."

"Oh, why did you drop in here?" stamping in annoy-
ance.

"Hang it! When a fellow is the sport of fortune, he
must be dropped somewhere when she gets tired of him."

"Oh, if I knew!" growled José, wringing his hands.

"*Patienza,* as the good monks of the Good Works say,"
observed the uninvited guest, slowly, throwing up the
other foot on the other knee, and chafing it leisurely. "I
am going to tell you, for it is a relief to be able to dis-
course without haste, after playing mum-chance many
hours. I was strolling about the country—pretty rugged

out this way—when I spied a newly-painted carriage
come along. 'Oho,' said I, 'another of those upstarts
setting up a coach and pair. I wonder whom the king
has given letters patent to?' But, judge of the jump I
gave on seeing my own arms on the panel——"

"Your arms?"

"Quartered with the Round Tower of that old derelict,
the Marquis of Castello-Rotondo. I reasoned that, as it
was not mine, but still of my family, I ought to see its
destination. It stopped out there, at a miserable, sneak-
ing back entrance for so sumptuous a turnout. I
learned from an obliging footboy, whom I certainly shall
recommend to his master or mistress for promotion, that
it was the Countess of Bazan's equipage! She has taste!
Of course, when a man finds his wife's coach at a gate,
he is privileged to enter where she abides. Hence, my
dropping in. On account of my garments having lost
their gloss and being torn with thorns and sullied with
smoke, I hesitate, for I am really timid, dear coz, to cir-
culate in this gay mansion, but I must wish good-morn-
ing to my wife, and explain why I abruptly quitted her.
Where is the countess, my fond kinsman, for I am
pressed to disappear again, unless you are so much of the
king's-man that you have called in that cursed edict
anent the duelists."

"It stands." He drew a free breath, for it was plain
that the man, with every appearance of a hunted one,
had not heard of the pardon. "Before I can do anything
for you, I ought to hear your plans for the future."

"To see my own lady, and her papa and mama, who
will, no doubt, be in the skies to welcome me. I suppose
this is her house, given by her parents. In that case, I
am at home"

"You dreadnaught, you are everywhere at home,"
sighed his relative.

"I am taking possession. I wonder if it is free of mortgage—eh? For I think I know a Lombard, in the Jewelers lane, who would lend fairly upon this."

José quivered with rage, which he dared not evince at this obstacle arising to oppose all his schemes. But the king was near, and it would have been pretty bold to send this man again to death while the royal pardon was lying on his breast. He was knitting his brow and wrestling with his disappointment, when the old marquis ambled into the room.

"My guests never were so happy," ejaculated he, not seeing other than the prime minister at his entrance. "They do nothing but toast my wife and the Countess of Garofa."

Cæsar rose and gave the old noble a careful bow, which, by its utter elegance, foiled the tarnished wedding-suit.

"My wife, the countess, is a toast, is she? Hound my, cats! I can sympathize with her, for I came pretty nigh to being a toast myself not so great a while ago."

The host stared at the speaker, who he but dimly recalled.

"Where is my lady?"

"I declare," exclaimed the marquis. "This must be the son of my old friend, who was at King Philip's court. You are Don Cæsar of Bazan, I believe? Yet, I heard that you were dead."

"I am convalescent," returned the dashing don, with supreme politeness.

Don José made haste to draw his muddling old confederate to one side, and felt like administering a sound shaking.

"Not a word—not another word," hissed he, in a voice which showed his unusual concern. "Show no astonishment at anything you see or hear, and do as I wish."

"My future! Oh, the pet dogs——"

"They shall be yours." Leaving the other stunned with the important promise, he returned to his cousin, who evinced no sign of stirring.

"Such sacred rights as yours must be respected, and shall be here," said he, firmly "Your wife, the countess, being here, you shall meet without impediment or delay. Let me have the honor to conduct her to you!"

"A mint of friendship this, cousin!" exclaimed the count, his eyes filling with bright tears, for he saw again the beautiful Maritana no longer in tawdry rags, but as the bride, than which he had never known a more perfect vision of loveliness. "What, marquis, are you going to leave me! No, participate in my pleasure, for if I have found a wife of super-excellence, you, I hear, have found a peerless daughter."

"My dear son——" began the marquis, in perplexity as to how far he might go without Don José's permission. "To find a son like you for my old age, in addition to such a daughter, is like meeting with two sticks when one looked forward to walking about with one."

"A stick, am I! Well, this is pretty complimentary!"

"Don't agitate yourself, boy!" continued the marquis, on seeing Cæsar pace the room. "I know of old what it is to face a young and beautiful bride! I had the advantage of you thirty years ago!"

Don José had returned, leading in the Marchioness of Castello-Rotondo, trying to look as if she had emerged from a dip in the Fountain of Youth. He darted a knowing glance, and gave a warning gesture toward the marquis.

"Cæsar, I have the pleasure to present to you the Countess of Bazan!"

"The countess! my countess?" uttered the expectant one, abashed at the wrinkled face. "I remembered her as willowy—but this form is elderly! I ought to have remained at the convent—I did not know what I was hastening to!"

The marquis was paralyzed by the substitution which the minister performed with matchless effrontery. As the old dame smiled upon the young man, spite of his dilapidated toilet, her husband chafed.

"Gad! she simpers as if she liked the discourteous trick under my own roof!"

"I know that one often plucks the thorn for the rose," moralized Cæsar, under his breath, "but this is a hag of sixty—no wonder she wore an inch-thick veil!"

The young gallant turned to the host, and added in a low tone:

"As you are better acquainted with this mansion than I, will you kindly point out the shortest cut, out upon the king's road?"

"Don Cæsar," said José, "the countess is prepared to fulfill such duties as are prescribed to her!"

"It is useless!" returned the happy one. "I do not claim any sacrifices on her part! I should prefer another warrant of execution to my marriage certificate! Make it out!" Retreating a little, and being stopped by the old marquis, he said:

"Old fellow, you have had long experience, but did you ever fall in with such a gorgon! Is she not frightful?"

"Tastes differ, my son! This young rake has had his sight perverted as badly as his morals—he cannot see a beauty in any one, now!"

"The countess awaits your determination," persisted José, in the belief that the stream had turned in his favor; "she is ready to share your fate and fortune!"

"Heaven's will be undone!" cried the cavalier. "Lady fair, I will not take advantage of an accident, though

charmed at the generosity of one willing to share the lot
of so poor, so dunned, so black a libertine! to live with
you? ah, better for you I should wed the gallows!"

"The lady knew your low condition when she consented to the union," observed the minister.

"Did she? and did she know that—ahem! if that old
fossil accepted this beldame from the gypsies as his
daughter, and not his long-lost grandmother, then I—
but," added he loudly, "I am not going to be outdone in
generosity. Lady, I will not take you from those to
whom years of diverted affection must be offered! I free
you from every tie which would hold you back from
those to whom your charms, your lively company, and
your simplicity, must recommend you! Did you ever,"
he went on to the marquis, to give himself a countenance,
for this was a Medusa, after his anticipations, "ever see
such wrinkles?"

"Wrinkles, you pert fellow! where you see wrinkles, I
see dimples, egad! wimples—I mean, dinkles—hang it!
this perverse cousin of Don José's drives all sense out of
me! But I must not break out and lose my temper—
and the lapdogs!"

"Perhaps, lady," resumed Don Cæsar, trying to cover
his retreat with honor, "at some distant time, some very
distant time, I may——" The marchioness turned toward him with such vivacity that he drew back as if a
tigress was making its spring. "No, I can never shorten
the distance between us! My poor old friend of my
father," proceeded he, as he again consulted the vacillat-
ing noble, "as a reverend counselor, let me ask you if
you would, on any worldly consideration, entitle that venerable left-over from the Deluge, a wife?"

"This is too much! you malapert. If you do not approve of caviare to the general, you might abstain from
scoffing at it before others!"

"Oh, do not let me stand in anybody else's way! Marry her off to some other fool!"

Don José had pacified the marchioness, who was not highly pleased with the erratic conduct of the young count.

It was necessary to end the imbroglio.

"Don Cæsar, you will know," said he, "that the object of this marriage was to transfer your title and no more?"

"That is a bargain by which I am willing to stand!"

"At your nuptials you had not ten minutes to live!"

"Oh, for the only happy ten minutes I have enjoyed!"

"The countess does not care for you!"

"Wonderful fellow-feeling in man and wife!"

"You cannot shake off the chains, but they will wear more lightly if gilded! Your wife has become one in a rich family—you still possess nothing?"

"My own steward could not estimate my financial standing more exactly!"

"Quit Madrid forever, and you shall have six thousand piasters yearly!"

"Six thousand only for ridding the capital of the bugbear of the burghers, the nightmare of the cits' marrying mammas, the terror of the money-lenders and the despair of the tailors! It is dog-cheap!"

"Ten thousand then! eh, marquis!

"I would give half out of my own purse to be quit of so dull and indiscriminating an Esau!" said Castello-Rotondo, eagerly.

The marchioness said nothing, but she curled her lip till the red flaked off, in her expressive disdain.

"At ten thousand, going, going, going—no, I am not yet gone! Quit Madrid, the place of my birth?"

"The place where were incubated your debts!"

"Ah, it is true! It is no longer my home, but that of my dupes, my creditors! I can break their coffers by going! This decides me! And my last injunction should be, cousin, do not wipe out my liabilities!"

"You must also renounce all rights acquired by your marriage!" pursued his relative, warily.

"Forego the bliss of the fruit when it ripens—ah! it is seedy already—it is a bargain, coz!"

"Will you put your hand to paper to that effect?" said the tempter, delighted.

"Dictate!"

The marquis opened a flap of a table and showed within material for writing. Don José led his cousin, without any exertion, to the seat before it. He dictated:

"Don Cæsar of Bazan, Count of Garofa, etc., pledges his honor to quit Madrid forever!"

Cæsar paused at the word and sighed; he was not thinking of the lady at their elbow, but of his creditors, whose last hope would thus flee with him.

"And renounce the Countess of Bazan, his wife!"

Cæsar did not glance at the lady; he was indelibly impressed with her appearance, and wrote textually without a pause.

"Never to claim the husband's place?"

"Oh, never—the longest possible never!"

"You have only to sign——"

But at "the Cæs—" he ceased, for a footman, passing in the antechamber, was heard calling out:

"The coach of the Countess of Bazan waits!" And, thinking his mistress might be in this side room, he ventured to push open the door. It was due to this that Cæsar, looking up, naturally perceived a ravishing apparition out there.

Like a queen, surrounded by her minions and squires, Maritana, in her splendid dress, worn with the air of inborn gentility, slowly sailed down the passage, acclaimed by the young gallant whom she had fascinated in her new part as deeply as when she had danced and clinked the tambourine on the plaza.

"Maritana!" shouted Cæsar, springing up and drenching the paper with the over-set inkdish. "What do I see?"

José flung himself across his path. The marquis hurriedly shoved the door back and eclipsed the dazzling vision.

"Stay—your signature! You have pledged your word!"

"Fraud! I see the trick!" He rent the splashed paper into shreds. "So much for that infamous document!"

"My poor girl!" moaned the marchioness, trying to remember in what attitude one should fall, if executing a ladylike and juvenile swoon.

"Bring in the footmen!" said José to the marquis.

The old man disappeared with his wife, foreseeing a tempest and glad to be out of its reach.

José held his ground before the closed door.

"You must remember that you are a doomed criminal," said he, red in the face, but white in the lips, struggling between fury and doubts, "and that when those servants arrive, one word from the prime man in Spain, would be the death signal for you!"

"Ah, a rogue has a rogue's mind! By help of San Jago, we may yet come out with flying colors! I can cope with you better when you drop the mask!"

The patter of feet was heard in the corridor. There was a trumpet blast in the gardens, and it was to be surmised that the soldiery, at hand when the royal presence was immediate, would be at his minister's orders.

"Flight is still possible," said he, his eyes bloodshot. "I will aid my kinsman on one condition!"

The reckless rover drew himself up to his full height. At that time he was brim with nobility, and his fine

honor emerged unsullied from the contest with mercenary moves.

"No more shameful propositions," said he, haughtily.

He took a forward step toward the lobby, where had
passed the retinue of beauty and fashion, enframing his
wife—the real one. His Maritana!

"Be warned," stammered Don José, for he felt powerless with all his might against this man to whom death
was an old and idle tale. "Follow your wife another
pace and it will precipitate you to destruction!"

"My wife!" cried Cæsar, with exultation. "You lend
me the spur! It is, indeed, my darling wife—my long-
loved Maritana! Give free passage to the Count of Garofa going to present his devotion to his countess, or I
shall owe the law another life!"

He was weaponless, but such was his intrepid advance
that his opponent feared to draw on him, and being pushed
aside as if he were a lackey, stood trembling with con-
flicting emotions, as the daring one burst open a wing
of the door and flew out of the room. At the last words,
the corridor had been choked up with servants and a few
of the royal guards in half-uniform. If the stranger had
been in any other garb than the Church's, no doubt they
would have seized him without any explicit orders. But
the cowl was sacred as a crown—the gown as appalling
as the steel coat, if not inspiring the terror of a hundred
years before, in faithful Spain. All fell back, and some,
with force of habit, bowed to receive the benediction.

Cæsar reached the top of the great stairs, when his
enemy, recovering from his panic, dashed out in the same
course.

His way was impeded by the throng, and, foaming at
the mouth as one in an epileptic fit he could just falter:

"That man! Pursue him! Soldiers, if he resist, fire
upon him!"

But even so soon the fugitive had descended the noble stairs by the schoolboy trick of sliding down the broad and polished balustrade. From the bottom, beside the fat hall porter's chair, he sent back a demoniacal shout of laughter.

"But a priest—a priest, excellency!" objected the lieutenant commanding the guards.

"Fire on him like a boor!"

But the desperate man, light and active as a buck, had already cleft the mob of footmen on the steps and vanished as if his previous unearthly friend, by superstition, had once more flown to his aid.

CHAPTER XVI

José of Santarem quitted the brilliant grounds with nothing but the shadow accompanying him.

In all his ascent of that path replete with difficulties which the statesman knows, he had never been so clearly aware of his treading between the precipices.

Maritana, spite of her ambition, was no longer the same ductile metal since she had perceived by instinct that it was Don Cæsar, her first and only love, who had stood beside her in the prison chapel.

Don Cæsar was not only not dead but capable of crossing his course at all undesirable moments. It could not long be concealed from him that the king had granted him pardon.

"As for the king, this selection of our Lord Don Philip," mused the politician, as he rode mechanically, "I cannot make of him what I will, I fear. He is dough that has become stone. He imitates his sire so well at times that I perceive that he may do a great deed, almost a good one, out of something naturally commendable in his heart. He forgave Don Cæsar in the teeth of his own edict, because he was clement. He would strike me from my place if he knew all, because he would see it was justice. He is generous, for he has, for this whim toward the gypsy girl, let me open purse after purse, and he will not fiddle over the details. But the amours of a monarch are ephemeral! Besides, the queen would never be pushed off the throne to make way for even a marquis' daughter. She will remain queen and Maritana will never reign, like

the fair Gabrielle in France or Jane Shore in England. I
must fan his flame; not throw cold water upon it!"

He was compelled to match his cousin in speed, and he
was backed with unlimited means.

Maritana, put in the carriage, and escorted strongly,
was on the way to the destination which he had chosen.

The king, whetted by the brief glance at her, arrayed
as became a king's fancy, was notified by a sure messenger where he might find the lady without any further
hindrances to the suit.

The queen, retired to the palace of Aranjuez, which is
on the border of what is called Toledo Province now, was
also apprised by a confidential courier that Don José, carrying out his promise to inform her on her husband's ab-
sences, would this night convey proof of that infidelity.

Double, treble traitor, not believing at last that Maritana would be his tool or that anything in his power
would reduce Don Cæsar to submission, he concluded to
make the queen such a proposition as in her jealousy she
would accept.

"She shall ruin the king and accept my sole guidance.
I will see that the king occupies the throne no more and
that he is relegated to a monastery! Into his place I will
lead over the frontier the new Charles the Eighth, who
will, for my breaking down barriers that the emperor con-
siders impassable, reward me with the prime ministership
in perpetuity and a bonus of a princely revenue! I have
my eye, too, on half Andalusia being sliced off into a
principality whereupon I should be Prince of Sevilla!"

A night bird screamed and his horse tripped. But he
was too absorbed and, on the whole, relieved by his plan
to notice the omen.

At the gateway, where the horse had halted and his
escort looked inquiringly at him, a man, armed with an
arquebus, confronted the party.

"'Santarem!' I compliment you on your good ward, Lazarillo!" cried Don José, assuming a pleased tone as he was helped out of the saddle by his groom.

Lazarillo, for it was the page transferred to the prime minister's private service, gave the word for the porter to open the door, but only the master entered.

In the hallway he paused and shook off the dust, asking impatiently:

"Is the house in good condition?"

It was one of those small houses like a fort, more Moorish than even in Morocco, with small windows and thick walls, capable of standing a siege without great guns to batter it. It stood in a grove of chestnuts and had a small garden walled in. Broken potsherds glittered on the coping, embedded in cement.

"The house, my lord," replied the young varlet, smiling, "is fully fitted, though the time was short. On the other hand, there was an army of furnishers. I could no less than goad them on, since the tenant was a lady and one in whom your excellency takes a deep interest."

"Boy, her welfare is second to none!" said he, enigmatically.

"Oh, is it the queen?" muttered the bright youth. "What mysterious intrigues! It is bad for the poor, humble finger which gets into the hinges of these palace doors!"

"Has the dame arrived?"

"Yes, my lord; and she was shown at once to her suite of rooms, on the next floor."

"Did her servants remain——"

"They took the horses and carriage straight away—I presume back to Madrid."

"Don't assume anything."

"Am I to announce your lordship?" said the youth, timidly.

"Oh, no, I have no curiosity!" but his tremulous lips bel' d him.

"Can you recall the *caballero*, a little pale but with grand manners, who used to call at my private house in the royal road?"

"For once or twice I saw him, despite a mask. I can, no doubt, recall him—he had a lofty air, though cold!"

"Besides, he will bear a token. He will say 'seven' to your challenge of 'Carlos.'"

"Joy," thought the boy. "It is the king, our master! Oh, my good lord is going to reconcile the king with the queen—this is some lady of hers who is to conduct the reunion!"

"You seem merry?"

"Master, I am like the poacher's boy—he begins to laugh when his master prepares the springs and traps— he knows there will be a feast when the capture is made!"

"You are the lad after my own heart! Good! It is a trap! But the game steps in willingly!"

"I am to admit the pale gentleman?"

"And no other."

"If they present themselves?"

"Use, to good advantage, the fine arquebus with which I see you are supplied. You understand it?"

"I was a gunsmith by trade, sir!"

"Good! Yet you may tell the lady that I have called."

He lingered at the door after he had dismissed his followers to a little distance to await him. While so engaged, he heard a peculiar blast on a hunting-horn at a distance. The notes were those sounded when a royal stag is sighted in a chase.

"Aha!" said he, joyously, "all flourishes famously! It is my king—my dupe!"

In the hall the porter bowed to him; on the stairs two footmen holding candles bowed. On the landing a third servant, also with a candle, indicated in silence the entrance to the lady's rooms.

Maritana must have been waiting, for what was to come, with impatience no longer to be controlled. For at the sound she opened the door with her own hand.

She receded and showed her disappointment, though what more desirable visitor she could expect is a puzzle.

Love hopes the impossible will come; thus it is that it is never surprised.

"Ah," said she, curtesying to conceal her vexation, "the Marquis of Santarem!"

"Only the marquis. I am happy to see that you are luxuriously lodged, but it is but a hovel to the casket which should comprise such a jewel. Is there anything lacking?"

"Nothing, nothing, I thank your lordship!" she formally returned, as if to abridge this interview.

"So your brilliant visions are realized?"

She bowed.

"You have a title not surpassed, an *entourage* of splendor, and the homage of all who near you! I think I have kept my promises as the wizards of your early acquaintance seldom do!"

"You have done so, my lord marquis. Do to the state, which longs for peace, what you have done for poor Maritana, and the country will long bless such a premier!"

"Ah, do you study politics? Cease—it is a study which makes the brain acne, which causes one to shed tears while shedding blessings on the ungrateful people!"

Maritana surprised him by weeping.

At this unexpected mourning he felt not only that he had a heart, but that she owned it. She had continued to spell him, although expediency told him that he must not be the king's rival—not because he feared him, but because to love another than the queen would hurl José from his elevation, only to be fortified by her.

"Do you think, then, that I am ungrateful to the queen, whose faithful agent you are?" sobbed she. "But I sigh amid all this gaud and glitter for the hours when I was free and happy!"

"I doubt you, lady; you sigh for the hour when you first assumed the trammels of matrimony! But I do not read your heart to cross its impulses! I have come to usher in one who will dry your eyes and exhilarate your dwindling heart! Farewell—I cap your dreams—I present your beloved mate!"

Maritana wiped her eyes. In that brief interval when the cambric passed over her sight a change took place: where the minister had stood another figure replaced him.

Maritana was under the eyes of Carlos of Spain.

This time, confused and oppressed, because it was not Cæsar who faced her, he had the leisure to contemplate so much loveliness, which the transient grief only enhanced, as a veil of spray redoubles the vivid gleam of the waterfall.

Carlos had a bright side to his passion, not commonly seen on his prematurely grave visage. He was handsome of his saturnine kind and equal to the ideal which many women as fair as she worshiped.

"Maritana!" said he, in his sweetest voice, such as his queen had not recently heard at that pitch.

Incensed by the fleeting view at the Castello-Rotondo's he was ravished by this uninterrupted meeting.

If Don José had demanded anything now he would have had the ready assent.

The voice, however, gentle and winning, made her quiver.

"Why do you not speak? Ah, each day will be a new life to me! But you do not approach!"

On the contrary, she retired, slowly but steadily, like a peasant girl held in the bushes by a reptile's fascinating eye, moving back and praying for assistance.

He followed and took her hand; it was cold. He looked into her eyes; they were lusterless. He looked at her lips; they fluttered, and her words were scarcely, audible; she could not articulate.

"What a chilling greeting! Has Don José given up to me one of those wax images into which the necromancers instill a passing breath of life?"

He was so angered that if his mymidon had been present, this time, he would have sent him into a dungeon.

"Are you not happy, thanks to me?"

"Happy!" was the hollow echo. "How can I answer you? Everything is so strange around me! My sudden discovery of parents—my still stranger marriage! I may be noble, but still something tells me that between us gapes a gulf as wide as separates the baseborn and the hidalgo. I feel that you are Don José's superior! I dare not raise my eyes to one who daunts me! What makes him speak to you with bated breath?"

"Fear me! your bound one! your courtier! fear?" but the haughtiness in his accents was uncontrollable. He wished to command affection on finding that it was not spontaneously his. "Oh, girl, you are wronging love by regarding me with such feelings! Your devotee adores you, and would sacrifice so much to hear that this love is returned, like his is offered, unstintedly!"

He snatched up her hand and kissed it, though the coldness again repelled him.

"By all the saints who wear crowns," cried out the disconcerted monarch, "there is deceit here—has that José deceived me?"

"I believe," said Maritana, lifting her tearful eyes, "that it is I who have been deceived."

He looked at her, deigning to inquire and so far give his confidence.

"I have been deceived by that ceremony. That man who stood beside me was not your wraith—but one I knew! A gentleman outlawed and penniless, but ever brave and high-minded. His sword was no longer gilded, but it flew out at the call of the weak and oppressed. He might have been the king in the ghetto—he was bowed down to by the gypsy, who does not bend his head to every one, let me tell you! While his voice spoke up for the injured and friendless, it was also leader in the general mirth. An eagle with the tune of a lark—a wanderer like myself, my heart accompanied his in its erratic flights! I had no substantial reason then to suspect my birth was equal to his, but I hoped that as we met upon the level at the holy altar, he would remember that I had held my worthiness in the past, and he might expect his wife to stand as firmly in the future."

"You married to be blessed in this world. You shall have your intention accomplished. My word on that! Every luxury shall minister to you. My love shall be so prodigal that you must return my unique ardor!"

She had retreated as he advanced, till the tapestry on the wall was flattened to it by her pressure.

"Do not touch me!" gasped she, with a beginning of loathing at his cowardice, which smote him acutely.

"I understand," said he, lowering his hand and stiffening himself with wounded pride. "You do not love me; not because I am unworthy—but because you love another! Maritana, your tribe are known to pretend with unparalleled art! Your heart beat for gain, for the pleasure of beguiling, with no true passion or earnest desire! Have I raised you so high to leave you usurping an undeserved position? Oh, do not think that I would throw you down from your pedestal, owed entirely to me!

Enough that now you must go to your chamber! You will learn before long what duty you owe your lord and master!"

He pronounced the words so commandingly that she shuddered as when the herald announces the will of the despot.

"Sir, you have reason for your anger, if you have been deceived," returned she, gently, for she felt that she was causing sorrow, and she was compassionate to a brother-sufferer. "I obey you for methinks that is a duty, indeed! I obey the lord and the master!"

The king watched her leave the room with relentment.

"Has Don José let her know too much? Is she yielding or defying? Why should I hesitate? I will declare myself rather than lose her!"

But he was stopped in the first step he was taking by the explosion of a firearm under the window.

It was a critical time. Autocracy was tempered with assassination. It was foolish, in the conquest of a girl, to run the fire of a regicide on whose gun depended the succession of the throne.

Nevertheless, overcoming his short trepidation, he bravely proceeded to the window in order to look out and perceive the nature of the attack. But hardly had he set his hand to the frame, which opened in halves, than another hand outside seconded his in the act.

The opening disclosed a manly figure, which thrust one leg over the bar, and was followed immediately by the other. From the intruder, who instantly closed the sashes, came a gay voice, saying, without his looking at his helper:

"Thanks, my boy! That is a vile way to salute visitors of importance! That marksman has carried away my new hat and feather! What the devil have I done to draw all shots into making me a target?'

This natural inquiry would have allowed any one acquainted with the most recent vicissitudes of Don Cæsar de Bazan to recognize that gentleman.

The king passed by him, and now, with his back to the window, could only stare.

"Oh, I beg your pardon, sir!" continued the irrepressible don. "I took you for a brother to that awkward menial."

Carlos did not resent this renewed impertinence otherwise than by questioning sternly:

"A visitor—why enter by that casement?"

"Because, simply, they had double-locked the door."

"I am in no humor for jesting!"

"No?" said the other, combing his locks with his fingers, *a la* Gitano, "what a loss! I am, always!"

"What is your motive?"

"I was driven——"

"What devil drives——"

"An angel! My motive is pardonable in any gentleman's and Spaniard's eyes. The moon is just peeping out! By its ray I spied a very pretty face at the next window, through the bars. I wanted to ask my way—to heaven—of which she seemed an inmate."

"Audacious—you would speak with her?"

"Sooner than to a churl! I went up to the door where your porter, on whose rudeness I do not felicitate you! refused me admission. How was I to get in?"

"Get out!" said Carlos, testily.

"His very words—I wager he is instructed by your blunt lordship! I made the circuit of the house—the walls are topped with broken glass, and I would not damage my clothes any more! I spied this window, to which approach was not difficult when one has been a sailor and has scaled the carved poop of an East Indiaman treasure ship—but never mind that! I mounted to the breach and you, with a kindness which redeems your surliness, opened to me. Your lackey's shot carried away my best hat! Give me the address of your hatter in the city, and an order for a new one, and I will wear it in your honor!"

"Sir, this is an insult!"

"You are right! Hospitality, one of the saints, I believe, was grossly insulted in bombarding me!"

"What business have you with this lady?"

"Business! you will not press—it is private—I wish to see her—to speak her, as we say at sea! That is the kernel of it."

"Impertinent! I desire you to quit this room!"

"After having given your varlet the time to reload his barker? Then you, if you are the master——"

"I am the master of this house!" said Carlos, haughtily.

"Then the most complete means of your making amends for your guard's rudeness would be to walk down with me on your arm!"

"You will more probably be walked out between the arms of my servants——"

"If you are master, then, I shall appeal to the mistress!"

"Do you know there is a mistress?"

"I saw a lady who is not accustomed to be the second in any house—I allude to the Countess of Garofa and Bazan."

"Do you know a real high lady like that?"

"Oh, my toilet? Oh, that is nothing—for I wore no other when I last parted with her esteemed father, the Marquis of Castello-Rotondo!"

"I say," went on the king, imperiously, "do you have the honor to know the countess?"

"Well, slightly, for our interview was just ten minutes

in duration. But since you are the master—may I know your name?"

The king was seized with a sudden thought as he was about to betray himself, goaded by this peerless impudence, and he replied:

"I am Don Cæsar de Bazan, Count of Garofa!"

His hearer, as we have begun to know, enjoyed a coolness rarely to be found in a dozen ordinary men, but at this declaration he puckered up his lips in a whistle which he did not sound. He made the eloquent gesture of offering the boaster a hat, which, we also know, he did not possess at the time.

"Don Cæsar de Bazan?" repeated he, overwhelmed, but not by the effect the speaker supposed.

He gloried in the revelation, for it was startling: two phœnixes had arisen from the ashes of the original bird.

The pause was broken by the entrance, rather rudely, of Lazarillo: he carried his still smoking gun in one hand and in the other the instruder's hat, which had a hole through it and the plume broken.

The mutual recognition of page and transient master was quick, but with the silence of prudence which the boy had learned and in which the other had been a proficient since long.

"A fellow at whom I shot while mounting the wall and whose hat——" began Lazarillo, to cover his impoliteness.

Cæsar snatched the hat, and curiously examined it.

"Thanks, my boy! Call on me for a Christmas present!"

The king did not heed this paltry episode.

"Now that I have satisfied you, sir!" said he, sternly; "accommodate me with your name!"

"This unknown can give me points in bravado," thought the other; "what an unblushing rogue!"

Lazarillo, while pretending to hold his gun in a defensive pose, whispered to Garofa:

"Good heed! It is the king!"

At this portentous disclosure, Cæsar understood all from a slight experience in this sort of clandestine amour familiar to courtiers. But thanks to his incredible self-command, not a tint appeared on his cheek, not a crease corrugated his brow, and not a spark glittered in his eye.

"My question embarrasses you," continued the king, which remark was not creditable to his powers of observation. "I demand an answer!"

"It is forthcoming!"

With a lordly—nay, a kingly gesture—he waved Lazarillo from the room, and, seating himself, while he clapped on his recovered sombrero, replied with incomparable dignity:

"If you are Don Cæsar of Bazan, I am the King of Spain!"

"What?" faltered the other. "You—king——"

"King of both the Spains!"

"You?" still protested the monarch, aghast at this counter-check.

"As surely as you are Don Cæsar of Bazan!" reiterated the gallant in a voice both pleasant and taunting. "This will teach him to play with pointed tools!" thought he, delighted with his discomfiture. "Ah, it would astonish you, or any one, to see majesty unattended at the door of a pretty woman who is not the queen! But I assure you that there is nothing in it to surprise you. I was in the humdrums! Our royal quacksolver gives it another and a more euphonious name, but it is the blue-devils all the same! Kings require relaxation elsewhere than in the cloister where my great ancestor sought it. But not a word of this amiable royal caprice," continued he, lifting his hand chidingly. "Still, with a man of your fame for gallantry, I may rest satisfied it will go no further! You will not betray our secret, will you, Cæsar?"

The monarch almost cowered before this airy and sarcastic persiflage. He kept trying to remember who this could be whose manner was, while flippant, quite courtly, feathering the sharp shaft.

"Let me see—I ought to recall something of our Don Cæsar! He flourished in the court when I was younger than of late! Of course, a sovereign is bound to remember all his subjects, especially those whom he ought to cherish with pride. A brave fellow in the camp, and a gay one in the court! I would that I were of his humor! He went a-duelling in sight of our royal commandment, and spitted a captain in the guards! It should teach me to hire none but masters-of-fence for such a post, and not a mere master of offence! His overset was humiliating to my colors, but it spoke volumes for the sprig's dexterity! Ah, I missed my man when I did not offer him the captaincy of my body-guards! But I understood that he was shot for breaking the law, in the Corregidor's courtyard."

He rose and strutted up and down the room, making his heels ring before, returning to face his baited prey, he went on:

"Do you mind answering me one little question: Being Don Cæsar, what right have you to flaunt your recovered liveliness in my kingdom? You cannot be tried twice for the same offense, but you can be shot twice! That is in the annals! But, bless you, last of the Bazans and Garofas! we are not the sanguinary tyrants to betray you!"

"Your majesty forgets himself——" began the other.

"That is possible. The keeper of the king's morals has

gone hunting with the royal remembrancer! But what has our majesty forgotten? other than his purse—I have not a dollar! by all that is coinable!"

"You forget that Don Cæsar might readily be alive, since he received pardon in full from your majesty?"

"Oh, did he?" He was moved.

"I have the best of reasons for affirming that his pardon was duly issued, with all the forms, and that it reached the prison in time——"

"To save him?"

"Well, it got there at eight——"

"And he was shot at seven!"

It was the king's turn to utter an emphatic "Indeed?"

"Yes, and very deed! I have the best of reasons for affirming that!" resumed the mock monarch. "He has grounds for pleading for an indemnity against so slow a messenger!"

"Still, you see that it would be useless to shoot at a pardoned offender!" said the other.

"As useless now as for me to wear a title which does not belong to me."

"Gracious, don't say now that you are not the King of Spain?"

"No? you half-suspected it, eh? Am I right?"

"Then you are——"

This time, there was a knocking at the door. Lazarillo was not going to make the blunder of entering without notice another time.

"I sniff *alguazils*—the watch!" muttered Don Cæsar. "Well, a pardoned man at his wife's door need not fear an army of tipstaffs! I am——"

"Sire!" said Lazarillo, venturing to interrupt, as he conceived the importance of his tidings, and kneeling down to the king, "a special courier——" He handed him a sealed packet.

The king had no sooner read this message, than he turned pale and he muttered "Treason!"

He was informed that the queen, come to Aranjuez, knew of his absence at the Marquis of Castello-Rotondo's, and was seeking him there and elsewhere. The "elsewhere" was what pierced him to the quick. He had no time for jesting now.

In this perilous instant, when he was the shuttlecock for Austria and France, to have another bat in the air, eager to strike him, was disheartening.

He beckoned imperatively to Lazarillo, whom he only knew, from his position in the house, as Don José's trusted servant.

"See that I have a horse ready. And do not let that man quit your sight. Learn his true name and condition, and keep him on the leash!"

The young man nodded respectfully, and exchanged a glance of sublimated intelligence with his former master, who did not hinder the king's hasty departure.

CHAPTER XVII.

"YOU ARE MY HUSBAND."

The page turned round, as the door closed, and they heard the quick steps on the stairs, and surveyed the intruder with wondering eyes.

"Can this be you, dear lord?" faltered he, half between joy and dread.

"Yes, I am the man whom you, I think, rescued from an unpleasant death—by musket balls! I did not like being bored!"

"Yes, I used my experience as a gunsmith to some profit," confessed the youth, complacently. "I drew the balls from the hand guns, so that unless you were perforated by the wads, you would remain unhurt. I was so pleased when you took the feeble hint I ventured to give you, and dropped at the command to shoot."

"Excellent, the hint, for I assure you that I meant to fall like a soldier, stiff and firm; perforated."

"Only I regret that I had a chance myself to spare you and yet I fired with ball!"

Cæsar smiled and put his finger in the bullethole which ventilated his hat.

"Yes, you came but now very nearly to being my executioner!"

"But how could I dream that it was you, sir?"

"I did not think you did—for you would never get your arrears of wages if you had drilled me in the head. Now, are you going to execute the royal orders as faithfully this time—expel me?"

"Why, it is the royal order, as you say!" and the boy drolly scratched his nose.

"If I refuse—if I resist, for I have lost my yielding disposition! the thorns and briars on my road recently have teasled my hair the wrong way!"

"Resist, then! my arquebus is unloaded, and you can take down one of those swords from the trophies."

"I act on your hint!" and the don, as if he had only come into his own, carefully selected the best of the swords, which, belonging to another age, decorated the wall in a panoply.

"There is no one to oppose you. The servants are country loons chosen for their stupidity, and they take their orders from me, whom Don José left in sole charge."

"You are a good page in my good books, henceforth!"

"I am Don Cæsar of Bazan's most faithful and obedient servant!" returned he, bowing.

"Should I ever obtain riches——"

"Retain me in your service, my lord, I pray thee, until then—and after——"

"Service? you shall be major-domo—cock of the walk! and a dozen lackeys shall wait on you, hand and foot! But, Lazarillo," he went on, lowering his voice and impressing even more depth of feeling to it, "what about this lady in this house?"

"She is in there."

"I wish to see her—to apologize for my walking in here under fire of your cannon! Yet an odd timidity—can you arrange to announce me?"

"I think, my lord, that the noise has excited her curiosity. No doubt she hears us, and—on my faith! she is coming!"

He ran to the inner door and opened it just as, on the other side, Maritana laid her hand on the door handle.

It is vain to try to express her surprise when, in this stranger, noisily making good his entry, she recognized

her old-time defender, her partner during the dancing-
time and the life-partner decided by Don José, when he
thought to cut short his life.

"I am going to quiet the servants," said the page, softly
leaving the room, with gladness, though he did not like
the serious aspect of both the persons thus brought together anew.

"Well, lady fair," said Don Cæsar, with a voice imperfectly controlled, "we meet at last!"

Spite of the tone being cool, she showed pleasure.

"I managed the meeting not without some trouble and
danger. I have been blown up, chased like a werewolf,
hunted by police, peasants and soldiers, and fired on by a
tolerably good, though young marksman. A high price
to pay for this interview."

"Still jesting, Don Cæsar?"

"Ever jesting—I shall no doubt die with a joke chok-
ing me, and another will be found in my brain like the
fowl's string of embryo eggs! But I am no longer the
carouser, the breakneck cavalier, the dancer and the
merrymaker to the court of his ill-kempt majesty of
Egypt, but the Count of Garofa, your husband, my lady,
the countess."

"I knew it was you all the while!" she broke forth,
passionately.

"I thought you would, if any one, though I began to
doubt. But, Maritana, I know all."

"Then, tell me, for I am bewildered."

"You thought my death was certain!" She looked
puzzled. "But that did not check you on the road to the
title you coveted since long back! When you left the
altar set up very appropriately as far as I, an outlaw, and
you, a gypsy, were concerned, in a jail, you listened for
the horrid sounds which were to bring death to me and
liberty to you!"

The Spanish Dancer.

A Paramount Picture.

She stared horror-stricken at this unexpected censure.

"It was a light price to pay for a name and rank which, however, thus you consigned to infamy!"

"Why, this is bitter falsehood! I have never wronged my husband's memory, even in thought." She answered his haughty and severe glance with a tender one. "But, say what you will and in any key—I am blessed in my belief being confirmed by your lips that you are in fact my husband, for another claimed to have stood by me at the font, and has since called himself the true Don Cæsar!"

"I know that! I have met the impostor! Little did I think that I should ever be robbed, and then, by the King of Spain! Oh, mockery! he has a string of titles as long as from here to Trafalgar, and yet, insatiate tyrant, he grasps my poor countship for what influence lies in it!"

"What do you mean by the king?" She shuddered to think that she had divined what presence was under that lofty and frigid mask.

"Oh, the winner!" returned Bazan, with forced lightness. "Royal wooers do not a-wooing go in vain!"

"Wait! let us stand on firm ground. Your word against the king's. How am I to know to whom I was given by Don José? I would not ask him, for he is a liar!"

"I agree with you, though he is my kin! His royal friend makes two of a kind—that is the latest court news —straight as my sword."

"Do you remember what words you parted with— at the altar?"

"I said something like 'I devote to your ladyship the rest of my existence!' I grant that they are unlike the last phrases which the old historians rounded off the last moments of their heroes with, but it has the advantage, such as it is, of being perfectly sincere."

"Those are the words my husband uttered in my ear—you are my husband!"

But he did not hold up his arms to embrace her.

"You are forgetting that I am above all a loyal subject! Rat it! one does not shake off allegiance because a king has winked at his loved one—a royal brooks no rival, so that I must join the ranks of the enemies of Spain in order to play at evens—perhaps, on the battlefield, I may strike at the helm which is surrounded by the crown!"

"You would not turn traitor to do that! Oh, Don Cæsar, husband mine!" she entreated, fervidly, "that would poorly repay my sufferings. If you hear me, you will not condemn me again, for you have, though I blame you not, judged me already. Do you not remember when our dancing pleased the queen?"

"And the king, and all the rest of the royal family!" jested he.

"A nobleman came to me thereon and professed an interest in my welfare——"

"Old Rotella-Castondo—or whatever the old idiot's title is—but overlook that—the old donkey—don—is your father!"

"No, it was another—he told me that he was commissioned by the queen to carry out her commands and to raise me to the elevation of countess. The means employed were——"

"Creditable and honorable—they would be," sneered Cæsar, "if, as I sharply suspect, this go-between was my dear cousin—whom heaven confound and bring down!"

"Yes, this time honorable, since I believed that in wedding you, I made one happy who had professed a love for me! It was one for whom I felt more regard than for any other m-m-man I ever m-m-met!" she sobbed.

"If you are the marquis' daughter, you would not be a right gypsy—so you may not be deceiving me?" said the other, relenting.

She knelt and grasped his hand, weeping on it.

"Oh, my poor companion, my dear husband, I have been greedy in my pride—I did crave a lifting out of the slough! But I have been punished for rising, like the glowworm which is set upon the wall, where it is seen better by the admirer, but, when the sun comes, it is withered up into a dry shell! I carry, like a gitana still, the steel to preserve my honor with life—but be thou the judge and the executioner, since we are united, and slay me if I am unfaithful!"

"Fearful conditions, Maritana!" said he, pressing his brow and veiling his eyes.

The doctrine was inculcated in him early that the king was the master, the possessor of all his subjects owned, as well life as honor, as well wealth as loved ones! Blacker than the death by the shots, by the rope, than all, was the scene of the scaffold draped with black, the burning brazier to consume the regicide's hand under his own eyes, the horses neighing and striving at their halters, which should tear the culprit to pieces, the heads-man with his knife to sever the joints, the pyre to burn up the very ashes of the "parricide royal."

"It is murder," thought he, as if the judge over his fate had spoken. "And to kill a king is the worst of murders!"

"Do you think that I dare not abide the issue," continued she, still kneeling but ceasing to weep. Indeed, her eyes were beaming up to him, as if he were looking down into two patches of sky. "Oh, my dearest lord, you know not what passion has grown to, which blossomed at the

altar, but had its green leaf and its bud when we were
proscripts together and all the world our enemy! Since
then, the hours of fear and self-reproach which I have
undergone have made your image an idol to my heart of
hearts!"

There was a flow of eloquence in her which seemed impossible in one brought up among the degenerate herd.

He caught her up and embraced her as if they had been
parted for an eternity and this was the last and only time
they should meet.

He believed her.   He became eloquent in turn and
poured out his resolve, formed ever so many times, but
being without an object, never begun in execution.   He
promised her that the racketty adventurer was no more
that he had died under the blank cartridge of the arquebusiers and that it was Cæsar, Count of Garofa and
Bazan, who survived, bent on removing the blemishes
from his coat, and becoming wholly worthy of a woman
so beautiful and so true.

Suddenly there was an alarm. Lazarillo had again
fired his gun, but as they heard the ball whizz past the
window, they conjectured that it was a warning merely—
that he had fired in the air.

They heard it as if it were a death-knell, however.

They heard, too, the regular beat of a drum, and a fife
piped the notes to its dull burden.

There was no need to peep out to ascertain the cause.

"I see soldiers," said Cæsar, trying if the old sword he
had taken would play easily in the sheath. "It is a bad
lookout!"

"If there be time, flee! Save yourself!" cried Maritana.

"Flee when a king replaces me at your door?" queried
he, with blazing eye and reddened cheek, from which
hers drew the flame.

"I can die here as well as if I saw you slain, and then put myself to death," said she, steadily. "Let us think!"

"Oh, others have done the thinking—that scoundrelly José, for example—I must act. As long as my heart impels my hand, and this blade clings to the handle, I shall do!"

"No, this is rash. I cannot live without you, so we both must be saved! I see no hope but in my sole friend! Cæsar, to the queen!"

"The queen?"

"She promised me her aid. As one offers a high price for a toy that momentarily pleases! She has forgotten you, as her lord his plight!"

He had become misanthropical by the pressure of misadventures.

"Tell her that I am in danger!"

"Oh, you do not know great people—they are so small! Yet I will do that! But I shall be plain: she shall know what detains her lord! Then, she will rescue you!"

"Now, go!" said she. "There is only Lazarillo under the window by which you scaled, and he——"

"He will miss me again?"

"I know how much I ask of you, who would sooner trust to a yard of steel than five feet of woman! But this is not seeking succor of a woman—it is a queen to whom you offer your arm to avenge! And redeem your wife in shameful captivity."

"By the spirits of all my forefathers back to Adam, I will bring you help!"

He boldly ran to the casement, opened it as boldly, and, indeed, spying not a soul but the page beneath, climbed over the bar and let himself slide down by the iron projections of waterspout, ornamental brackets and doortops to the ground.

Lazarillo pointed to the wall, in a spot, whence he had

cleared away the spikes and broken glass, and the young man bounded up a ladder, bestrode the parapet and jumped down.   Lazarillo could not see more of him, but Maritana did at her higher point.

Cæsar, as if fresh from the pillow, darted off at the same time as a company of soldiers, sent to make the hold stronger, were admitted at the gateway on the road.

"The queen," muttered the woman, incredulously, "may not be a kind heart, but she must be jealous, and I will rely on her jealousy rather than her promise to please!"

She went to the nook where a sacred image opened out its arms holding the Redeemer, and she fell there and prayed.

CHAPTER XVIII.

A DESPERATE RIDE.

Poor, blind mortals that we are! It is one of our bitterest afflictions that our horizon is so bounded, that our prescience is so dim and that we have none of those instincts by which wild beasts extricate themselves from traps which seem infrangible.

Cæsar had hardly begun his fresh journey when he lamented that he could not foresee what was to happen.

He was stopped by hearing a horse neigh and others whinny for the companionship. He plunged off the highway into the underbrush and carefully proceeded.

He soon spied a group of horses, forming a circle, since they were picketed by the head. Two or three men in arms guarded them. They had probably come with the soldiers seen to enter the lone house, but they had dismounted in order not to be embarrassed with their chargers in becoming the garrison around the lady.

"Oh, if I could detach one of those horses!" thought he, worming his way toward the place with gypsy ingenuity, of which he had imbibed his share by habitual association.

At last, near enough not to be seen, but yet to see all that happened, he reviewed the petty camp with a soldier's keenness and judgment.

"Oh, these petardiers," said he, wondering.

The petardiers, antetypes of the grenadiers, were men charged with the desperate deed of blowing up obstacles, such as town gates, breaching walls and firing houses condemned as scenes of murders, treasons and atrocities, which should leave no trace.

He knew the uniform, marked by scarlet and yellow lace; and, besides, in a metal case, over which one stood guard with a short musket, no doubt reposed some of the bags of powder, which were their main instruments.

He counted them. There were six petardiers and their corporal; three or four others might belong to the cavalry, of which the force had entered the house. These remained to care for the horses.

Don Cæsar sighed again and again for the horse by which he would lessen his fatigue and shorten the time to reach his goal.

All at once a bright, an infernal idea seized him.

"The Duke of Egypt has set me on this track!" muttered he. "I will attempt it, for those fellows are nodding—they have been roused in the barracks from slumber, after a hearty meal. I believe that now I experience the novel sensation of being in love with my own wife. All will come easy for me. It is a great blessing to have an angel on the earth playing success to you."

Groping in the wood, he soon discovered one of those long saplings which, after growing tall in the hope to catch a little air and light over the heads of the immense forest-monarchs which loaded Spain at the period, die and dry off, but still retain toughness and elasticity. The one he seized was, as he conjectured, easily snapped off at the root. He had thus in his hands a long wand, terminating with gradual tapering and fine finish in a tip like a rush.

It required great dexterity and the strength of wrist which he displayed in his fencing bouts to manipulate it.

He dragged it with him, point foremost, and the butt noiselessly glided over the dead leaves, which lay thick over untold depth of vegetable detritus.

He approached the camp from leeward, and was delighted that the horses did not neigh any more.

'All he could remember of Arab cunning and gypsy patience came to his aid.

Thrusting the interminable rod before him, he let it slide, well hidden by the grass and weeds, toward the spot where the sentinel watched the case of explosives.

Its advance was without sound and unseen. Nothing would mar the experiment but the chance step of a soldier toward it, and his being tripped up by it. Even then it would not be immediately suspected that a human hand had introduced it there, and the daring operator might make his escape.

"I shall be no worse off than before," thought Cæsar, methodically pushing the stick onward.

Once he gave up all as lost. The fine point had met some obstacle, which snapped it partly off. The sentry heard the sound, for he looked off over the site of the mishap. He could not see the adventurer, thirty feet aloof, and he resumed his half-somnolent watch.

This forming at the end of the pole a slight hook helped a good result. When Cæsar audaciously touched the case of ammunition with it, this hook fastened itself in the strap by which the canister was carried. In consequence, when he gently drew it back, the thing followed the impulse.

He suppressed his joy and continued the movement. The case aided him by rolling on the uneven ground, and only stopped in its revolution by entering into the embers of the half-burnt-out fire.

Cæsar had done all he could.

"If the ashes are hot enough, they will fuse the metal or dissolve the solder, and out will pour the heated powder."

He thanked Providence, for he believed that the petards had been brought to blow up the house in case there had been more than one invader there and the place had to be stormed.

"Poor Maritana! she was almost living over Vesuvius!"

Having done with the long pole all that he intended, he crept in the same cautious mode in another direction and placed himself near the horses. He still bore upon him the knife which had served the sham monk to open his sackcloth when a "dead man" in the Good Works Monastery, and this was all he required for the second stage of his exploit.

Luck was with him. Nobody noticed the case smoldering in the embers until too late.

"Alerta!" cried a sleeper, awakened by accident, as he perceived that the canister had apparently been kicked into the imminent bed. "The powder—it is in the fire!"

He himself sprang to remove it before too late, and he might have succeeded by the skin of his teeth, to quote the popular expression, but at his first step he stumbled on the pole and measured his length, his hands failing to reach the case by a full foot.

At the same moment the heated object began to hiss, and the outbreak instantaneously followed.

The powder caught as it spread in a sheet, and the fire, almost dead, became a glowing mass.

The cinders, charcoal and ends of unburnt logs flew, blazing, and the glade was lighted up as at noonday!

"Chaos returned!" muttered Bazan, darting through the retreating soldiers, who did not try to drag their daring companion by the heels from where his hair singed.

He had previously singled out the best of the horses, a fine Andalusian of Barbary stock, somewhat light, but up to his weight. It was saddled for war, and he had no difficulty in slinging himself across the back.

He galloped before he thought of sitting up and set-
tling in the seat.

Hooked to the pommel was a carbine, as it would be
called now, such as the officers of some doubly-armed
corps carried then in addition to their swords; it took
the place of the modern revolver.

The moment he sat up, a volley was fired on him, but
it was too hurried to be of avail.

"Fools!" said he, "do you not know that I am in-
vulnerable!"

He disdained to return the shots.

He looked back, but without slowing; the glade was a
flame through which the soldiers were seen hindering the
other horses from running away after breaking their
halters, and helping their comrades out of the trap, beginning to burn where the fire had caught dry and
resinous branches.

He heard the bell at the lone houses tolling; it was
feared there that the fire was a movement of an enemy
coincident with the intruder's escape.

"Pooh! they will not revenge themselves on a
woman!" he reasoned to correct his impulse to return.
"I must speed on my mission. I am bearing not merely
the fate of my love, but that of Spain! A kingdom will
be divided unless I can prevent the breach opening."

He had some hard riding to do over short cuts from
roads to roads, and some of those tortuous rivulets to
cross which fed the headwaters of the Tagus. He reveled
in the pace, however, since it distracted his mind.

No one accosted so desperate a rider. The peasants
saluted; the forest-rangers flung themselves back not to
be ridden down, and the petty constables simply withdrew into the bushes until he had swept by.

If he had been challenged, he meant to call out: "Errand of the king!" which had power to clear the high-

way. As for the other sort of detainers, the vagrants and gypsies, he was in possession of the charms to drive them afar. A word that he was going to get help for "their sister," the dancing-girl, would have sufficed.

It was thus that he covered over twenty miles, which had brought out the good qualities of the Barb.

Then pity seized him; he left the animal at a post-house, declaimed his quality as Count of Garofa, and demanded of the postmaster, on royal service, his best horse. He was bearing a message from the king to the queen at Aranjuez.

His costume was so rich that in spite of its being soiled and reduced to shreds, the postmaster believed the plea, and "charged it to the crown." With a fresh horse he traveled the rest of the journey without delay. He stopped at the old bridge on the Tagus, and, taking to walking, proceeded toward the palace.

It was impregnable to an army. It was terribly imposing and forbidding. It was, then, on a high land, little dominating over the deeply wooded country, bristling with fir-trees and pines, which had succeeded the oaks and chestnuts felled for its timber-work.

The vales had been deepened by the extraction of stones for the walls and towers; these quarries were half-filled with water, in which crawled monstrous reptiles. All was repellent; the turrets, carrying brass culverins, loopholes for guns, ramparts with wall guns, iron portcullis, turning-spikes on the copings, wide moats flooded with black water, and sentinels at every point; to say nothing of patrols which continually made the circuit and appeared here and there where there was a connecting bulwark.

"Holy Mary, I shall never scale these walls of Babylon!" he groaned, despairingly.

Like a wolf, he began to prowl around the circumvallation, growling and snarling like one.

"I wager that Don José has been before me and put the watch on the *qui vive!* It is guarded as though the French had crossed the Duero! Oh, if only he had the key to that gate, and its possession was on the point of his or my sword!"

Speaking of swords, at that moment his own, borrowed without thought of how the belt would fit him, loosened itself like a snake and, assisted by his stumbling, jumped out of the casing and not only fell on the ground, but rebounded and continued the flight like a living thing.

Inanimate objects have these provoking traits at times.

It slipped along and downward, and he feared for a space while he pursued, that it would disappear in the ditch.

Luckily or unluckily, it met with a hole, such as the monster rats bore in such moist hillocks, and vanished, as if a kobold's hand gripped it and pulled it into this burrow.

"By my life; what a disaster!"

Unarmed, a swordsman is not a tithe of a man. He dropped on his knees and thrust his hand and arm into the cavity, at risk of being stung by some venomous thing.

But at the pressure of his knees, the edge of the pit began to give way. Before he could catch at anything to restrain his following the blade, which still eluded him, he was standing waist deep in a hole, wet and slimy.

"My clothes have stood a deal, but they are finished this time!" he humorously moaned.

But he spied, by a gray beam of light, the sword lying on brick pavement, a little below where he had been checked.

"Oh, it is a subterranean passage!" said he, not sure whether he ought to rejoice or not. "I must have my sword anyway, whether it is the abode of an imp or Gnaw-well, the rat king!"

On stooping to pick up the weapon, he perceived that it was on the floor of a tunnel stretching before him some twenty feet.

It was large enough for him to walk through, if he bent nearly double.

Here was no mystery; it was simply one of those covered ways which, bored under the moat, enabled a forlorn sortie to be made by a garrison if driven to that extremity.

Time and a late inundation from the mountains had scraped and washed off the earth from the surface and bared it so that the least shock, such as his step had given, revealed the secret.

The vaulting was excellently done, for the cement, of Roman make, had prevented the least drop trickling through from the moat overhead.

He could walk up to the palace walls without being wet-footed.

He advanced, after girding on the sword more securely.

He was in the castle wall now. The masons had simply perforated it at this point and filled up the gap with two impenetrable iron doors.

"Much be my gain!" muttered he, for this seemed a block to any further progress.

Indeed, it would be a poor commander of a fort who, having a secret egress in case of the worst or to execute a sortie, should let his mode of communication set his defenses at naught, by falling into the knowledge of the foe.

He was so sure that he had no power to shake the

shield that he did not so much as lay his hand upon the iron.

But looking up with that appeal to the powers above habitual to the Christian, he perceived that above his head the vault was greatly high.

The dark accumulated here and gave the altitude increased scope.

"It is the bottom of a well—a dry well," he thought. "This is singular."

His eyes, accustomed to the gloom, then could distinguish that the upper portion of this vault was an oblong inclosure of marble, white, but looking gray.

"It is much like a sarcophagus!"

He began to reflect on what he had heard of the palace.

He had never been in it; his comrades of the guard and court had brought back no reminiscences of the mountain refuge.

"It is a *retiro* without a story!" bewailed he. "I am in no man's land."

Suddenly the great box overhead became illumined softly. The effect was beautiful; the chest was not of marble, but of alabaster. The pellucid gleam was soothing to the eye after so much lack of light.

He could discern that the object over him was an empty tomb of colossal proportions, sculptured finely within. The slab was set without cement and closed with its weight, so that no light could penetrate the crack.

After the light appeared, no sound followed.

He drove his sword into the interstices of the stone blocks and mounted on the handle, clinging to the asperities of the masonry as best he could.

Thus his head was within the tomb; he could make sure that his conjecture was correct.

He was startled by hearing close to the marble, but still invisible, the hard breathing of a man who was pursuing some labor to which by his panting he was probably unused.

He was digging with a spade in the earth, at one end of the structure.

"What idiot is this? Making a grave when there is a tomb already to his hand which would hold a family!"

It is needless to say that his curiosity did not induce him to put an inquiry to this grave-digger.

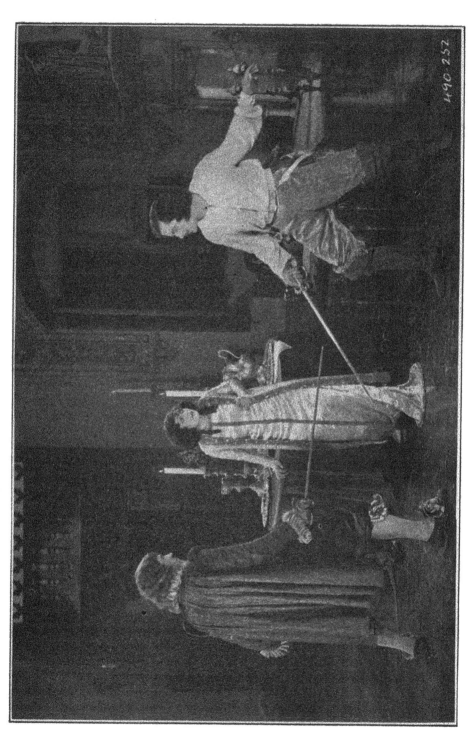

490 252

A Paramount Picture.

The Spanish Dancer.

CHAPTER XIX

THE TRAITOR'S DOOM.

Our hero had prudently pulled up his legs and propped himself within the sepulcher, and it was none too soon. The delver, assisted by the ground being tenacious and giving way in a lump, dropped it almost in a block. At the foot of the alabaster tomb, a great gap appeared, the dirt falling to the bottom, whence Cæsar had lifted himself in time.

The digger looked in and down, and sighed with delight at the success of his undertaking.

"Abundant," said he, laughing under his breath.

"Great powers!" thought the hearer, "it is my precious cousin."

This sufficed to seal his lips. His desire to pierce this mystery was sharpened.

Don José, satisfied with his work, shaped the orifice a little regularly, patted it to firm it with the flat of the spade, and proceeded to cover the whole with some planks. The light came through their crevices, however, and Caesar began to believe that he should not be longer in the dark, at least.

"There it is," murmured the plotter, easily; "the queen may come now and I will engage to hurl her down the hole if she assumes the virtuous and indignant tone with me, and does not accept my proposition in its entirety."

He went away, leaving the light, and Cæsar dwelt in horrible perplexity.

Nevertheless, assured by the quiet and conceiving that the treacherous minister had gone to conduct the queen hither, he ventured all upon one die.

He worked his way to the hole, as a chimney-sweep moves, with elbows and knees, and removing one of the planks, b ldly risked his head through the aperture he made.

He looked up and around in one of those imitations of classical round temples which had their vogue under the artistic Popes.

Columns and pilasters, some antique, others modern, upheld a very good vault in the style of the ancient "lanterns."

All was still; a rope torch burnt steadily in an iron socket by the open doorway. Cæsar climbed out and replaced the plank.

The tomb was not used as such; it served as a table for an immense group of marble, partly antique, partly restored.

A giant with merely a lion's hide wrapped round his loins was struggling with the several heads and arms of a monster, which might have been the sculptor's idea of an octopus; at the back and side, seahorses and mermen struggled, too, but which was friend and which foe to the wrestler was disputable.

Garofa's classical lore was not stupendous; he examined the statues without interest, and said:

"Hercules and the Hydra, I think."

Truth to tell, he was thinking of the struggle which he felt to be impending.

"I am in the grotto, and my devilfish is returning!"

He went and concealed himself in the creepers and woodbine which formed a screen between two of the columns.

He heard voices in the darkened gardens, at the far end of which the castellated walls arose; the gleams of light from the torch streaked the darkness as they were emitted between the stone uprights.

In one of these long rays the watcher saw two figures approaching.

"It is my cousin, and he is leading the queen by the hand!   The Santarems are in the lead, still, by Jove!"

With all show of deference, almost humility, the marquis led the great lady within the artificial temple.

The latter was not wasted, or blighted; passion had warmed and enlivened; she, perhaps, had a more animated expression since jealousy stirred, than since she had discovered that her husband was false.

She pretended a heedlessness to her risky position of according interviews of this private, ruinous nature which bewildered the count, one who with all his levity and scorn of conventionalities, had the Spaniard's esteem for rigidly constraining women.

"Your lordship could not have chosen a fitter spot for our meeting," said she, with a sad smile; "for this is the remains of the Temple of Fidius, god of treaties, disinterred in the ruins of Tusculum.   The Pope Clement sent the pieces hither as a present to King Philip; but as they did not arrive until after the king's death, the fragments remained in their packings, until his successor, a Medici, fond of the arts, sent to Philip the Fourth this group, representing Hercules and the Hydra, or a sea monster, which was set up here under the restored fane by the Grand Duke of Florence's own sculptor, Piero Lacca."

José had listened without more than glancing at the relics.

"The Grand Duke Ferdinando had better have attended to his own realm falling into ruins than set his artists to repairing those of old!" said he, incisively. "His estate, between the empire, France and the internal dissensions, was in the same danger as overhang us."

"You said that you bore news concerning my gypsy *protégée?*" said she, disconnectedly.

"Oh, that is a minor matter! Anything to obtain this serious interview! Your majesty knows by the gazettes which I forwarded to you by a safe hand in what misery, this kingdom ferments?"

"It is like that strong man in the many arms of the Hydra, but, take patience, it is strong and it will surmount them!"

"Not without aid! Hercules did pretty well, but he was but a demi-god—it would require the gods to relieve us of our foes! Instead of this prince, becoming young again by his turn of the tide, beguiled by necromancers and their agents, we must have a leader whose hand will strike powerfully, and not let a woman hang on it! Hercules at the feet of Omphale! Faugh!"

"Omphale! Not Dejanira? Not his wife? Do you mistake?"

"I mean, my lady, that Carlos is enthralled with a woman whom he is going to meet, going to a house out of the way, without attendants, alone!"

He paused to give this dose of acid time to scorch its way in, to the bone.

"You will conduct me there!" said she. "At once!"

"Oh, there is no haste—for, at a word from you, it is he who will be parted forever from this decoy! In a monastery he will not meet gypsies any more!"

"This woman is a gypsy, eh?"

"In the heart, if false papers seem to prove her a Christian born. But what matters all this? Can I write to those who eagerly await the reply that Charles will be forced off the throne to give place to the appointee of the empire and France, and good wishers to Spanish prosperity; ay, and propriety?"

The queen made a wild gesture.

"A fig for these state intrigues—at this time," said she, monopolized by her jealousy. "Let the two Charleses fight out their contest for the crown! Let me punish this viped which has stolen into my confidence—but, yet you have not named her!"

"I thought your majesty guessed, from having felt a dread of her from first sight—aversion, hatred! It is that dancer who capers on the royal mantle, spread under her feet as a carpet!"

"Maritana? You do not say that Maritana thus repays me for my offers to lift her out of that ditch!"

"Oh, she is out of the ditch without your generous hand!" replied José, in an irritating tone. "That stupid old Castello-Rotondo has already been promoted for recognizing her as his child! He would have recognized a rag doll, to be made keeper of the king's spaniels!"

"Maritana, the Countess of Castello-Rotondo?"

"Oh, better than that, which is her born title, thereby, for she has been married to the Count of Garofa, one of those complaisant panderers who would put his hand to any deed by which the king could cover his duplicity and iniquity!"

"A mock marriage?"

"All these proceedings are a mocking of your majesty, to be sure!"

She went up and down, and at each turn smote the marble columns with her fan.

"The king must be punished—these, his instruments of my woe, must be imprisoned, slain!"

"All your will be done, majesty! Only give me the written warrant!"

"I, the queen! Write—seal—sign——"

"I understand—you are not yet regent. Well, is there not a little slip of paper with the king's sign-manual which could be filled out for the chastisement of these wretches who aim at your peace?"

"I should have thought that the prime minister would have been plentifully supplied with these orders in blank?" said the queen, suspiciously.

"Oh, my rank sits newly upon me—besides, having an idea that I would not approve of this treachery to his wife, he does not accord me the confidence which I praise your majesty for!"

"Well, I am no second-rate liar," thought the listener, "but this cousin can give me cards and come out first by far!"

"Well, I can find the warrant," said the queen. "In return, will you not guide me to confront this impudent disturber of my domestic peace?"

"Assuredly. After this is confirmed, your majesty will listen to what has been arranged if your consent is ours!"

"When I return, equipped for the journey—and, on the ride, we will come to a final understanding—I do not say agreement, yet!"

"She loves her husband," muttered José. "This is untoward! I can do little with her! I must throw her over—that is, under! and by letting the king conserve his plaything make my bond stronger with him. Let Charles, the would-be Eighth, manage his own approaches, then, as long as the Seventh is subservient to my enterprises!"

He had ushered the queen to the doorway, and she rapidly disappeared in the garden.

"She must die," sternly said José, thinking himself alone. "But I will not lay my hand on the Lord's anointed! This pit hole will let her through to the ground, where she will break her crown!"

"Here is a bloodthirsty premier for you!" thought the

hearer. "And yet, for the sake of the family, I must never boast of what a serpent I snapped in twain."

"Ten minutes to go to her rooms, ten to dress, ten to return, and within five she disappears in this grave, under the care of Seniors, Hercules and the Tritons! In half an hour one may overturn a succession!"

"In less, one may upset a villain's pet schemes!" interrupted Don Cæsar, stepping out and between the entrance and the plotter.

Satan touched by Ithuriel's spear could not have expressed on his convulsed features greater desolation than Santarem's wore.

"You!" his lips shaped without a sound issuing. "You again!"

"It is I! You have heated a furnace by which you will singe your beard! You would war with women, would you? Destroy Maritana and also our queen because they balk your atrocious projects!" He drew the sword.

José drew his.

But his antagonist dashed it from his hand.

"The sword? Flatter yourself, double traitor and coward that you are, to perish by the gentleman's weapon?"

Trembling with terror and thwarted hopes, fury enkindled into making him heroic, José dashed to recover his weapon. But on the way he perceived the bar with which he had broken the ground for the pit. On seeing this, Cæsar contemptuously took up the spade, sheathing his rapier. "You are a clown, and you should be combatted with a clown's weapon!" said he, scornfully. "I know all your ignominy! I am ashamed that you are tied by blood to us! I shall not only kill you, but bury you in this heathen temple, so that your soul will wander forever unannealed!"

The contest with the unaccustomed arms was rude as

that of antediluvians. Bar and shape-shaft clashed, and terrible blows were delivered and parried.

The spade-blade was knocked off, and the bar was bent.

"Oh, this resembles cudgel-play," said Cæsar, recovering his loquacity as this became a more reasonable match. "Look! this is for plotting against our lord the king!" He struck a blow which would have cleft his skull or broken the staff but for the bar held up with both hands. As it was, José bowed to the knees.

The marquis began to groan with rage and pain. The other, bent on punishing, was striking him across the shoulders and the back at opportunities which his growing weakness and blind fury gave freely.

"This is for my wife!" said the count.

The blow was a swinging one, with both hands coming together in the strike. José bit his howl in two, for fear of bringing assistance, which he could not hope would be his, and threw the bar at his foe.

Cæsar warded it off so that it fell against the statues and beheaded a Triton.

The head rolled down and bounded on José's foot.

"Your head will lie beside it next!" said Cæsar. "See how chaff and corn fly asunder at the stroke of Justice!"

But the tried stick broke at the blow on the other's bruised shoulder. He staggered back and, finding he had, in the changes of the duel, reached the spot where the iron bar had fallen, stooped to pick it up for a final effort.

Cæsar grasped it at the same time. They faced each other, the iron between them. By his hand in this position, José felt the other's sword rap his knuckles. He uttered a joyous exclamation. With incredible renewal of fierceness, considering his bruises and loss of blood, he let go the bar with one hand, grasped the sword and drew it to him.

Not expecting this, Bazan, losing his balance at the dropping of the iron at one end, swerved round a little. His breast was exposed to the lunge which was coming like lightning, when the heels of the villain, even as he began to laugh victory, were sinking between the planks which he had placed loosely over the hole. He threw up both hands to recover his poise, but Cæsar had swung the bar out from his grip.

The stroke met the sword in its passage and carried it with it, so that, with his neck severed, Don José fell into the pit.

There was a horrible, dull crash. Then, absolute silence.

Cæsar drew back, as if shot to the heart. He had forgotten about the pitfall dug for another, and the disappearance had seemed providential.

He kicked the parted planks close over the yawning gap as if he had committed a murder without justification.

He retreated to the door, when he heard light, hurried footsteps.

"Oh, madam, do not go further! There is blood—of a traitor in there!"

"Don José's?"

"Our poor marquis would have been a misleading guide! He has met with the cure for ambition! The only genuine remedy!"

The lady peering within the rotunda perceived the detached head of the statue—it looked ghastly.

"Oh, that? That is a harmless head—his is turning to stone and has reached Treason's goal—the dirt and dust. Allow me to replace him!"

"You! Wait! I have seen you—you were with those gypsies?"

"I was with them, but not of them—my descent forbid! I am Don Cæsar de Bazan, Count of Garofa, and it is I who will conduct you to my wife, Maritana of Garofa, who, I assure your majesty, to whom Heaven accord long life to see how truly I speak, will bless you for coming to save her from a treacherous plot against her, against your majesty and my lord the king!"

CHAPTER XX.

The explosion of the petards had brought all the soldiers in the residence of Maritana to the doors, where they were joined by the petardiers and their comrades. Ruefully, out of blackened lips, they reported by their corporal to the lieutenant the loss of their horses, which were scampering over the countryside.

They could not account for the casualty, but Lazarillo could give a fair conjecture. He went to comfort his mistress, and assured her that her courier had no doubt got off on one of the stampeded horses.

Nevertheless, though she had parted with her beloved, showing a firm countenance, it fell when the page announced the visit of the king.

Lazarillo dared not remain, but he went with the less distress on knowing that Maritana retained of her former attire that knife in her garter without which no true Gitana, or false one, travels.

The king had inquired of the page less about the tumult of which he had heard little, than of the intruder. The youth confidently answered that he must have fled through the gardens and over the walls before the soldiers came to mount guard.

Maritana saluted the visitor with such formality that he bit his lips with vexation.

"Who has dared betray me?" demanded he, throwing off the mask.

"Your majesty," boldly replied the countess, "he that betrayed you is the same who counseled you to commit a meanness congenial to him but beneath a monarch!"

"Whom do you allude to?"

"The Marquis of Santarem, ostensibly!"

"Ah!"

"He has made a mock of your majesty, as he did of heaven, by that deceit at the holy altar!"

"Well, girl, I am your king. In sooth, my spirit has revolted at this trivial cheat. Now that you know who speaks, listen to me."

"My lord, all is waste—all is lost—there is no love possible in me for you!"

"All is lost, but the last thing one loses is hope!"

"Oh, I hope; but that is almost forbidden to you!"

"What still may I hope?"

"That you will escape the penalty for your connivance with your prime minister! If in public matters he is villainous as in private business, then all will go ill with Spain!"

"The penalty! I incur any penalty!"

"The severest, for you besmirch your queen! This suit ill suits one who has no right to complain of your consort! I implore you to leave me while it is yet time!"

"Bah! come all! Come death, since it is of my own choosing! I cannot leave you—you, who are the only one I ever loved!"

"Carry your love where it is claimed. Show me only generosity, mercy! Spare me and this will be the brightest jewel in a crown!"

"Oh, it is for you to claim jewels—I will have one token that I was not scorned!"

He thought that she would appeal to the Madonna, and he was prepared to pluck her from that refuge, but, instead, she stood erect and, drawing a dagger from her knee, with a rapid movement, which was resolute and not devoid of grace, she threatened him, not herself.

It was no plaything, but one of those Navarese *navajas*

which can kill a bull by a slash across the throat and a boar by a stab in the back of the chine.

But he was more wounded by the repugnance which tempered her derisive smile.

"What!" said he, "am I loathesome to you?"

"You are nothing to me—all my existence is bound up in one who must find his wife worthy of him or fit for the grave!"

"Of whom speak you?" queried he, only too well guessing.

"Of the Count of Garofa!"

"That Don Cæsar of Bazan! That blackguard!"

"Ah! if your white guards were as fixed on honor!"

"Why, he is dead!"

"Not at all!" interposed a voice.

Don Cæsar entered jauntily by the door which Lazarillo, in some degree emboldened by his return, held open to admit him.   The corridor was filled with soldiers and servants, but the king was perplexed at recognizing the uniform of the Queen's Halberdiers.

To add to his uneasiness, he heard quite a hubbub at the roadside; a number of horse rode up and rapidly dismounted.   The house seemed thickly besieged.

This fellow who so audaciously advanced might be the leader of one of those royal kidnaping expeditions not unprecedented on the annals.

On seeing him, Maritana sheathed her dagger and appeared fully reassured.

"My husband now will protect me!" said she.

The king looked at "her husband," who, with the utmost unconcern for his presence or his feelings, slammed the door in the many faces and locked it, and, doing the same with the inner door, took out the keys.

"What are you doing, sir?" demanded he.

"I have fastened the doors so that no one can enter—

and my page has orders to drive those back who might, as courtiers will do, glue their ears to the keyhole!"

Don Cæsar had laid his hand on his sword, and he spoke fiercely, too, like one with whom the sword had always determined debates.

"My lord," began he, "if my wife's persecutor had been a soldier and a peer of myself, I fear that I should have denied him the honor of an encounter! I believe that I should have dispatched him as we do a thief who enters our dovecote at midnight—off-hand! For in such a case one does not look for reparation, but revenge! But we are here in face of a king, though a misbehaving one —I must disarm my revenge!"

He drew his sword, but it was to present it to the king, by the point.

"Yes, you are speaking to the King of Spain!" said the other, mastering a host of contesting emotions.

"To whom else would I speak in this strain? As we cannot always subdue the will or restrain the naturally-prompted hand, I will render both powerless!"   He threw away the rapier.   "But there must be atonement!"

"Must?   Atonement?   But, go on—your audacity amuses me!"

"Cæsar," said Maritana, in a low voice, "remember that his wife loves him! and she is my patroness!"

"Yes, it is a loved king—but his subjects, his nobles, will not long love a king who gives up his love for unequal sharing! Your power and that of your minister are combined against this poor, weak creature and her humble champion, but she has sought the protection of her patroness, the queen!"

This time the hearer quailed, and shook like a tower, long battered at, at last receiving the stroke which affects the heart.

"You see in me the queen's messenger from her palace of Aranguez."

"You, the queen's messenger——"

"Better—or worse! The queen's *avant courier?*"

"Ha!"

"Yes, you shall hear all! The palace was strictly guarded. You should applaud her captain of guards, your governor of the castle. Denied admission, I ferreted out an entrance unknown to the uninitiated. But how useful to a traitor!"

"Oh, you ran into danger!" uttered Maritana.

"Pshaw! your husband is getting bullet-proof! I harbored myself in a Grecian temple——"

"The Temple of Hercules and the Hydra——"

"Yes, the same, only Cæsar has killed the Hydra!"

"Cæsar? No, no!"

"My story is the modern version, and will elucidate, my lord! There came to confer, in this classical Ear of Dionysius, two persons, courtier and lady of the court, whose remarks were worth my listening to, and your majesty's heeding."

"Courtiers?" said the interested monarch. "High degree?"

"The highest! One was the First Man of the Kingdom——"

"Oh, Don José?"

"And the other, the First Lady of the Land!"

"My queen!" dismally.

"The queen!" said Maritana, joyously.

"The minister offered in plain words to make the lady the regent until Charles of Hapsburg should assume the throne as the Eighth of Spain!"

"I will have José's head for this suggestion!"

"It is already at your disposal, being detached from his body very timely, it now appears."

"They plotted such treason; they two?"

"Oh, that was a trifle to what was next to come! The minister said that, meanwhile, by way of diversion, he would pilot the queen to this very house in the woods, where she would find that her husband was whiling away the tedium of state in preferable company!"

"Who dared to watch my movements——"

"The ex-minister of police! the late minister of state!"

"The late? 'tis false! If it were true!" He rushed to the door, but Cæsar held up the keys in his face, and jingled them.

"Traitor!"

"I remarked that reparation must accrue to me! Do you understand me now?"

"On your allegiance—open that door!"

"You cannot leave, for it is just—what wrong one does another should be reflected upon himself! I learned that among my practical tutors, the gypsies, who have several such jagged saws in their workshop."

"Shall I command that door to be broken in?"

"Scandal; my lord, does not want too many witnesses. That is how kings, who were memorialized as saints, have been thrown off their pedestals by posterity, which such witnesses enlightened, later!"

The king buried his face in his hands.

All that he would have made Don Cæsar suffer, he had turned upon his breast. He dared not cry for help. And at any moment his injured wife would condole with this other injured wife.

He rose and commanded Cæsar to open the door.

The retribution was excruciating.

"Take up your sword, sir!" said he then, in a strangled voice.

He drew his own, and Maritana gathered herself to leap between.

"A king no longer, for your claim—your treason equal-izes us! Defend yourself, or you will make me an as-sassin!"

"It will be too late!"

"Too late for what? To save my fame unto my wife?"

"Pish! I was not thinking of that! Too late to punish my cousin!"

"He must die, and you—but you first! Defend or I strike!"

"When did a Spanish nobleman hesitate in revenging an insult to his king and his queen? Think you I would spare even my dear relative, one who would have made my dishonor the stepping-stone to his rise, and your in-carceration in a convent the smoothing of his road to the premiership of a foreigner? No, sire, I have taken your deathsman's place. Your honor is preserved, with your throne, and your fame! It is now your turn to deal with mine!"

He knelt on one knee and pointed to Maritana, who stood with firmness and eyes directed heavenward to await the decision.

Carlos did not longer hesitate; the deliverance from José, whom he had never liked, pleased him so that he hardened his heart to its individual loss. He did not look at Maritana, who returned him this indifference in full coin, by the way, but held out his arms to the pleader saying graciously enough, although it was a trial:

"Rise, Count of Garofa!"

Bazan gave one key to the lady, who used it to enter her own rooms, and he opened the outer door with the other.

An endless stream of courtiers poured in, and more would have come if the room had been capacious enough.

They seemed surprised, for the word had passed that

there might be some shocking deception in this mysterious abode.

"It is the king!" was the cry.

"Certainly, it is the king," returned Charles, putting on that summer-day face of monarchs who wish to hide contrariety, "we have inspected the country seat of our well-beloved Don Cæsar, Count of Garofa, and esteem it meager accommodation for such a lady as his dame! So we desire him to move into the palace of the Governor of Valencia!"

"Governor of Valencia!" repeated the surprised courtiers, mystified.

"Yes, gentlemen," observed Don Cæsar, to such as he caught the eye of and were known to him, "the force of merit makes its modest way, you see!"

Then, turning to the king, and leaning on his armchair with the assurance of an old favorite, he placidly remarked:

"If the governor's mansion at Barcelona, for Catalonia, is not immovable, I should prefer his residence, my good lord!"

"Why Catalonia?" queried the king, with more surprise than susceptibility.

"Only that it is farthest from the capital, and so forfends my pursy creditors, ahem!"

"Your creditors? Why, you may draw on my privy purse to annul your debts before you take office, of course!"

"Hear, my king! you do not know that that would require the state treasury!"

"You are appointed Governor of Catalonia, then, and to defray your expenses, we transfer to you all the appointments which should proceed toward our late prime minister and which, with his estate and possessions, are forfeit to the crown!"

"The late prime minister?" muttered all voices, amazed at the absence of the Marquis of Santarem from this peculiar "inspection."

"Why, yes," said Don Cæsar, clapping his hand to his brow as if a sudden cutting recollection brought a cloud over his good fortune, "my poor cousin, while inspecting the Grecian temple at Aranjuez, fell into a hole, incautiously left open by a bungling workman, and broke his blessed neck!"

Comment was checked upon this abrupt piece of news by the entrance, at the same time, but by different issues, of the queen and Maritana, who had conjured up a toilet of surpassing brilliancy; but perhaps her sudden and unmarred happiness had something to do with that splendor.

The greeting was warm to both, and the more sincere to the beauty of the Castello-Rotondos.

The queen looked sharply at her husband, but, debonnaire as any gallant gentleman who had called on another gay and careless gentleman to congratulate him on also finding a wife, he was joining the hands of Maritana and the new Governor-General of Catalonia.

"Between ourselves, my dear," said he to the queen, "I believe this reformed Count of Garofa is an irredeemable profligate, but I do this to get him away from our capital of temptations, and his charming wife is a *protégée* of your own, to whom, for your sake, I ought not to refuse anything!"

The queen smiled on Maritana, and, to this day, until we reveal it, no one suspected that the queen's great amity for the Garofas sprang from her trying to make the countess her cat's-paw.

"But never mind that little insignificant gypsy," went on the king, "let us haste back to the summer palace, where we will pass the Festival of the Trinity together like old lovers, for I wish to consult you on the vacancy to be filled, left by that poor Santarem, who really was useless as a statesman, since he would go poking his nose into the dust of ages over classic busts and torsos!"

Lazarillo accompanied them.   When he outgrew being a page, he returned to his first love, that is, the care of arms.   Curator of the arsenal, he became keeper of the royal armory, and for diversion not only defended his charge so well during a landing of the Corsairs that they fled to their ships, but, mustering all available fighting men, embarked in an improvised fleet and pursued them. Coming up with them, off Majorca, he drove some galleys ashore and sank almost all the rest.

For this exploit he was knighted.

In a local history, still in MS. in the city archives, a note states: "The leaden statue in the Fish Market is erected to the memory of Don Juan Lazarillo, Knight of the Order of St. Jago, captain of the coast guard, and was paid for by the ransom money of certain Turks (Algerines, in fact), captured by this valorous soldier in the victory off Cape Formentor.   Don Juan was the inventor of that humane plan by which, one cartridge being blank in the guns of a firing party of soldiers used at an execution, each can cherish the illusion that another hand than his fired the fatal shot."

He had the pleasure of teaching the son and heir of his beloved master the manual of arms, with a "firelock," which, by his improvement, had superseded the arquebus of his boyhood.

The Count and Countess of Garofa, reigning like prince and princess in the remote country, had no quarrel with happiness.

But one day the lady said to her mate, whose justice (!), economy (1!) and devotion to his fireside (11!) had endeared him to his subjects:

"What could have induced you to go so far from Madrid when the king did generously wipe out your debts, Cæsar?"

"Oh, the king has a long arm, saith the proverb, and it was out of his reach I wished to be. He would guess by my happiness what a treasure was escaping him in you!"

THE END.

There Are Two Sides to Everything—

—including the wrapper which covers every Grosset & Dunlap book. When you feel in the mood for a good romance, refer to the carefully selected list of modern fiction comprising most of the successes by prominent writers of the day which is printed on the back of every Grosset & Dunlap book wrapper.

You will find more than five hundred titles to choose from—books for every mood and every taste and every pocketbook.

Don't forget the other side, but in case the wrapper is lost, write to the publishers for a complete catalog.

*There is a Grosset & Dunlap Book
for every mood and for every taste*

RUBY M. AYRE'S NOVELS

RICHARD CHATTERTON
A fascinating story in which love and jealousy play strange tricks with women's souls.

A BACHELOR HUSBAND
Can a woman love two men at the same time?

In its solving of this particular variety of triangle " A Bachelor Husband " will particularly interest, and strangely enough, without one shock to the most conventional minded.

THE SCAR
With fine comprehension and insight the author shows a terrific contrast between the woman whose love was of the flesh and one whose love was of the spirit.

THE MARRIAGE OF BARRY WICKLOW
Here is a man and woman who, marrying for love, yet try to build their wedded life upon a gospel of hate for each other and yet win back to a greater love for each other in the end.

THE UPHILL ROAD
The heroine of this story was a consort of thieves. The man was fine, clean, fresh from the West. It is a story of strength and passion.

WINDS OF THE WORLD
Jill, a poor little typist, marries the great Henry Sturgess and inherits millions, but not happiness. Then at last—but we must leave that to Ruby M. Ayres to tell you as only she can.

THE SECOND HONEYMOON
In this story the author has produced a book which no one who has loved or hopes to love can afford to miss. The story fairly leaps from climax to climax.

THE PHANTOM LOVER
Have you not often heard of someone being in love with love rather than the person they believed the object of their affections? That was Esther! But she passes through the crisis into a deep and profound love.

GROSSET & DUNLAP,   PUBLISHERS,   NEW YORK

EDGAR RICE BURROUGH'S NOVELS

TARZAN THE UNTAMED

Tells of Tarzan's return to the life of the ape-man in his search for vengeance on those who took from him his wife and home.

JUNGLE TALES OF TARZAN

Records the many wonderful exploits by which Tarzan proves his right to ape kingship.

A PRINCESS OF MARS

Forty-three million miles from the earth—a succession of the weirdest and most astounding adventures in fiction. John Carter, American, finds himself on the planet Mars, battling for a beautiful woman, with the Green Men of Mars, terrible creatures fifteen feet high, mounted on horses like dragons.

THE GODS OF MARS

Continuing John Carter's adventures on the Planet Mars, in which he does battle against the ferocious "plant men," creatures whose mighty tails swished their victims to instant death, and defies Issus, the terrible Goddess of Death, whom all Mars worships and reveres.

THE WARLORD OF MARS

Old acquaintances, made in the two other stories, reappear, Tars Tarkas, Tardos Mors and others.   There is a happy ending to the story in the union of the Warlord, the title conferred upon John Carter, with Dejah Thoris.

THUVIA, MAID OF MARS

The fourth volume of the series. The story centers around the adventures of Carthoris, the son of John Carter and Thuvia, daughter of a Martian Emperor.

GROSSET & DUNLAP, Publishers, NEW YORK

FLORENCE L. BARCLAY'S NOVELS

THE WHITE LADIES OF WORCESTER

A novel of the 12th Century. The heroine, believing she had lost her lover, enters a convent. He returns, and interesting developments follow.

THE UPAS TREE

A love story of rare charm. It deals with a successful author and his wife.

THROUGH THE POSTERN GATE

The story of a seven day courtship, in which the discrepancy in ages vanished into insignificance before the convincing demonstration of abiding love.

THE ROSARY

The story of a young artist who is reputed to love beauty above all else in the world, but who, when blinded through an accident, gains life's greatest happiness. A rare story of the great passion of two real people superbly capable of love, its sacrifices and its exceeding reward.

THE MISTRESS OF SHENSTONE

The lovely young Lady Ingleby, recently widowed by the death of a husband who never understood her, meets a fine, clean young chap who is ignorant of her title and they fall deeply in love with each other. When he learns her real identity a situation of singular power is developed.

THE BROKEN HALO

The story of a young man whose religious belief was shattered in childhood and restored to him by the little white lady, many years older than himself, to whom he is passionately devoted.

THE FOLLOWING OF THE STAR

The story of a young missionary, who, about to start for Africa, marries wealthy Diana Rivers, in order to help her fulfill the conditions of her uncle's will, and how they finally come to love each other and are reunited after experiences that soften and purify.

GROSSET & DUNLAP,   PUBLISHERS,   NEW YORK

KATHLEEN NORRIS' STORIES

SISTERS. Frontispiece by Frank Street.

The California Redwoods furnish the background for this beautiful story of sisterly devotion and sacrifice.

POOR, DEAR, MARGARET KIRBY.

Frontispiece by George Gibbs.

A collection of delightful stories, including "Bridging the Years" and "The Tide-Marsh." This story is now shown in moving pictures.

JOSSELYN'S WIFE. Frontispiece by C. Allan Gilbert.

The story of a beautiful woman who fought a bitter fight for happiness and love.

MARTIE, THE UNCONQUERED.

Illustrated by Charles E. Chambers.

The triumph of a dauntless spirit over adverse conditions.

THE HEART OF RACHAEL.

Frontispiece by Charles E. Chambers.

An interesting story of divorce and the problems that come with a second marriage.

THE STORY OF JULIA PAGE.

Frontispiece by C. Allan Gilbert.

A sympathetic portrayal of the quest of a normal girl, obscure and lonely, for the happiness of life.

SATURDAY'S CHILD. Frontispiece by F. Graham Cootes.

Can a girl, born in rather sordid conditions, lift herself through sheer determination to the better things for which her soul hungered ?

MOTHER. Illustrated by F. C. Yohn.

A story of the big mother heart that beats in the background of every girl's life, and some dreams which came true.

GROSSET & DUNLAP,   PUBLISHERS,   NEW YORK

BOOTH TARKINGTON'S NOVELS

SEVENTEEN. Illustrated by Arthur William Brown.

No one but the creator of Penrod could have portrayed the immortal young people of this story. Its humor is irresistible and reminiscent of the time when the reader was Seventeen.

PENROD. Illustrated by Gordon Grant.

This is a picture of a boy's heart, full of the lovable, humorous, tragic things which are locked secrets to most older folks. It is a finished, exquisite work.

PENROD AND SAM. Illustrated by Worth Brehm.

Like "Penrod" and "Seventeen," this book contains some remarkable phases of real boyhood and some of the best stories of juvenile prankishness that have ever been written.

THE TURMOIL. Illustrated by C. E. Chambers.

Bibbs Sheridan is a dreamy, imaginative youth, who revolts against his father's plans for him to be a servitor of big business. The love of a fine girl turns Bibb's life from failure to success.

THE GENTLEMAN FROM INDIANA. Frontispiece.

A story of love and politics,—more especially a picture of a country editor's life in Indiana, but the charm of the book lies in the love interest.

THE FLIRT. Illustrated by Clarence F. Underwood.

The "Flirt," the younger of two sisters, breaks one girl's engagement, drives one man to suicide, causes the murder of another, leads another to lose his fortune, and in the end marries a stupid and unpromising suitor, leaving the really worthy one to marry her sister.

ELEANOR H. PORTER'S NOVELS

JUST DAVID

The tale of a loveable boy and the place he comes to fill in the hearts of the gruff farmer folk to whose care he is left.

THE ROAD TO UNDERSTANDING

A compelling romance of love and marriage.

OH, MONEY! MONEY!

Stanley Fulton, a wealthy bachelor, to test the dispositions of his relatives, sends them each a check for $100,-000, and then as plain John Smith comes among them to watch the result of his experiment.

SIX STAR RANCH

A wholesome story of a club of six girls and their summer on Six Star Ranch.

DAWN

The story of a blind boy whose courage leads him through the gulf of despair into a final victory gained by dedicating his life to the service of blind soldiers.

ACROSS THE YEARS

Short stories of our own kind and of our own people. Contains some of the best writing Mrs. Porter has done.

THE TANGLED THREADS

In these stories we find the concentrated charm and tenderness of all her other books.

THE TIE THAT BINDS

Intensely human stories told with Mrs. Porter's wonderful talent for warm and vivid character drawing.

GROSSET & DUNLAP,   PUBLISHERS,   NEW YORK

JACK LONDON'S NOVELS

JOHN BARLEYCORN. Illustrated by H. T. Dunn.

This remarkable book is a record of the author's own amazing experiences. This big, brawny world rover, who has been acquainted with alcohol from boyhood, comes out boldly against John Barleycorn. It is a string of exciting adventures, yet it forcefully conVeys an unforgetable idea and makes a typical Jack London book.

THE VALLEY OF THE MOON. Frontispiece by George Harper.

The story opens in the city slums where Billy Roberts, teamster and ex-prize fighter, and Saxon Brown, laundry worker, meet and love and marry. They tramp from one end of California to the other, and in the Valley of the Moon find the farm paradise that is to be their salvation.

BURNING DAYLIGHT. Four illustrations.

The story of an adventurer who went to Alaska and laid the foundations of his fortune before the gold hunters arrived Bringing his fortunes to the States he is cheated out of it by a crowd of money kings, and recovers it only at the muzzle of his gun. He then starts out as a merciless exploiter on his own account. Finally he takes to drinking and becomes a picture of degeneration. About this time he falls in love with his stenographer and wins her heart but not her hand and then—but read the story!

A SON OF THE SUN. Illustrated by A. O. Fischer and C. W. Ashley.

David Grief was once a light-haired, blue-eyed youth who came from England to the South Seas in search of adventure. Tanned like a native and as lithe as a tiger, he became a real son of the sun. The life appealed to him and he remained and became very wealthy.

THE CALL OF THE WILD. Illustrations by Philip R. Goodwin and
Charles Livingston Bull. Decorations by Charles E. Hooper.

A book of dog adventures as exciting as any man's exploits could be. Here is excitement to stir the blood and here is picturesque color to transport the reader to primitive scenes.

THE SEA WOLF. Illustrated by W. J. Aylward.

Told by a man whom Fate suddenly swings from his fastidious life into the power of the brutal captain of a sealing schooner. A novel of adventure warmed by a beautiful love episode that every reader will hail with delight.

WHITE FANG. Illustrated by Charles Livingston Bull.

"White Fang" is part dog, part wolf and all brute, living in the frozen north; he gradually comes under the spell of man's companionship, and surrenders all at the last in a fight with a bull dog. Thereafter he is man's loving slave.

GROSSET & DUNLAP, PUBLISHERS, NEW YORK

Lightning Source UK Ltd.
Milton Keynes UK
UKHW020640241218
334505UK00007B/307/P